ARCANA
RISING

ALSO IN THE ARCANA CHRONICLES

KRESLEY COLE

ARCANA RISING

THE ARCANA CHRONICLES

VALKYRIE PRESS

NEW YORK   BASIN TOWN   STERLING   REQUIEM   FORT ARCANA

Valkyrie Press
228 Park Ave S #11599
New York, NY 10003

ISBN 978-0-9972151-5-1
ISBN 978-0-9972151-4-4 (ebook)

Published in the United States of America.

ACKNOWLEDGEMENTS

I couldn't have published ARCANA RISING without a team of dedicated professionals. Thank you so much to everyone who gave their invaluable assistance!

All things medical: Dr. Bridget, who's been medically fact-checking me for more than fifteen books.

Helicopter research: Nicola Schenker with Reykjavík Helicopters. Nicola, that trip was spectacular (next time I'll try the shark). And many thanks for letting me record what an alarm sounds like!

Formatting and proofing: Amy Atwell with Author E.M.S. Two words: you rock.

Translations: Amy Williams with World Translation Center. Lightning-fast turnaround on multiple languages and dialects.

Story editing: Joal Hetherington, Kristi Yanta, Charlotte Herscher, and Barbara Ankrum, all of whom delivered keen insight and essential feedback. My next manuscript in on its way....

THE FIELD OF BATTLE

During the Flash, a cataclysmic flare, the surface of the earth was scorched to ash, and bodies of water evaporated. Virtually all plant life was killed, most animals as well. The majority of humans perished, with women hardest hit. After months of total drought, rain began at last—then fell constantly, until the first flurries of snow. The sun has ceased to rise, leaving the world in endless night. Plague spreads.

OBSTACLES

Militias unify, consolidating power. Slavers and cannibals hunt for new victims. All are bent on capturing females. The Bagmen (Baggers)—contagious zombies created by the Flash—roam the Ash (the wastelands), wailing for blood.

FOES

The Arcana. In every dark age, twenty-two kids with supernatural powers are destined to fight in a life-or-death game. The winner will live as an immortal until the next game, the fallen reincarnating. Our stories are depicted on the Major Arcana cards of a Tarot deck. I'm the Empress; we play again now. In my sights: Richter, the Emperor Card, who massacred an army, possibly murdering my ally Selena and Jack, my first love.

ARSENAL

Knowledge of the game will help me survive it. My grandmother is a Tarasova, a wisewoman of the Tarot, who can help me develop my Empress powers: regenerative healing, the ability to control anything that roots or blooms, thorn tornadoes, and poison.

I'll need all of these abilities to challenge the Emperor. But to defeat him, I'll call on an alliance of killers—rogues, witches, knights, and warriors—with nothing left to lose. . . .

1

DAY 382 A.F.

Death kept taking me farther from Jack. I stretched my arms out, fingers splayed toward the heat of that seething pool of lava. "He can't be dead," I sobbed. "Can't. *NO, NO, NOOOO!*"

"You want to follow the mortal?" Aric demanded. "Get your revenge first. The Emperor mocks your pain."

I could hear that fiend in my head—laughing.

The red witch exploded inside me, a force that could *never* be contained. I shrieked, "You will *PAY!*"

As the Emperor laughed, Death murmured in my ear, "I have your grandmother, *sievā*. That was the gift I spoke of. We'll teach you how to kill the Emperor. You'll avenge Deveaux."

"Don't you understand? Jack's not *DEAD!*" I screamed that over and over. "He's alive!"

With my mind teetering on the brink, I spied something in the skies above us. I gaped, disbelieving.

Real? *Un*real? Just before oblivion took me down, a mountain of water curled over our heads, racing toward that hell of flames.

Circe's towering wave. Taller than a skyscraper. —*Terror from the abyss!*—

—*Quake before me!*—

Circe's and Richter's calls boomed in my mind, jolting me back from the blackness.

"Come!" Aric snatched me into his arms and sprinted from the clash. "When they meet, the blast and then the flood . . ."

I stopped fighting him; the need to turn Richter's laughter into screams clawed at me, which meant I had to survive.

Aric gave a sharp whistle; a horse's nickering answered. Thanatos. With me secure in his arms, Aric leapt into the saddle, and spurred the warhorse into a frenzied gallop.

We all but dove down a slope—passing the mangled body of my own dying mount—then charged up the next rise.

I gazed over Aric's shoulder as that tidal wave crested above Richter's lake of lava.

Heaving breaths, Aric kept Thanatos at a breakneck pace. Up another mountain. Down another slope—

Circe struck.

A hiss like a giant beast's. A detonation like a nuclear bomb. The shock wave was so loud my ears bled. As loud as the roar preceding the Flash.

The air grew hotter and hotter. The world rocked as a blast of scalding steam chased us.

BOOM! The force sheared off the top of a mountain behind us. Boulders crashed all around as we careened into yet another valley. Still we rode.

"Surge comes next," Aric grated.

The ground quaked from the weight of an ocean of water. I could hear the flood roaring toward us. *"Aric!"*

He got as far as he dared, as high as he could. "Hold on." Clutching me tight, he dropped from Thanatos, who kept galloping away. Behind the cap of the tallest mountain around, Aric braced for impact. He wedged his metal gauntlet between boulders, wrapping his other arm around me.

Gaze locked on mine, he yelled, *"I'll never let you go!"* We each sucked in a breath.

The searing water hit. The explosive impact ripped me from his chest, but he caught my arm, clenching his fingers above my elbow.

Death's grip. The ungodly force of that flood. My watery scream ...
Aric never did let me go—
My arm ... gave way.
Separated.

DAY 383 A.F. (384?)

How long had I been carried in this furious current?

Days and nights. Nights and days. With no regeneration. One of my shoulders ended in a ragged stump, skin fluttering like fringe. My collarbone was broken, my cheek, my nose. Ribs cracked. Skin scalded.

Rain pounded, the snow a memory. Blinking against the downpour, I zoomed past mountain peaks ... the hulks of old high-rises. ... Barely keeping my head above the surface.

Aric, where are you? Had he lived? Or was he dead like Jack?

No, I refused to believe Aric was gone too. He was the Endless Knight. He was invincible.

Would he believe *I* had died? Probably about to. He would make sure to win this game, enduring endless nights to reunite with me again.

Dizziness. Spinning ... in a whirlpool? A vortex had caught me! *Circe, why are you playing with me?*

Maybe because I'd betrayed and murdered her in past games?

Spinning, spinning ... like the ball in a roulette wheel. The whirlpool was too strong! "J-just f-finish me, Circe!" My stomach lurched. When I heaved, water flooded my mouth, nearly choking me.

Sinking?

Sinking!

My lungs screamed for air. My deadened legs kicked. I sucked in a gasping breath at the surface.

Wails. I squinted. The whirlpool had trapped Bagmen! On the opposite side of the vortex, four of the zombielike creatures spun with me. Their wasted skin glistened, chunks of flesh missing. Their eyes were pale as chalk—and filled with hunger.

The circle tightened. I screamed when their grasping hands missed my face by inches. They snapped their teeth at me, desperate to bite.

To drink my blood.

For so long we'd thought they craved liquid in any form. All this water around them, and what they truly preferred was inside me. *Bloodlust.*

I was prepared to die. *Not* to be transformed into a Bagger.

The whirlpool spun faster, faster. Ever closer to them. Closer . . . One snatched my jacket!

I kicked, breaking its grip. The next rotation would be my last—

We drifted apart, the vortex weakening. How? The current swept us toward a church bell tower, the water dividing around it. Survivors, three men, clung to the tower. The bells rang in the night.

The Baggers went right of the steeple; I shot left, struggling toward it with one arm. *Can't catch hold!* One man held out his hand for me. I screamed as my claws scrabbled across the slate roof.

Adrift. In time, the current quickened again. A mountain loomed. Instead of parting to the sides, the current rushed straight for the center. Would I be bashed against the side?

My eyes widened when I saw the path of the water drop—into a tunnel. I was heading right for it!

Seconds later, I was swept down into that pitch darkness. Total black. *Can't see, can't see!* I kicked to keep my head above the surface. For air—and to hear.

Wails echoed off the tunnel walls. I jerked my head around, unable to pinpoint the sounds. Debris battered me. Things moved against my legs. Were Bagmen below me as well? I whimpered at the thought.

I bumped into something afloat. With a cry, I latched on to it with my remaining arm. I clung, bobbing like a cork. My skin was so numb I couldn't tell what it was.

The blackness lightened to murk, and rain drummed my head again. Out of the tunnel!

I blinked at my raft. Blinked again. A skull-and-bones tattoo? A bloated belly. I was clinging to a headless, limbless body.

"*Ahhh!*" I flailed away, but it seemed to follow me. I kept my eyes on that corpse as it floated alongside me for what might have been days—

I collided with something hard. Metal gouged my skin. I craned my head up: a cell tower! The current trapped me against the structure, pinning my back and arm.

I couldn't move. A pinned insect. The tower groaned in the waves, swaying.

More Bagmen sped toward me. I was completely vulnerable, laid out for a bite. If they turned me into a zombie, would I float forever?

Maybe that was how the game would be won. By an Arcana who would never quite die.

The Baggers thrashed to reach me, pale eyes frenzied. The flood defended me for once, sweeping them away like twigs.

Ah, God, a *house* rushed toward me. Adrenaline flared; I gritted my teeth and somehow twisted my body to face the tower. With one arm, I climbed the service ladder.

I imagined Jack climbing out of that lake of lava unharmed. We would both reach the top. He'd be waiting for me there, offering his strong hand and his heartbreaking smile. *Missed you, bébé.*

Another rung higher. Memories surged like Circe's wave. Agony ripped at my chest as I recalled my last words with Jack. He and I had marveled at the snow. At tiny drifts of falling white.

Another rung. The house bore down on me . . .

It passed the swaying tower within inches. I wouldn't be so lucky next time.

Lucky? I laughed into the wind.

At the gusty top of the tower, I coiled my arm around the ladder and laughed till I sobbed.

Jack is dead.

2

Tess.

My eyes shot open, my shaking arm tightening around a ladder rung. Tess had the power to go back in time!

Jack might be dead. He didn't have to stay that way.

She and I had saved his sight by reversing time; we could save his life! And Selena's. We could save Jack's entire Azey army. I just had to reach Tess.

She, Gabriel, and Joules had been a couple of days out of Fort Arcana. The three would have heard the attack, would've returned.

I had to get back there. How? I didn't know its location—or my own. I believed the fort was in northern Tennessee. Or Kentucky. Ish.

The storm had dwindled, the winds not as fierce, and the water had receded until the depth looked to be no more than a few feet. Which meant I teetered a hundred feet in the air.

From this height, I craned my head around. In the gloomy dimness, I spied rocky foothills to my left. To my right, I could just make out the remains of a town. I could determine my location there.

Energy filled me, my mind sparking with purpose. The stump of my arm finally twitched with regeneration, my scalded skin beginning to heal. My glyphs radiated like a spotlight, a beacon in the black.

With one arm, I started climbing down. Muscles so stiff. Each time I released my grip, I had to lean into the tower to balance my body, then painstakingly place my feet lower down. So slow.

And every moment since that massacre counted. Each second that Tess went back in time drained her of life; she'd nearly died when I'd forced her to go back just eleven or so minutes. With my claws sunk into her arms, she'd withered away to a husk, her hair falling out, her bones jutting.

How much time had passed since the Emperor's attack? I could have been unconscious for hours—or days. How far away had the flood carried me?

Why hadn't Circe killed me? Didn't matter. *Gotta get to Tess.*

I would need so much more from her than minutes. But I could work with her until her power bloomed, until she could withstand the demands of her ability.

What if I got her to reverse time by days, yet we still missed Jack by an instant? We needed to go back long enough to take out the Emperor before he struck. We could get Circe to attack him sooner!

I frowned. I'd heard Richter's evil laughter in my head ... *after* Circe's flood, not just before. How had he survived? If the Priestess couldn't take him out, was Richter invulnerable?

I couldn't worry about that. Not yet. Aric had killed the Emperor in a past game, so he knew Richter's weaknesses. My grandmother would be a wealth of information as well. Because of Aric, she was alive and safe at his castle.

With their help, I could learn how to destroy Richter. For now, I just needed to get to Tess. *On a clock. Tick-tock.* No time to waste descending one rung at a time.

Sucking in a breath, I closed my eyes and let myself pitch backward, free-falling from the tower.

Falling ...

Landing ...

Pain!

Rebar jutted from my side. *Shit, shit! Don't panic. . . .* I forced myself to examine the wound. Wasn't as deep as I'd thought, but I was trapped on the ringed metal. *No time for this!*

I huffed in breaths through gnashed teeth, then pushed with my arm. The bar scored me inside, inch by ragged inch, till I freed myself. I struggled to my feet, reeling for balance. My wobbly legs didn't want to hold me. Each breath was agony.

If I could take one step, it'd be one step closer to Jack.

I took that step. And another. And another, until I was slogging through filthy water toward the town. I wound around debris—and half-submerged Baggers trapped under storm wreckage.

That could've been my fate. How close those Bagmen had come to biting me! No wonder Aric had held on to me so tightly.

Aric, where are you?

No answer to my telepathic call. No Arcana voices at all.

Baggers snapped their teeth at me as I passed. For each one I could see, how many were concealed? Would I step on one? Like a Bagmine?

Focus. In this situation, Jack would keep his cool and work out logistics. Everything depended on me reaching Tess as quickly as possible.

When Aric had abducted me from the Hierophant's mine, I'd believed Jack had died, and I'd decided to live for vengeance. But this time, I would simply refuse to believe he was gone.

I swung my head left and right, searching for any clue about my location. As I trudged, supplies floated past me—food, bottles of water. I never would've passed by these treasures when I was on the road with Jack, but I didn't have my bug-out bag, nothing to stow them in.

I'd lost it when I'd lost my arm.

Jack's training still resonated within me; I needed survival gear. To save him, I had to survive long enough to find Tess. So I snagged a floating tackle box and found a utility knife inside. A good start. I shoved it into my jacket pocket.

Something was already stuffed inside?

I gave a cry. The red ribbon! The ribbon he'd taken from me a lifetime ago, the night before the Flash. The one he'd saved and carried for more than a year. I was supposed to give it back to him when I chose him above all others, when I was ready to make my life with him.

I'd intended to.

Jack was . . . dead.

Not forever.

Something else was in my pocket . . . His letter! I snatched it out. The drenched paper disintegrated in my trembling hand, and I could only watch it. He'd left me this letter, urging me to go with Aric, to live in a place with sunlamps and food and safety.

Because I love you, Jack had written. *This might be the most noble thing I've ever done. Noble, for the record, cuts like a blade to the heart.*

Why had I never told him I loved him? In all the months I'd known him, I'd never said those three words.

I didn't grieve the letter, because I was going to go back in time. It would never have been lost. I shoved the ribbon back into my pocket. One day, I swore to God, I would give it to him. I pushed on with even more determination.

Finally I reached a cluster of brick buildings—the only things left standing here after the firestorm of the Flash. I limped toward the middle of them. In what must have been the town square stood a monument: a man on a horse with trash wrapped around him. Wasn't it always a freaking man on a freaking horse?

By the light of my glyphs, I read the plaque: GREEN HILLS, INDIANA

My heart stopped. My glyphs sputtered. *Indiana.???*

A completely different state from the fort's location. Reaching Tess might take a week—*if* I had transportation, fuel, and directions.

I sagged against the monument, and tears welled.

Crying is a waste of time, Evie!

Tick. Goddamn. Tock.

I wiped my wet sleeve over my face and raised my chin. My plan was still sound. I'd find Tess, and then I wouldn't rest until she could reverse time—by months. By years! Hell, I'd go back to before the Flash and save my mom and Mel!

Step one was getting a vehicle for the journey. Step two: fuel. Step three: directions.

I had a mission. I would be like Lark, with her single-minded focus. I would have strength and fortitude. I imagined myself as a horse with blinders on, seeing only the road before me. Nothing else mattered. I would bury my grief and destroy anything that got in the way of my mission.

Vehicle.

Fuel.

Directions.

Any vehicle near this town would be sunk, stuck, or swept away. I needed to get out of the path of that flood. I needed highlands. I turned toward the foothills.

I ran.

Holding my injured side, I fought the resistance of the water, moving my legs through sheer will.

I ran until I splashed out of the edge of the receding flood. I headed upland toward the line of rocky hills. A road snaked through them. I followed it.

My deadened legs tripped. I lurched forward; only one hand to catch me. I face-planted onto a shelf of stone.

Tick-tock. I scrambled back up. Spat blood. *Blinders on.*

I ran.

3

DAY 389 A.F. ?

"Who let the dogs out? WHO? WHO? WHO?"

Even over the freezing winds and drizzle, I heard a song blaring from over the next rise.

Maybe I'd gone crazy and was having—what had the mental-ward docs called it?—an auditory hallucination. Likely. I hadn't slept in days. Hadn't stopped running.

Get to Tess. Get to Tess. Get to Tess.

Though I was filled with purpose, my glyphs had dimmed, my abilities on the fritz. Regeneration was agonizingly slow—my arm had regrown just a couple inches, and the wound in my side still gaped. My broken bones weren't knitting. Exhaustion threatened to consume me.

But my mind was all-powerful. My mind told my body not to stop, and it obeyed. The ribbon was a talisman that kept me moving.

Aric had said I possessed untapped potential. I drew on anything—everything—I had. I reminded myself that Demeter had scoured the earth looking for her daughter, never resting. My search for Tess would be just as relentless.

I ran toward the music. Music meant people. People meant victims I could rob.

Over the last several days, I'd become one of the bad guys, a black hat, threatening the few survivors I'd encountered (even though all I could manage was the merest show of a vine).

Do you have a map? I would steal it from you.

Food? Hand it over.

I like your backpack. It's mine now.

To keep myself alive for Jack, for Aric—and for Richter—I'd become the monster lurking in the shadows.

As a black hat, I understood so much better how Baggers, cannibals, and militias worked. *Always seek out people; they'll have something you want.*

I had no qualms that I was stranding or starving others. As I told them, "Tick-tock. On a clock. None of this will ever have happened." Because I was going to reverse time.

Thanks to my thievery, I now wore a hooded poncho over my jacket and one of a pair of fingerless gloves. On my back was a bug-out pack with gear: MREs for another couple of days, a knife, glow sticks, and salt for Baggers. . . .

I trudged up that hill, digging with one hand into the muck, fighting against streams of water. Between breaths, I said, "You there, Circe?"

The more I thought about that epic clash, the more I realized the flood had been the unintended aftermath of her attack on the Emperor.

While her tidal wave had vibrated with her presence and hostility, the flood had been violent but . . . lifeless.

Controlling a wave like that couldn't have been easy for her. Hell, I'd nearly poisoned Jack with my powers. Tess had almost died from hers.

Deciding that Circe hadn't been trying to murder me, I'd hailed her in puddles. She could see and hear from any body of water. She would know where Aric was.

She'd never answered. No one did. I hadn't heard a single telepathic Arcana call. Unless I'd been running in circles—possible—I should have covered a lot of ground. Had I not neared any Arcana?

Damn it, we were supposed to converge!

I tried again: *Aric? Tess? Gabriel? Joules?*

Nothing. I was tempted to hail Matthew—but he had *allowed* the massacre.

Yet he'd also taught me about Tess's time traveling: "Sometimes the

World spins in reverse. Sometimes battles do too. The word *carousel* means *little battle*."

Maybe all this was an exercise to enhance Tess's unimaginable power? He might have known all along that I would bring Jack back! Matthew always did things like this.

I called for him. Again, nothing.

As I ran, fears threatened my single-minded focus. Even Aric—the king of the airwaves—hadn't responded to me. What if he'd been injured? What if the Emperor had been able to side-step Circe and advance? Surely I would sense if other Arcana had died.

Focus, Evie. Every second counted. *On a clock.*

I topped the rise and narrowed my gritty eyes. In the valley below me, fog made a blanket. Some distance away, lights dimly shone beneath it. The music came from that direction.

I skidded down the mucky slope to the bottom. At the base, the air felt warmer, almost sultry. I ran.

Deeper into the valley, I made out more details. A mall-size parking lot was situated off a highway, filled with scorched cars. Baggers must be roaming that foggy vehicle maze; wails carried in the night.

I charged into the lot. The mist thickened around me, right when I needed to see. Shit! I should be terrified—in a murky maze, surrounded by Bagmen—but I didn't have time. I put the blinders on.

A structure came into view at last. Bowls of oil fires lit a soaring wall. The music thumped from just beyond.

A coliseum? The Flash-charred arena had withstood the apocalypse! A new song—"Welcome to the Jungle"—boomed from inside, the lyrics clear: *"I wanna watch you bleed. . . ."*

Real? *Un*real? Was I dreaming?

Then I sensed something that made my thorn claws tingle. *Can't be right. Going crazy.* With a hard shake of my head, I ignored it. *Focus, Eves.*

Vehicle.

Fuel.

Directions.

This place was a genius location for a settlement, with a built-in defense—lurking Bagmen. The lot reminded me of the minefield fronting Fort Arcana. Jack's brilliant idea. *Blinders.*

So who lived here?

I slowed. Damn it, I couldn't deny my senses any longer. Somewhere nearby . . . plants grew. A lot of them.

How? Even if the earth hadn't gone fallow, we'd had no sunlight.

I jogged around the coliseum, trying to home in on the plants. This unseen collection must dwarf even Aric's extensive nursery.

Their nearness fueled me, exciting the red witch, that dark, murderous part of me. When my body vine budded from my neck, I yanked back my poncho hood. The vine divided behind me until it flared like an aura.

Or a cobra's head.

A wail came from behind me—the Baggers had caught my scent, trailing me. One was on my heels. As the music blared, I straightened and stiffened a vine—then jabbed the creature through the head.

". . . feel my, my, my serpentine. I wanna hear you scream. . . ."

Another Bagger lunged; I struck again. Putrid slime coated the vine. I let it fall off, growing a new one.

I could see a brighter glow just around the curve of the coliseum; following it, I came upon a line of military trucks. Perfect! I needed the keys to one and as much fuel as I could transport. Which meant I needed the guy in charge of this place trapped in my vines—with my poisonous claws at his throat.

Voices sounded. Ducking between the trucks, I sidled around one and spied two shirtless men guarding an entrance. They carried machine guns and didn't seem at all concerned about the nearby Bagmen roving the fog.

In my weakened condition, a direct attack wasn't wise, but if I "surrendered" . . .

The good thing about being a female A.F.—no one wanted to shoot me unless forced to.

Logistics: I could only raise one hand, so they might think I was reaching for a weapon and fire. A gunshot wouldn't kill me, but it'd draw more guards and Baggers.

I commanded the vines of my cobra's flare to slip down and twine into my empty poncho sleeve, puffing it out. I moved my green arm; looked like the real thing. Perfect.

In past battles, I'd tried to limit the body count. Now I cared only about what actions would be *quickest*. Once I completed my mission, none of this would have happened.

I limped into view, working the damsel-in-distress angle. "P-please help!" I cried, both arms raised—the green one emitting poisonous spores. "Can you help me?"

The two guards swiveled and gawked at me. One said, "A female!" and ran to apprehend me. The other reached for his radio.

Neither completed his action before he dropped.

Pulling my poncho hood back up, I strode past their bodies and approached the entrance. I peeked inside; no one right there, so I slipped in.

Lining a dark corridor were cells filled with what must be two hundred men. Past the cells at the far end of the curving hallway was an open doorway. Light, heat, and music spilled through it.

I could tell I neared those plants! My claws budded and sharpened, and I felt the first real tingle of regeneration.

No one had seen me back here in the dark. All eyes were trained in the other direction on two more shirtless men guarding that doorway.

Whimpers and murmurs rippled from the cells: "What happens now?" "Has anyone escaped?" "What will they do to us?"

Nothing good, I wanted to answer.

Since the Flash, I'd been caged by a militia, shoved into a serial killer's laboratory, dragged down into a cannibal's subterranean pantry, and forced into a house-of-horrors torture chamber.

These prisoners weren't headed for a pleasant destination. Would they be slaughtered like cattle? Or used as target practice as some faction mowed them down?

I sidled closer to the cages. In one, a boy of about nine was crying while an older guy—looked like his granddad—tried to comfort him. But the grandfather was clearly just as wigged out. The kid called him Pops.

I eased over to them, keeping a low profile until I got more intel. "What state are we in?" I asked Pops.

He jolted, maybe because he'd just heard the voice of a rare female; or because I was strolling around *outside* the cages. "Indiana."

Still? Damn it! "Who runs this place?"

Overhearing our hushed exchange, a burly guy with a bandana over his head turned toward me and said, "Solomón, the leader of the Skins."

"Skins?"

Pops said, "Those are Sol's fanatical followers."

Bandana added, "They consider us the Shirts." Shirts and Skins. As in football? *Who makes up this shit?* "Sol's been rounding up survivors all over the state."

"Why? Why put you in cages?"

"Because Sol likes games," Bandana said. "For entertainment. You'll see soon enough."

A guy sitting beside Bandana asked me, "Don't suppose you know how to hotwire electronic cell locks?"

No, but I could slip a tree between two bars, growing it till the metal bent. Maybe I should free these prisoners.

Then I remembered the lesson I'd learned from Jack and Aric: *shackled person* did not mean *good person.*

Besides, these men roaming free presented too many new variables and would slow my mission. In an altered future, I never would have been here anyway.

How to get to Sol most quickly? If I turned myself in, those guards might not hand me over to their leader right away, might even mutiny to keep a female for themselves.

An electronic whirring sounded, and all the cell doors opened. No one was brave enough to be the first to step out, to try an escape.

The two shirtless guards—Skins—started down the corridor, guns at the ready. One of them called, "You men are about to make history!"

In Sol's *games?* If these prisoners were part of his entertainment, then my best hope of access to him might be to join them. I slipped into Pops's cell, blending with the others before the guards passed. The pair ambled to the other end of the corridor.

"Everybody out and start walking," the second guard called. "Any of you still in a cage when we roll through gets shot. Better hightail it out before then." They were driving us toward that entrance?

Men hurried to exit, and I joined them. Playing along—for now—seemed quickest. Still, impatience had me by the throat.

Bandana edged closer to me. "I could look out for you, little girl," he said. "If we live through this."

I frowned at my new suitor. "You're optimistic. And I don't need you to look out for me."

Bandana's friend smirked. "You say that now, but wait till the blood starts flowing."

That was my problem; I *couldn't* wait. The red witch bayed for it.

Pops murmured, "You should announce you're a female. You'll be spared whatever's about to happen to us."

I could *feel* that we were approaching those plants; I had to stifle the urge to run ahead of all these men. "I'll be just fine."

Bandana met his buddy's gaze and twirled his forefinger at his temple. He thought I was crazy? *That's fair.*

"You don't seem scared," Pops said. "Do you know something we don't?"

His grandson stared at me with owl eyes; I winked at him.

Bandana asked, "You packing something under that poncho?"

I had a sleeve filled with vines. If I weren't so impatient—*could these guys be slower?*—I might've laughed. "You could say that."

As we passed more cells, injured men crawled toward the exits. Others desperately dragged the unconscious. From the stadium, Queen's "We Will Rock You" pounded, seeming to mock these prisoners.

Behind us, those two Skins swept up the corridor, making good on their promise. Gunshots boomed in the echoing space; all the Shirts seemed to duck at once.

"*. . . you got mud on your face. Big disgrace. . . .*"

Another shot, and another. Those guards murdered the unconscious, the injured, the slow.

I shuffled along with the herd of prisoners until we emerged onto what had once been a football field. Now a pasture. With *real grass.*

I swept my astonished gaze around the interior of the coliseum. Crops covered the bleachers on three sides, pots filling the rows like terraced gardens. How??? I craned my head up, expecting to see priceless sunlamps, but I spied none. Maybe this settlement kept the lamps under lock and key, only bringing them out when needed.

I'd figure it out later. Once I went back in time, we could sic Jack's Azey army on this place. They'd raid the crops, free any caged white hats, and relieve Sol of his sunlamps.

For now, I had a ready-made arsenal to use against my new adversary.

Along the sideline at midfield was a large stage, decorated with swaths of purple cloth. Purple banners with gold lettering—Latin words?—hung from posts.

The movie Gladiator *called. Wants its props back.*

What had to be a thousand shirtless men occupied seats in the stands flanking that stage. They were drinking and raising hell, singing along to the music. All of them were well-fed and muscular, their skin scarred but uncommonly tan. How many sunlamps did this faction control?

As we marched to the center of the field, the ground grew wet, then wetter still, until my boots squelched. I glanced down: I was ankle-deep . . . in blood.

From the opposite side of the arena, a parade of guards—some with crude weapons in hand—emerged in a line. Like the home team from its locker room.

I blinked in disbelief as they neared. They were . . . Bagmen. *Hundreds* of them.

They filed around the field, surrounding us. Yet they didn't attack, just stood idly at the edges. Why were they not wailing, trying to bite us? Who—or what—was controlling them?

With a terrified yell, one prisoner turned and sprinted back toward the corridor. Two Bagmen took him down with more strength and speed than I'd ever seen in them.

The man screamed as they drank. Their slurping sounds put everyone on edge.

The stadium's loudspeakers crackled, and the song transitioned into "Seven Nation Army."

"*... A seven nation army couldn't hold me back....*" My thoughts exactly.

As the music boomed, a platform ascended from below that stage. Little by little a man in his early twenties became visible, first his head— he had black hair, dark eyes, and a handsome face—and then the bronzed skin of his nearly bare chest. He was tall and built, wearing only a knee-length toga.

Two Baggers flanked him, a male on one side, a female on the other, both well-dressed in normal clothes.

A gasp hissed through my lips when an image flickered over him— an Arcana tableau: a child wrapped in a waving red pennant, surrounded by sunflowers and summer wheat. In the blue sky above, the sun had a face, and it was menacing.

Sol. Sun. I'd found the Sun Card. My lips curled. *I'm gonna serve it to you....*

4

Sol raised a hand, and everyone fell silent, the music fading. "Welcome to Olympus! I am El Sol!" he bellowed. Spanish accent? "In a world of darkness, I bring you light!"

With his sun-kissed followers and crops a-growing, Sol must be able to emit sunlight. So how would that ability affect me? Charge me up or dry me into a husk? I racked my damaged mind to remember. I hadn't heard this card's call. Had he heard mine?

The men in the stands drummed their feet, chanting, *"Victi vincimus."* Whatever.

They quieted when he yelled, "Hail the Glorious Illuminator! Next to me, all is shadow."

The men chanted, "Next to him, all is shadow."

"I am your god!"

Wow. Even Guthrie, the Hierophant Card, had considered himself only a shepherd guiding his flock. El Sol believed he was an actual deity. Considering his toga and his coliseum lair, I'd wager a *Roman* one. Were we to be his sacrifices?

I pinched the bridge of my nose, muttering, "Crazy-ass Arcana." But could I really talk?

Once Tess and I returned from our trip back in time, maybe I'd just shatter into little Evie pieces.

For now, I would be opting out of the sacrificial part of tonight's program. I had a mission. Sol stood between me and my three goals.

Which meant he stood between me and Jack. Sol might as well be murdering him in front of my face.

My claws sharpened. I'd already linked with every plant in this stadium. Would I be strong enough to fight off so many Skins?

The Shirts could be just as dangerous. Word seemed to be spreading among them that I was a female.

Sol continued, "Only worthy gladiators will find a home amid the riches of Olympus! Prepare to battle for your place!"

I had to give it to him: he knew how to put on a show, a real entertainer. In my present mood, this performer was about to break a lot more than his leg.

The would-be gladiators all around grew antsy as they comprehended their plight—a fight for survival. How many died in each contest?

No wonder all those Skins were big and scarred. To earn their spot in the stands, they'd had to emerge alive from a free-for-all.

I might not *have* to take Sol out. But I *wanted* to. What was one more icon?

No, focus! Tick-tock.

Sol waved his hand, and the Bagmen lurched forward. They deposited those crude weapons on the field—pikes, hoes, axes—then returned to the periphery, as if they were being choreographed. The Sun must have control over them, the way I controlled plants! Which made sense—after all, Bagmen had been created by solar radiation during the Flash.

When the sun had shone at night.

Among the Shirts, gazes darted and fists clenched, men readying to fight. When should I strike? Would I have enough spores to knock out a thousand Skins? And what about the Bagmen?

Sol raised his hands, and his body began to . . . glow.

Empower me or burn me up?

All around me the Shirts gasped in shock. Sol's followers lifted their faces and basked as light radiated from his body—stronger and stronger in intensity. It grew so bright, I nearly cried out. I closed my eyes, bracing myself. . . .

When my glyphs shivered, I opened my eyes. Soon those swirling lights on my skin were shining almost as brightly as Sol. The Sun was supercharging me! But no one noticed; they were all too busy staring at him.

I shoved my hood back, and vines flared behind my head, cobralike once more. My claws dripped with poison. My broken bones and wounds were mending faster, faster. The vines in my sleeve made way for my growing arm as flesh built on itself. Already to my elbow!

Deep within me, the red witch stretched and purred.

The bleacher crops stirred in readiness. I could turn this into a bloodbath if I chose. Jack had been one of my last links to humanity, to goodness. Until I recovered him . . . the red witch might slip her leash.

A supercharged Arcana. With zero humanity. And an icon up for grabs. If only taking down the Emperor could be so easy—

I frowned. Richter. What if he wasn't invulnerable after all? Maybe . . . I simply needed a portable solar battery. I could take *Sol* back in time with me on Tess's carousel. But could I control the Sun enough to keep his powers in check? What was the *extent* of his powers?

Sol dimmed his light, then he and his two pet zombies took seats on the stage. Suddenly, a game buzzer sounded.

Yelling men ran for those weapons. Fights broke out. A melee erupted around me. The crude weapons made murder a grisly business. Blood spurted, hacked limbs dropping.

Behind me, Pops's grandson cried hysterically. I tossed a vine toward him and Pops. It branched out in front of them—a shield of green.

Attention back on Sol.

He'd linked his fingers with those Baggers' on either side. Did Sol *care* about those two? If so, I could use that. But first I needed a distraction.

As I'd learned to do in the Lovers' basement, I snatched another vine from my neck and lobbed it in the direction of the Bagmen guards on the periphery. My own grenade; I fueled it from within me. The vine spread, forking out to climb up bodies and spear skulls. Bagmen dropped like dominoes.

Nearby Shirts jerked back from me. Good. I was about to need the room.

I invoked the red witch—and could almost pity my enemies. *I AM the red witch,* some part of me thought. *Evie is a sliver of ME.*

Other Baggers mobilized to locate the threat, shoving through the mass of men.

From my cobra's hood, I straightened the end of a huge vine, another spear. It shot outward, jabbing a Bagger through the eye.

More creatures turned toward me, wailing as they attacked. I speared another one and another. Soon I was using two spears. Three spears. *Ten.* Like a hydra.

I'd never felt more monstrous. Glowing. Vicious. Claws overflowing with poison.

Shirts yelled and dove out of the way, more afraid of me than anything else in this place. Bandana stared at me with revulsion and fear.

I smirked. *But I thought we were gonna date?*

One green spear pierced a Bagman, then caught the two behind him. Dead zombies piled up. The stench almost made me retch.

The red witch craved her carnage, demanding total control. But my mission was too important to give her free rein.

Struggling to focus on what mattered, I sent barbed rose stalks creeping toward the stage. Sol didn't notice as green slithered up his chair and his companions'.

Stalks suddenly coiled around their necks. I used them to lift the two Baggers high into the air.

Sol yelled, "Nooo! Stop!" He clenched the stalk around his throat and pulled, so I tightened all three barbed collars.

The Bagmen on the field ceased their attack. The melee slowed, until everyone was staring at my handiwork.

With a flick of my hand, those terraced plants swelled. The Skins in the bleachers reacted too late; from behind them, a surge of green overran them, my own terrifying wave. The vines snared them, a vast living net. The more the men struggled, the more trapped they became.

A spotlight seemed to shine from Sol's eyes as he swept his gaze over the crowd to identify his attacker.

I stepped into that light and moaned. God, it felt *amazing*.

"Who are you?" he demanded, bleeding fingers curled around his collar. "*What* are you?"

My gore-covered vines cleared bodies out of my way as I strode toward the stage, closer to that delicious sunlight.

Even with all these plants, I'd only been able to regrow half of my arm. Now I raised the stump to his spotlight. My flesh regenerated before our eyes. Even my icons returned.

Gasps and whimpers sounded from all around me.

I flexed my new fingers and claws. Rolled my wrist. With my restored hand, I pointed at Sol. "You're coming with me."

5

"I'm the Empress, and you're my prisoner."

When I continued forward, a different beam shone from Sol's eyes. This one did nothing for me, nor *to* me. But the men closest to me screamed. A few balled up and rocked in the bloody grass. One sank to his knees, battering his fists against his head.

Sunstruck? Had Sol just maddened them? Power number three.

I tightened the Baggers' collars; the pair wailed in the air. "Try anything else on me, and those two will lose their heads."

"Wait!" Sol raised his palms, dimming his gaze. Accent thick, he said, "I've stopped. Just don't hurt them, *por favor!*"

"They'll be safe as long as you do what I say."

His eyes were panicked. "Anything!"

I beckoned him with a crooked finger. Still collared in rose stalk, he descended the stage to the field, his Birkenstocks squelching in the blood and Bagger slime.

When he stood before me, heat radiated from him. He was even taller and more built than I'd thought, so I used another stalk to bind his wrists and tightened the one around his neck. Blood ran down his neck and bronzed chest.

Taking a page from the Lovers' playbook, I told him, "Your collar—and the ones on your two pet zombies—are pressure-loaded. If I die, or go crazy, or lose control in any way, the three collars will snap closed, beheading you."

Brows drawn, Sol asked, "What do you want from me?"

"A truck, with all the gas it can carry. You and your two Baggers will be coming along as my hostages. If we get to my destination safely, I might not kill you."

"Where are you taking us?"

Unfortunately, I had to reveal where I wanted to go; couldn't reach it otherwise. "To a place called Fort Arcana. I want you to ask your men if anyone has ever heard of it."

"*I* have heard of it."

I narrowed my eyes. "Continue."

"From captured Azey soldiers. That's the Army of the Southeast—"

"I know who the Azey are." Jack had been marching them down to Louisiana to establish a settlement around Haven. A refuge.

"These soldiers camped across the river from this fort." He was telling the truth! "We plan to raid it in the future."

Good luck with that. "Where are those men now?"

"Didn't survive."

Shit. "How far is the fort?"

"Two days."

Days! So many minutes! "Do you have a map?"

He shook his head. "But I know the way."

I should probably get him to draw a map anyway, but we didn't have time. Besides, navigating was not my strong suit. "Why should I believe you?"

He shrugged, wincing as thorns dug into his shoulders. "If I don't get you there in two days—barring unforeseen roadblocks—you can kill me."

I rolled my eyes. "Can I? Thanks for the okay." I had a thousand other questions for him, but I could interrogate him on the way.

He gave me a strange look. "Even if I had a map, I like the idea of being useful to you."

"Good. You can drive."

What do you get when you mix two Baggers, a bloodthirsty toga-wearing card, and a half-mad Empress?

Road trip A.F.–style.

I was about to be living one of Finn's jokes....

With Sol's Skins trapped, the Shirts had overrun the crops, Pops and his grandkid among them.

I'd freed a few Skins to supply us for the trip. Oh, if looks could kill . . . I'd dared to threaten their god, and they were pissed. I'd created a rose crown, a skittering halo above my reddened hair, to remind them of my own power.

Then I gave orders.

The only trucks Sol had were the large military ones I'd seen parked outside, so I commanded his followers to fuel one up and pack it with tanks of gas and water. I ordered a couple others to bring me packaged food for my bug-out bag and to find out what day it was.

I'd been rocked by the answer: 389 A.F. I'd lost a week. Add another two days to get to Fort Arcana.

Tick-tock.

Now as we awaited the truck provisioning, I told Sol, "We're heading outside of your safe, warm coliseum. You'll need layers and boots." He was wearing Birks, for fuck's sake. And a *sheet*. A useless wristwatch rounded out his ensemble.

He cast me his first smile. "Concerned for me, *querida*?" I'd bet he could be a charmer when not homicidal.

Same could be said for me. "Your frostbite or hypothermia will slow me down." I pulled the matching fingerless glove from my pack and drew it on. Before I concealed my hand, I noticed him noticing my icons, but he didn't remark on them.

"I'll suffer neither condition," Sol said. "I'm forever warm."

Must be nice. I recalled shuddering atop that antenna tower. "Glass can cut your bare feet."

He glanced down. "They aren't bare."

"With your first step out into the Ash, mud suction will eat those sandals." I surveyed him. "What about jeans? Denim would protect your legs from falls. And I don't know how bonebreak fever spreads, but I wouldn't want to be going commando if we pass a plague colony."

He swallowed and subtly narrowed his stance.

"You must have a bug-out pack you want to bring."

"Bug-out?" Sol blinked at me.

Had Jack felt this much frustration at my cluelessness? "A backpack. With survival gear. To keep you alive."

Unconcerned shrug. "I suppose I could prepare for a more rugged environment. Care to come back to my apartments and dress me?" He gave me a heated look, and I almost laughed.

Barking up the wrong oak. He had no idea how untouchable I was. "Get one of your men to collect some clothes and boots. If he's not back before the gas cans are loaded, you can raid corpses like the rest of us."

He waved a Skin over and gave him the orders. Then he turned to me. "What will you do to my worshippers?"

Really? "They all committed murder—just to walk around without a shirt." Most of them remained under my net.

"You heard them say *victi vincimus?* That's Latin for *conquered, we conquer.* Some of them might have killed in self-defense."

Maybe some were good; maybe some weren't. I answered, "Maybe some can get loose. Maybe some can't." None of this mattered anyway! "We're on a clock."

One of the Skins signaled that the truck was loaded.

I ordered Sol, "Load your pets into the back, then get in."

With a wave of his hand, the two zombies marched up a loading ramp. I gestured to one of the Skins to close it, and Sol and I climbed into the cab of the truck.

He settled behind the wheel. "Now that we're traveling together, shouldn't I know your name?"

"No."

His lips turned down. "My worshipper isn't back with my clothes. After teaching me the error of my ways, you expect me to go without boots and jeans?"

"Not if there's a body nearby when we refuel."

"You can't be comfortable in your own wet, muddy clothes," he pointed out. "I can provide dry jeans and a sweatshirt. A warm pair of socks. What's the rush?"

Get to Tess. Get to Tess. Get to Tess. Eleven minutes on the carousel versus nine days. Thousands and thousands of minutes.

When I had forced Tess to reverse time and she'd narrowly survived, I'd been worried that she would hate me forever. But Joules had told me, "She'll be glad she helped. Lass likes to help."

That sweet girl had been *glad.*

Which meant she would be willing to *work.*

Together, we could do this! But I wouldn't stack the deck against us by adding unnecessary minutes. I told Sol, "That's my business." I used a rose stalk to lash one of his wrists to the wheel, the other to the gearshift.

He sighed. "I'm down with kink, but these bindings are quite painful."

"Oh dear. Are they?" I tightened them. "Go."

Clenching his wide jaw, Sol clumsily ground the truck into gear. Could he suck at driving worse than I did? I'd never even gotten my learner's permit—because I'd been locked up in a mental ward the summer before I turned sixteen.

After the Flash, Jack had driven most of the time.

In a grave tone, Sol said, "All you had to do was ask me to go with you. I would have, without your threats hanging over my head."

"Did you *ask* your prisoners if they wanted to fight for survival? Now *drive.*"

He shrugged and gave the truck some gas. We headed for the highway.

I watched in the side mirror as a shirtless "worshipper" sprinted after us with a duffel bag. He hurled it toward the back of the truck. . . . The bag landed well short.

This just wasn't Sol's day.

6

"Since you refuse to give me your name, what should I call you?" Sol asked. We were climbing higher into the hills, the road getting more treacherous. "O Great Empress? The Blond One? How about the Green Queen?"

I'd been staring out the window in silence, ignoring his attempts at conversation. As I took in one Flash-fried scene after another, I alternated from Evie to full-on Empress—leaf-strewn red hair, rose crown, dripping thorn claws, glowing glyphs—and back. At one point, I'd drummed my claws on the armrest with impatience, absently stabbing holes in it. Poison had collected.

Sol had shuddered in horror.

"Call me Empress."

"We're not on a first-name basis? Fine. You can call me Illuminator."

"Yeah. That will never happen, *Sol.*"

Snow began to drift down. Jack's words rang in my head, his voice over the radio when I'd ridden out to meet him: *"So this is snow. . . ."* A bayou boy, he'd never seen it before.

I'd been delighted by the clean white drifts. After a year of ever-present ash, the white had seemed like a blank slate.

With our voices linked, Jack and I had marveled at the snow.

My chest twisted so hard I almost screamed. *Blinders!* I fully believed that I would get him back. But the mere *idea* that we weren't on the same plane made me crazed.

Sol said, "I still can't believe the Empress is a real girl. For months, I've been hearing all these voices in my head, and then up pops one of them—in the very lovely flesh." He'd been hearing our Arcana calls.

Matthew had told me mine was louder than everyone else's. Apparently, my call had broadcast all the way to Indiana. Yet I'd never heard Sol's.

He imitated my voice, "'Come, touch . . . but you'll pay a price.'" He raked his gaze over me. "Who wouldn't pay it?"

Jack had. He would still be alive if he'd never met me. Or if I'd let him go after my battle against the Hermit Card.

Aric had paid over and over again.

He still hadn't contacted me. Maybe the Arcana switchboard was down once more. After all, I hadn't heard Sol's call from mere feet away. Which would mean I had no mental link to my allies and friends.

And no idea where my enemies were.

Or maybe I just couldn't consider the alternative: that Aric was too injured to respond. It wouldn't matter anyway, because of time travel. Once I went back, I would keep him safe.

God, I could go nuts thinking about this! For days, I'd had zero sleep and little food. I wasn't exactly tracking well. And the Sun's leer wasn't helping. "Are you done, Sol? Just pay attention to where you're going."

He wasn't done. "I saw an image flash over you. You had your arms open, were beckoning me." My Arcana tableau. "Some of the Azey soldiers spoke of supernatural people called Arcana. Even after so many baffling events—and my own powers—I scarcely believed." I hadn't either. "So if the voices are real, then the game must be too. I've heard enough to glean the basics. There are more than a dozen of us, right? And we're all supposed to fight? To take each other's—what are they called?—*icons*."

I could confirm that a hand marking accompanied each kill. Instead, I shrugged. I didn't trust this card whatsoever; keeping him ignorant seemed wise.

"You have icons, right? I thought I saw something on your new hand before you covered it." When I didn't answer, he asked, "Will there be other gods at Fort Arcana?"

Other gods. Ugh. Aric had called me a goddess, but he'd meant it figuratively.

"That makes sense," Sol continued. "This fort of Arcana must shame my humble Olympus."

The fort didn't look like much, but it was strong. Jack had built it with his own two hands. "Fort Arcana was constructed out of anything available by people scrapping for a better life out in the Ash. Not everybody got to stroll into a ready-made stronghold."

In a way, Sol was like the Hermit Card, a worm who slithered from one shell to another.

"Who started the game?" Sol asked. "What happens if you don't wish to fight anyone?" Casting me a significant look, he said, "I'm a lover, *querida*, not a fighter."

"No, you just make *others* fight. For your entertainment."

"I could've drawn you a map to the fort, and then you could have killed me. Why kidnap me? Because I helped you regenerate?"

"I have plans for you." If I was going to use Sol in the past to face the Emperor, would he need to be on Tess's carousel with us? Would more people make it harder for her? Maybe I could go even further back in time, then drive up to Olympus to snag Sol before the clash.

Time-travel conundrums made my head hurt. I'd figure something out. . . .

Sol said, "Plans for me? Like using, then killing me?"

Bingo. But I didn't want him to think his number would soon be up. "Drive faster."

"Again, what's the rush? We must be hurrying to meet other gods."

I was stuck in this cab with a guy who thought he was divine. "Why don't you concentrate on the road?"

"*Sí.* Okay." Two minutes later: "Where are you from? With that drawl, I'm thinking Deep South."

My heart ached to think of my native Louisiana. I tucked my hand into my pocket, touching the red ribbon.

Despite my silence, Sol said, "I'm from Barcelona. I came to the States for college. Do you speak Spanish?" Nope. Cajun French. "You don't talk much, do you?"

Once upon a time, I'd been bubbly and friendly to everyone I'd met. "Maybe I just don't talk much with murderers."

"That's rich, coming from you. I've learned enough about the game to say: takes one to know one, Empress."

"I've killed in self-defense. You forced others to kill for sport. Even children."

"Or perhaps I weeded out my followers based on their actions in that fight. I was well aware of the crying boy. My Bagmen referees wouldn't have allowed the child to be hurt, and anyone who'd targeted him would've been disqualified from Olympus."

"Yet there were no kids in your stands? Don't lie to me again." I tightened the Baggers' collars in the back.

When they wailed, Sol clenched the steering wheel, and sunlight flickered from his face.

Thanks for the top-off. My body vine sprouted from my neck, nuzzling my cheek.

He grimaced at the sight, then said, "I sent children and parents on their way."

I raised my hand to hurt the Baggers some more. I was glad I had *two* zombies to work with. I might have to gank one, just to show Sol I was serious.

"It's true, Empress! *Mierda!* I swear it's true."

Maybe it was. But... "What about those injured prisoners who couldn't get out of their cages fast enough? Your guards shot them in cold blood."

"A mercy," he said firmly. "Anyone injured A.F. is in a literal world of misery. Besides, I'd say eight out of ten of those men have murdered."

I couldn't quite disagree. I'd rarely met decent people out on the road. But that didn't give me an excuse to round them up and play games with them.

Didn't matter anyway. I wasn't going to befriend this card. Sol might be better than the Lovers or Richter, but that bar was as low as Circe's abyss.

"You threaten others so easily," he said, sounding hurt. "Without a thought. Why are you so cruel?"

"Bagmen aren't *others*. They're monsters." My mother would be alive if not for them.

"Not to me. They're my friends."

The Lovers had called their carnates *children*. "Then you're sick."

"And you're not? You're over there necking a slithery vine. For all I know, you could be the most evil of the gods. Maybe I should ally with other Arcana and take you out."

"Maybe."

"I've heard of one who could hand you your ass. Doesn't the Emperor control fire and volcanoes and earthquakes? He should be able to take on some measly plants."

Enough! "The Emperor is a mass murderer! For sport, he annihilated hundreds of men, women, and children—non-Arcana, people who had nothing to do with this game."

"Oh, really? And how do you know that?"

"I watched him do it! I heard Richter laugh as his lava burned them alive."

Right before then . . . *Jack and I had marveled at the snow.*
BLINDERS!

Sol frowned at me. "Why should I believe you?"

"Half a day's ride from Fort Arcana is a valley. You'll be able to tell that he struck." I pinched the bridge of my nose. "Why am I even telling you this? You don't have sympathy for innocent people."

He quietly asked, "How many people are innocent after the Flash?"

I hated that he had a point.

"Empress, from where I'm sitting, you're merely the *diablo* I know."

No, the Devil had been a totally different card.

7

I could hear the howl of the wind even through the bunker-thick walls of the electrical substation where we'd holed up. Jack always loved to stay in these—concrete cubes with steel doors and no windows. Good A.F. shelters.

Gale-force gusts had foiled my need to push ahead. The canvas on the back of the truck caught the winds like a sail; when we skidded on a patch of black ice, we'd nearly headed off a cliff. Guard-rail maintenance was a thing of the past.

Though I was racking up minutes I didn't have to spare, I figured I couldn't help Jack if I was in the bottom of a ravine somewhere.

I'd made a thorn cage inside for the Baggers, keeping them close for leverage. While I'd used flints to start a fire, my vines had dismantled a storage crate for wood. The smoke wisped upward and vanished through some crack or vent overhead. The flames were a reminder of Jack's death, but soon I'd have him back.

I glanced over at Sol on the other side of the fire. He was still sullen because I'd yelled at him. Sure enough, there'd been a fairly new corpse when we'd stopped to refuel. I'd ordered Sol to remove the dead man's boots.

The Sun had put up his nose. "That's disgusting. I'd rather go without."

I remembered when I'd been too freaked out to source sunglasses off a body. Or to retrieve a precious arrow out of a Bagger. How had

Jack put up with me all that time? "You hang out with slimy Bagmen," I'd pointed out, "and you're calling a corpse disgusting? Baggers *are* corpses."

He'd looked at me like I'd insulted his mother.

"Boots, Sol. *Now!*"

He'd refused, launching into a diatribe in Spanish, and things had gone downhill from there. . . .

Now I dug into my bag for a package of freeze-dried soup and a collapsible pot, courtesy of Sol's "worshippers." I'd always depended on easy-to-carry energy bars, but beggars, choosers, blah blah.

When had I eaten last? Couldn't remember.

I dumped the package into the pot, mixing in water from my canteen. After the last week, I'd never take having two hands for granted. I set the pot over the flames, and stirred with an all-purpose utensil.

Sol's stomach growled. "Are you going to share any with your captive?" He gestured to the soup with his bound hands.

"I might have, if my captive had offered to heat this room—and this meal—with his powers."

His lips thinned. "If you're not nicer to me, I'll make sure you get a Bagman bite. Maybe not tonight, or even this week. But someday."

I took the pot off the fire. "Try it, Sol. See where that lands you. I'm sure I'm immune." Well, five percent sure. At his frown, I said, "Poison's my thing." I started to eat, blowing to cool my first spoonful. *Pretty good.*

"Bagmen don't inject poison, venom, or even a pathogen. It's a radiation-based mutation. Like something you'd find in comics."

"I'll just take your word for it. Besides, I regenerate. I can't get sick," I lied. I had no idea how my body would react to a comic-book mutation. I hadn't caught bonebreak fever—but then, I hadn't had the plague injected into my skin via a zombie's mouth.

"One of my worshippers is a scientist," Sol said. "He's been studying Bagmen. Besides, I wouldn't order a bite to turn you—I'd do it just to be a dick."

"Ah. So I should watch my back for them?" I pointed to his caged pets. Silent and motionless, the two stared blankly ahead, gruesome with their creased skin.

"Those particular ones don't bite anyone."

The pot had cooled, so I drank straight from it. "Again, I'll take your word for it." *And your icon, if you don't shut up.*

Once I'd finished about half the soup, I gazed at his seemingly sincere expression. Maybe I shouldn't be trying to shut Sol up when I could be learning about an enemy. "So . . . does it make you tired to shine?" I took one last swig of dinner, then passed the pot to him.

He beamed. "*Sí,* it does." He drank the soup straight down, then swiped his brawny arm over his mouth. "The colder the weather, the harder it becomes. But I'm getting more efficient with practice, so I use less power. Soon I'll be able to light up the entire world, commanding a legion of Bagmen."

Good to have goals, Sol. I wondered if the Sun Card had possessed this kind of control over Baggers in past games, latent within him, but had never discovered his ability. After all, there'd been no zombies to experiment with, no Flash to create them. "How'd you figure out you could direct them?"

"I was attacked on Day Zero." His gaze grew unfocused, and he winced at whatever he was remembering. "I wanted them to stop hurting me, and suddenly they did."

So he was immune to their bites as well. "Why didn't your Bagmen react when you were shining? I thought they feared the sunlight."

"If they're not starving or dried out, the light doesn't seem to bother them too much. In fact, they are drawn to me, seeming to sense me, even ones I'm not controlling." He shrugged. "Unless they're simply attracted to what they fear."

As I'd been with Death? *Aric, where are you?* Silence. I glanced over at the two Baggers. "Can you talk to them in any way?"

"I can command them with my thoughts, see through their eyes, and hear through their ears. I can merge my mind with any Bagman within a certain range."

"You borrow their senses?" As the Lovers had with their carnates, and Lark did with animals.

"Sí." His eyes turned filmy white. "I can see the scorched Statue of Liberty through one Bagger's eyes. Another Bagger just limped down a highway exit for Disney World."

"What else?" Vincent had said his carnates had ranged all over, finding only ash and waste. "What about people?"

"Lots of fighting. Murders. Rapes." Sol's eyes cleared. "If you saw what I do every day, you would not have so much sympathy for the men in those cages."

Probably.

"Each week, my range extends, and I'm able to meld with Bagmen farther away. One day I hope to reach my native Spain." In a softer tone, he said, "Maybe my family survived."

"Would you know if they were . . . turned?"

He nodded. "It's likely they were. So many were transformed."

I thought about those boys in the Lovers' tent, the ones they'd purposely infected. I cringed to remember a half-turned boy crying over a trough of blood, fully aware of what was happening to him. I asked Sol, "What do you feed these two?"

"Blood. There will be a jug of it in the back of the truck. My worshippers would know to pack some."

And where had they gotten the blood? From the fallen men on Olympus's field? "Your pets don't smell as bad as some." Still, I grew red roses on their thorn cage to scent the air.

"The slime is what stinks. It takes a few days after it seeps to rot. I keep their skin clean."

"Why are these particular ones special to you?"

His gaze grew shuttered. "I don't want to talk about it."

"Fine." Switching subjects. "How did you get good soil for crops?"

"We harvested it from caves. If you get deep enough, it's still fertile."

He and his followers had figured out a way to cultivate crops, and they'd discovered the Bagger mutation. If Sol could be believed, then they were doing *some* good.

"We've been growing for about half a year, so no trees yet," he said. "No apples, pears, or oranges."

I'd grown Tess an orange tree to atone for nearly killing her. As if that would make up for the risk I'd forced her to take when she'd unleashed her power. At least my own powers couldn't end me.

Sol asked, "You don't need dirt to grow things, do you?"

I shook my head, figuring that reveal couldn't hurt.

"Do you have any seeds? Maybe apple? I could give you some sun, and we could have apples tonight!" he said, as if it were an apple-pie-in-the-sky dream.

I sliced my thumb with a claw, and started a tree. When it grew to a sprout, I said, "Be my guest."

Excitement lit his gaze—heated brown eyes framed with thick dark lashes. He beamed, sunlight pouring from his chest, arms, and legs.

I went heavy-lidded as the tree shot to the ceiling.

"Dios!"

I directed one of its limbs to him and one to me. We each plucked a shiny red apple. At his first bite, he groaned. "I don't think I'll ever get used to that."

I tasted mine. Not bad. "What did you do before the Flash?"

"I was a history student, and I ran a party promotion service with some partners. We hosted raves in abandoned buildings. Everyone thought we got paid to have fun, but actually a lot of work was involved."

"So you went from raves to bloody free-for-alls?"

He answered with a Russell Crowe *Gladiator* impression: "Are you not *entertained*???"

"You *didn't* just do that."

He shrugged.

"Why'd you go Roman?"

His eyes lit up again. I'd compared Aric's starry gaze to a sunrise, but Sol's blazing eyes were like high noon at the equator. His irises went from dark brown to backlit caramel. "I learned from my job: presentation is everything. And talk about a culture that understood presentation! The Romans had emblems, symbols, elaborate uniforms, pageants. They were ruthless, but had codes of honor. They adored warriors and contests. And they worshipped me."

Ugh! "FYI, you are not a sun god. We were enabled by gods, but we are not divine."

"Speak for yourself, *querida.*" He flashed me his seductive smile. "Kiss my lips, then tell me I'm not divine."

If I hadn't seen him hosting a death match, I would've found him charming. He was as playful as Finn, but also possessed a simmering charisma.

"In Roman times, one fighter with a sword could change the world," he said, his excitement making him seem younger.

"How old are you?" I found myself asking.

"Twenty-three. You must be"—he took his time checking me out—"twenty?"

"Seventeen."

His lips parted. "I've been lusting after a girl that young?"

I rolled my eyes. The effect was ruined by a yawn. The soup had warmed me, making me drowsy. Plus I hadn't slept in days.

"You look wiped out. Understandable, since you are a child, *pequeña.*"

"What does that mean?"

"Little one. You should get some sleep."

"With a hostage nearby? An evil hostage?" Not unless he was contained.

"Evil? I'm *layered.*" He grew serious. "Empress, what can I do to convince you that I'm not all bad? What will make you trust me?"

"Even if you're *half* bad, I still wouldn't trust you."

He was an Arcana. He might be targeting me for betrayal, the way Lark had. He might know more about the game than he was letting on, as Selena had done.

Hadn't I heard music drifting from Olympus right when I'd been on the jagged edge? It had drawn me straight to Sol's lair. *Beware the lures.*

With a wave of my hand, I stretched the Baggers' thorn cage over him as well, then released his wrists—keeping the collar in place.

How ironic that Sol wanted me to trust him—just as I'd wished Aric and Circe would trust me. But then, I'd once been as evil as they came.

I might not trust Sol. Or want to be his friend. But I couldn't *judge* him.

He tested his cage. "Red roses, *pequeña*? Only yellow ones are fit for a sun god."

The nerve of this guy. I glowered at him, just as irritated at myself. I'd had the briefest impulse to turn the red to yellow.

8

I shot upright with a scream, tears streaming down my face.

"Empress!" Sol was ripping at his cage, trying to get to me. "You're having a nightmare! Wake up, *pequeña!*" His skin glowed from emotion, and his hands were bloody from my thorns.

My gaze darted as I slowly recalled real life. *Substation. Sol as my prisoner. On our way to Fort Arcana.*

I buried my face in my hands when my tears kept coming. I'd stifled my grief so much, I should have expected it to bubble up as I slept.

In my nightmare, Jack had told me, "Why didn't you let me go? I'd still be alive. I asked you to set me free." Then he burned from the inside, lava pouring from his body.

His bellow of pain still rang in my ears. Followed by the Emperor's laugh. . . .

"What was your nightmare about?" Sol's skin dimmed, but my thorns had grown from his blaze of light.

"Th-the Emperor's massacre," I murmured. "Richter . . ."

"You fear another attack?"

"You would too. You should." Some detail was nagging me about Richter's escape from Circe. That night, had I heard a . . . helicopter? "Olympus isn't out of his range." Was anyplace?

"You screamed a name. Who's Jack?"

My tears came faster.

"Was he family?" Sol's brows drew together. "Or did the Emperor kill the man you love?"

I ran my sleeve over my eyes. "Richter killed him, and a loyal friend of mine, and an entire army." I freed Sol from his cage, mainly to have something to do.

He swiped his hands down his toga, the blood stark on the material. He'd hurt himself trying to help me. After tossing wood on the embers of the fire, he sat on the other side. "What happened to Jack?"

Unguarded, I found myself saying, "I was riding to meet him, to go away with him, starting a future together." *A blank slate.* "We were talking on a two-way radio . . . he told me he was going to marry me . . . and we talked about the snow."

"And then?"

"I-I was just about to tell him I loved him, was wondering why I had never said those three words, when I heard three other ones: 'Quake before me.' The Emperor's call. In seconds, the entire valley was a lake of lava. All those people, dead instantly."

Sol's lips parted. "Why would he attack so many?"

"Richter enjoys killing. He gets off on using his power to destroy. I'd been warned about him. No one is safe while he lives."

"But aren't we all supposed to kill each other?"

"Some of us have been fighting not to," I said. "We've made an alliance."

Sol seemed to consider this, then he said, "You must miss Jack very much."

"Every second." And each second took him farther out of my reach. Damn it, the winds still howled outside. Desperate for a change of subject, I said, "What about you? Have you been in love?"

"*Sí.* Before the apocalypse."

My hand shook as I raised my canteen for a drink. "Did your girlfriend die in the Flash?"

He cast me a playful grin. "You assume I was with a girl?"

Given the way he'd been flirting with me . . . yeah. "Did you lose your boyfriend, then?"

"I had both."

"You loved two people?" I handed him the canteen.

He took it, drinking deep. "Desperately."

God, I could relate. Sol and I now had something in common outside of the game. He'd probably just ensured I could never kill him.

"Bea, Joe, and I were committed." He squared his shoulders proudly. "Everyone doubted we could make a go of our trio, but we'd been together for two years."

I'd never met anyone who'd been in a relationship like this.

He tilted his head at me. "Will you judge me? Us?"

A bitter laugh spilled from my lips. "Are you joking?"

"Good, *pequeña*," he said. "Do you believe a heart can be big enough to love two?"

"I know for a fact that it can." The Lovers—for all their disgusting faults—could detect what was in a person's heart. Mine was divided evenly. "I'm in love with two." Jack was foremost in my mind right now, of course. I was crazed to bring him back because I'd *seen* him die. But I was plagued with worry about Aric too. Though his armor weighed so little, it would have to hinder him in the water. *What if*—

I shut down that thought. Going back in time would protect him as well.

Sol frowned, as if I might be pulling his leg. "Truly?"

I nodded. "Jack and Aric."

"So now you will be with Aric?"

"It's complicated." One of my favorite non-answers.

"*Sí*, it can be." He gazed into the fire. "I loved them so much."

"What were they like?"

Raising his face, he said, "Beatrice was this warm, affectionate angel with a backbone of steel. She volunteered at the hospital each Monday, reading to kids with cancer. She was brave and helped them be brave—but she would bury her face against my chest during scary movies." His eyes watered. He didn't seem to realize he was rubbing his chest, as if he could still feel her. "Joe was an ex-linebacker, law student. He planned to be a big-shot lawyer—but he couldn't knot his tie. I had to do it for him.

I'd bought engagement rings for them. Would have married them both."
Gazing past me, he said, "But then, on our anniversary, I got them . . . hurt."

Chills tripped up my back. "I don't understand."

"It happened on Day Zero. The three of us, business partners as well, were in a basement, setting up for a rave. I needed more supplies. Instead of getting them from the van myself, I asked Bea and Joe to go." His expression was stark. "I sent them outside of a perfect shelter—just in time to see the Flash."

My head whipped around to the Bagger cage. Oh, dear God, those creatures were his girlfriend and boyfriend. Joe, the law student, and Bea, the hospital volunteer. They stared at nothing, cracked lips moving soundlessly.

I'd threatened them. No wonder Sol had freaked out. In his mind, *I* was the monster.

For so long I'd been fighting Bagmen or running from them. I'd hated them for causing my mom's injury. But I'd rarely stopped to think that they'd once been people.

Maybe Sol wasn't evil. Yes, he delighted in blood-sport contests. But if I lost Jack *and* Aric, I would do far, far worse.

Sol's troubled gaze rested on Bea and Joe. "While I was alone down in the basement, I got sick, felt like I was spinning, and passed out for what must have been hours. I woke just as they were finding their way back inside. They attacked me, holding me down to drink."

I couldn't imagine how horrific that must have been. To see loved ones turned?

"Understand me: I would have *died* before I hurt them. I resisted, but I couldn't hit them. Then, as I told you, they obeyed me." He paused to clear his throat. "When more Bagmen descended into the basement, I began to suspect that the Flash had created countless legions like them. We emerged, and I saw all the world was broken."

I recalled my first look around after the apocalypse. If I hadn't had my mother with me . . .

Had Sol been all alone? I glanced at the Baggers again. No—not in his mind.

"Empress," Sol murmured, his brows drawn. "Do you think Bea and Joe could ever turn back?"

Never. Their bodies were too damaged, their minds gone. But I said, "Maybe none of this is permanent, Sol. Maybe they'll come back when the earth does. I wouldn't bet against anything right now."

He narrowed his eyes at me, all light extinguished. "You don't believe that. But you were kind enough to play along. . . ."

9

DAY 391 A.F.

Sol and I stopped at a fork in the road. One way was unpaved and rocky. The other was a highway, cleared of wrecks, but with litter all along the shoulders.

As if a large army had marched that route, pitching trash on the way.

"The area's starting to look familiar," I said. We were at the fork between the treacherous slaver route—the one Jack, Aric, and I had taken to the Lovers' hideout—and the Azey army's highway. "I think I know where we are."

Sol exhaled a relieved breath. "Ah, *gracias a Dios.*"

I frowned at him. "What?"

"Past that last interstate, I had no clue where I was going."

"You lied." I lowered my voice menacingly. "*You shouldn't make me angry, Sun.*"

"*Why are you whispering?*" he whispered. "One second you're crying, the next you're scary. Then you're really sexy. Then you're sexy/scary."

"You lied *to me.*"

"I didn't want you to kill me!"

I twirled my thorn claws at him. "Why shouldn't I now?"

"Because I make you stronger." Expression growing troubled, he said, "I wonder if someone like you *should* be stronger."

I lowered my hand. "Just head down the highway. Follow the trash. And don't lie to me again." The only reason I wanted more strength was so I could eviscerate the Emperor while he was still alive. I imagined using my claws on him, slicing him to ribbons. Or should I choke him in vine? Flay him with my thorn tornado—

"How much farther do you think it is?" Sol asked, dragging me from my daydream.

I shrugged. "We could be there late tonight or tomorrow."

"What will happen to me once we get to the fort? Will the other gods hurt Joe and Bea?"

"We're not . . . forget it." I let it go. "To answer your question, I won't let anyone hurt them—or you. If you behave."

"We will behave. I swear to myself."

"Swear to yourself? You. Are. Not. A. God."

He waved that away. "Tell me about your alliance. How do you expect to defeat someone like the Emperor? Can't he simply bomb your hideaway? Attack with his lava?"

Bingo. "We have advantages that I won't tell you about. And strength in numbers."

"Which Arcana are in your alliance?"

Most. Was Circe? Every time I passed a body of water, memories arose of our past. The more I remembered of her, the more I missed her friendship.

I told Sol, "I won't talk to you about strategy or strengths and weaknesses. Even if I trusted you were on my side—which I don't—you could get abducted. Richter could force you to talk."

"Empress, *you* are forcing me to get involved in this game. I don't want to fight. Especially not against a man who is as strong as a volcano."

"I don't want to fight either. I want revenge against the Emperor, but after that . . ."

After that, *what*? I had a connection to almost all the players left. But Aric had warned me that the game wouldn't be denied, calling it "a hell we've all been damned into." I hadn't believed him until Richter had entered the arena—with Jack caught in the crossfire.

With that in mind, my plan to run off to Louisiana had been ridiculously naïve.

After I brought Jack back, and we'd destroyed Richter, what would we do?

"You should come live with me at Olympus." Sol slid me a seductive look. "You could be my goddess queen. Together, we'd build the largest settlement on earth! With your crops and my sun, we'd feed thousands. Between your thorns and my Bagmen, we'd maintain order."

Order. Jack had wanted the same thing. I absently said, "That is something to think about. Well, except for the goddess queen part."

"Don't knock that part, *pequeña*. It's my favorite detail about our future. We would do our duty and repopulate the world. Because we are givers. I, myself, would be *devoted* to giving."

I quirked a brow at him. "No kids for me. Would you really bring children into a world like this?"

Eyes alight with playfulness, he said, "No. It was just an excuse to get in your pants."

"Ugh. Behave. Or you'll get a vine where the sun don't shine."

His jaw slackened; then he started laughing. Belly-laughing.

Despite everything, I felt my lips twitch. If he weren't a homicidal god-wannabe, and I didn't have a murderous red witch inside me, we might've been friends.

When his laughter died down, he said, "Back in the day, we would've made a great reality TV show. *The Sol and Empress Show*."

"The shit show," I muttered. The way I felt right now, *I* would've gotten top billing.

DAY 392 A.F.

"Drive faster!" I told Sol, all but bouncing in the truck seat. From the bridge, I'd spied Fort Arcana's outline up on the windy bluff.

I was concerned about the lack of lights, but maybe they were conserving after the massacre. Or they'd gone dark for cover.

Being this near the fort made me feel closer to Jack. Excitement welled inside me as I ran my fingers over the ribbon in my pocket.

When Sol got his first good look at the fort, his lips thinned with disgust. "*Pedazo de mierda.* What is this piece-of-shit place?"

I had my hand wrapped around his neck so fast, my claws dripping. "This is a place where people dreamed of having a better life. While you were holed up in your coliseum stronghold, others were out in the Ash fighting and scrapping for everything they got."

"I-I'm sorry, Empress."

I released him with a glare. "You're like the Hermit Card—you crawled into a ready-made shell. It cost you *nothing.*" Choking back my fury, I commanded, "Drive around that stretch of dirt."

At the edge of the minefield, a rutted trail meandered this way and that. Tire tracks. As if from a mass retreat. "Follow those ruts. *Carefully.* There are mines everywhere."

He swallowed, and drove along the trail. As the truck closed in on the fort's outer wall, we passed chunks of some charred animal. A huge one with frizzy black fur. "Oh, my God." Cyclops. Or half of him.

"What was that?" Sol's eyes went wide. "A giant dog?"

I muttered, "Something like that."

Tracks and furrows led away from the legs and tail, as if the wolf had dragged itself from its severed hindquarters. Why was his pelt riddled with bullet holes?

Who would've shot him?

Though a favorite of mine, he'd remained here to help Finn reunite with Lark once the Magician had healed enough to make the journey.

I reminded myself that the wolf couldn't die. Not as long as Lark lived. Cyclops could be holed up in the neighboring rock forest, regenerating. He might even pick up my scent, and then Lark would know I'd survived.

I told Sol, "Drive up to the entrance and park."

As we neared the gates, I replayed my memory of Jack riding through them with his chin up, his bearing proud. All the army soldiers had respected the legendary *Hunter*, as he'd been known. They'd made him their general. So many of those men had died.

Not permanently. *Not if I can help it.*

Sol had just turned off the ignition when the gates swung open, wind battering them against the wall. No one manned them. The metal groaned like a Bagman's wail.

"Come with me," I said, climbing from the cab. When Sol joined me on the ground, I stretched the stalks circling his wrists to bind his ankles as well.

"Is this really necessary, *pequeña*?"

"Really is, Sol." As I approached the wall, I cried, "Hello! Is someone here? Please answer me!" *Aric! Finn! Tess!*

I half expected to find Aric waiting here for me. Would I hear his horse nickering in the stable? Had Thanatos survived the flood?

Had Aric?

Of course, he would have. *So where is he?*

Inside, I swept my gaze around and found a ghost town. No fires, no animals, no voices. Just the blustery winds and desolation.

This place was a shell. Fort Arcana had . . . died.

Crates of supplies had been abandoned. The fort's inhabitants must've thought the Emperor would continue his path of hell straight for them.

Maybe some Azey South survivors were camped across the river? I hopped onto a plankway and ran to the tower. Sol hobbled after me, but I couldn't wait for him.

I climbed the stairs, then peeked from the lookout, hoping to spy a campfire, any sign of life.

Nothing.

I turned back to the fort. In one corner, I saw the orange tree I'd grown for Tess. Without sun, its leaves had already begun to brown.

Beside the tree was a mound of dirt. Was that a . . . grave? Whose? A horrible idea arose—no. *No.* I quashed it as I raced down the stairs and lurched past Sol.

I tripped over another plankway, blundering around empty animal pens. I passed Jack's tent and imagined I heard his deep voice saying, *"Ma fille aux yeux bleus."* My blue-eyed girl.

Heart in my throat, I slowed when the mound came into sight. The ground was trampled as if someone had been buried in a hurry. A single staff jutted from the dirt to mark the grave.

Tess's staff.

A cry slipped from my lips. No, no, that didn't mean Tess was buried here! Her death was my nightmare scenario: the one that couldn't possibly be.

The one in which Jack had been burned alive by a monster—and I could do nothing to save him.

Someone had just wanted to mark a burial, and her staff had been handy. She had left it behind on occasion. Only one way to be sure.

Sol had hobbled closer. Uncaring of his gaze on me, I knelt and started digging, stabbing my claws through the icy soil in a frenzy.

One foot down; two feet down. Three. Four.

I reached cloth and pulled on it. More dirt gave way to reveal . . .

A husk wrapped in a sheet.

Choking back bile, I peeled away the material and found what had once been a sweet girl named Tess.

Her body was like this fort—a shell of her former self. Without life inside.

My nightmare. One look at her wasted body, and I knew how she'd died. She had *already* tried to reverse time. To save Jack, Selena, and the army . . .

Tess had tried so hard that she'd lost control of her incomprehensible powers. *Lass likes to help.* She'd killed herself to bring others back. And she'd still failed.

Jack is dead.

I cradled what was left of Tess in my arms and mindlessly rocked her body like a doll.

From a distance, Sol watched grief destroy me.

10

I was covered in mud and out of breath, my muscles knotted. But I neared the top of that peak.

The one I'd stood upon while witnessing a massacre.

When I'd last journeyed to this vantage I'd been filled with hope, riding a hard-working mare that I'd never even named. Her remains must've been washed away in the flood.

What would I find atop the peak now? Having no idea, I trudged upward.

I'd remembered more of the Emperor's attack, and every detail confirmed that Jack had died. But I'd also told him I would never underestimate him again. Maybe I could find some clue, some hint that there'd been survivors.

At the very least, I had to see for myself his ... final resting place.

And so I gritted my teeth and climbed. Circe's flood had gouged this slope, making it much steeper.

What will I find at the top?

I'd told Sol to wait in the truck. Had I tied him down? I was so numb with grief that I couldn't remember.

As I searched for a handhold, I recalled the vision Matthew had given me before he'd disappeared. He'd shown me ten swords in my back—like the ten of swords Tarot card—vowing that the darkest days were ahead. He'd told me, "Matthew knows best."

On the way back from the Lovers' lair, I'd asked Selena what she made of his message. Her brusque answer: "That he's a freaking nutjob?" At my disapproving expression, she'd added, "I know that the ten of swords card means that somebody's about to be crushed by a merciless power—with no warning. I mean, *totaled*. It's supposed to represent rock bottom, when you can't sink any lower." Her dark eyes had grown serious. "Doesn't sound good, Evie."

Matthew had been preparing me for Jack's death. Or trying to.

The Fool had no idea. There was *no* preparing to have one's heart destroyed. Those ten swords had stabbed me through, piercing it.

He'd asked me what I would sacrifice. I hadn't been able to answer then, but I could now.

Not Jack.

I pulled myself higher. *What will I find at the top of this rise?*

The Fool had also begged me never to hate him. I would give him as much mercy as he'd shown me. He could have prevented Jack's and Selena's deaths, the entire army's.

All of those people had set off, filled with hope about a place called Acadiana. Jack would've made good on his promise of a refuge.

Matthew knows best? He'd ridden away like a coward before the Emperor attacked, telling Finn one last cryptic statement: *I've made peace with it.*

With letting my Jack die.

I blamed Matthew as much as Richter. One of those ten swords had been the Fool's. *He* had stabbed me in the back.

What will I find at the top . . . ?

I blamed myself as well. It should have been me. *I* had been fated to die.

At the very least, if I had listened to Circe's advice—leaving Selena in the hands of the Lovers—Jack and all those people might've been spared. Selena had died anyway.

I'd made those choices—I'd pretended to be a leader—so those deaths were on my head. Tess's was as well.

Last night, after I'd reburied her body, I'd run down to the shore outside the fort, where Circe and I had once talked. I'd yelled to the river, "I know you're here, Circe! Show yourself!" Nothing. "Have you seen Aric?"

She hadn't given me even a ripple on the surface. "You were right about taking out the Emperor!"

When she'd still refused to answer me, I'd waded into the river and kicked the water to provoke her. "Damn you! Why won't you appear?"

Silence. Even as my tears had spilled into her domain....

Finally, I reached the top. Gasping for breath, I levered myself up on my feet—and stared in shock.

The peak was no longer a peak. Circe's tidal wave must have flash-cooled Richter's lava because a sea of smooth black stone stretched from the top of this mountain to a distant one, across what used to be a valley. The drizzle made the surface shine.

"Mark this image," Aric had told me as he'd pointed to the cauldron of bubbling lava. "*Where* will you search for him?"

A sob burst from my chest. I'd watched Jack's murder.

No, I refused this! There must've been a way for him to escape. I fought to clear my dazed mind, to recall what I'd seen before the attack.

The long line of the army's caravan had inched across that valley, a glowworm in the dark. Cars and trucks had sprawled for about a mile, a fraction of the valley's length. Jack and Selena would have been riding at the forefront, but had turned back toward me when I'd radioed.

Jack and I had marveled at the snow. At tiny drifts of white. He'd marveled that I'd chosen him.

He and Selena might have ridden a mile or two at most before Richter had struck. Lava had buried the line of trucks from front to back—as well as this entire valley and several rises all around.

Even if Jack and Selena had covered ten miles, they still would've been in the middle.

Selena, the girl who'd just endured the Lovers' hell, had died. Part of me had *sensed* that kill. Other Arcana had as well, and Matthew, in his own way, had confirmed it.

She'd had superhuman speed, agility, and senses, yet she'd perished. And she'd been right beside Jack.

He's dead.

No one could have survived this.

That battle had left behind a vast gravestone. Buried beneath it were hundreds of victims. My Jack was buried there.

Why had I made the decision not to fight in this game? Maybe the game was punishing me for daring to challenge it. Or the gods were.

By trying to reverse time and bring back Jack, I'd challenged fate as well. And I'd failed.

Did that mean I *always* would? Could a fate ever be changed?

In a daze, I trudged across the stone. Roughly halfway across, I stopped. Here the wind blew even harder, the rain stinging.

With a sob, I dropped to my knees to mark Jack's and Selena's graves. How could I sum up their lives in a few short lines? They'd been so much more.

Flaring my claws, I began to engrave the rock, starting with Selena.

Then ... Jack. Sweating, bleeding, hyperventilating, I carved. Time passed. Who knew how long? Night rolled over into more night.

When I finished, I'd worn my bloody fingertips to the bone, and insanity beckoned as seductively as a blossom. I collapsed onto my back and lay between the two memorials, dripping blood on them.

I grew friendship ivy for Selena.

And honeysuckle for Jack.

I wondered if grief could be so strong it was fatal. My heart hurt so badly it must be bleeding out inside my chest. *I* must be bleeding to death. *Ten swords pierced me through.*

But something else was competing with my heartache, a thread of fury.

After Jack and I had watched the smoke plume from my mother's funeral pyre, he'd told me, "She died in grace. I only hope to go out so clean."

He hadn't. Because of the Emperor. Richter had laughed as he'd murdered Jack and all those people.

Richter would die. The red witch would annihilate him. Hatred made me rise. Hatred forced one foot in front of the other as I staggered away from the graves.

With each step, blood dripped from my ragged fingers, dotting a trail across the vast black gravestone. A tether from me to Jack.

As I neared the edge of the stone, I remembered those last moments with Aric, my new arm aching. What if he hadn't survived that searing flood? Maybe he wasn't invincible.

No! No Arcana had gloated over Death's death; none of us had sensed it.

Then I frowned. We were all disconnected now. And I didn't know *when* the switchboard had gone down.

What if he'd ... drowned? He might've called for me as he'd died. His lifeless body could be washed up somewhere along the flood's path. Maybe *that* was why Circe's river wouldn't answer me.

I'd assumed Jack's death was the worst that I could endure. Matthew might have been preparing me for *both* of their murders.

Dear God. Both.

I shrieked with fury and pain. As I screamed and screamed, rose stalks burst from my trail of blood, spreading until they'd blanketed the gravestone and the surrounding mountains.

If Aric lived, I had to find him. But how, when I was dying from grief?

I pictured a tourniquet around my pierced heart, stopping the bleeding and keeping me alive long enough to reach Aric and then to get revenge. Yes, I would twist the tourniquet, tightening it to constrict my heart, starving it of blood. Strangling it.

A bloodless heart couldn't *feel*.

Twist, tighten, constrict.

Numbness settled over me. My emotions shut down. Like this, I reasoned that Aric must still live. He had for so long. He was strong.

We might have simply missed each other over all this distance. The flood waters had parted often; he could have been carried in a different direction. I seized on that thinking.

Yes. This was what I needed. Numbness. Just until I'd completed my two missions:

Find Aric.

Annihilate Richter.

After that, I would release the tourniquet and let myself bleed out.

Jack and I had marveled at the snow.

THE FOOL
WHEREABOUTS UNKNOWN

My eyes flashed open.

The Empress's screams had awakened the dark in me. *Reverse, perverse.*

The Dark Calling.

Her smile was broken. It was time. *I always know best.*

12

THE EMPRESS

Sol sat at the edge of the black stone. As I closed in on him, I tilted my head. "You followed me. You were watching me." *The Sun's icon would look so good on my hand.*

He stood, his gaze bouncing from my eyes, to my reddened hair, to my bloody fingers. "You, uh, get everything taken care of?" He backed up a step. And another.

I advanced. "You should have escaped me while you could."

"I considered it," Sol said, as I struggled not to slice him. "But I'm trying to earn your trust."

The red witch ached for a kill. Until the Emperor's turn, this card would do. "By spying on me?"

He stumbled backward, nearly falling. "What did you carve?"

"Epitaphs. Have you ever written one? Ever summed up someone's life in a few lines?"

"No, I haven't."

"I'm going to pay the Emperor back for these murders." Aric and my grandmother would teach me Richter's weaknesses, and I would figure out how to use Sol as well. Which meant I didn't get to kill him.

Seething with displeasure, the red witch receded.

I had to get the Sun to Death. Maybe with this card strengthening me—and the help of every player in our alliance—we could take out Richter.

But then, our small alliance had recently dwindled by two Arcana.

The game seemed to be speeding up, building on itself. Right around the deaths of Tess and Selena, I'd met the Sun.

Were we spinning to an end?

How stupid I'd been to think I could avoid fighting—that Jack and I could live happily ever after. The Arcana did converge; I'd face them for the rest of my life. Unless they all died.

That doesn't mean I have to take them out, I thought, even as my claws tingled for Sol's vulnerable flesh.

"What will you do to the Emperor?" he asked.

"Vines will grow through Richter's body like veins, oh-so-slowly flaying him. Roots will burrow and feed on his organs. When he begs me to kill him, I'll force him to pick his next meal: thorns or pieces of himself."

Sol coughed. "Remind me not to get on your bad side."

"You and I are going on another little trip." Logically, getting to Aric's castle made the most sense. Then Lark could help me find him. I didn't exactly know the location of his home, but I'd made the journey from there to Fort Arcana not long ago. Matthew had given me directions; I would simply reverse them.

"Where are we off to now?" Sol said.

I smiled evilly. "Right to Death's door."

DAY 396 A.F.

"Are you sure you know where you're going?" Sol asked for the third time this hour.

I ignored him and kept walking.

Two days ago, the truck had died, probably due to Sol's driving. I didn't miss the ride too much though. The roads had gotten so bad that we'd bottomed-out every other mile. Each time, Sol and I had freed it with the help of my vines and his Baggers.

Pushing the truck shoulder to shoulder with zombies had been bizarre.

We'd been forced to continue on foot, trudging through mountainous terrain. Sol had found some clothes and boots at Fort Arcana, so he wasn't slowing me down. He, Bea, and Joe had restocked our food and water from the supplies there, while I had . . .

I frowned. Huh. I didn't remember what I'd been doing.

Now Sol asked, "*Pequeña*, can we stop for a moment?"

I kept walking.

Ever since the gravestone, he'd tried to be nice. He'd said consoling things. We'd politely shared food and water as we'd traveled the Ash together.

But I had nothing left. Bea and Joe showed more liveliness than I did.

Whatever burgeoning friendship—or at least understanding—between me and the Sun had disappeared.

Jack had been one of my last links to humanity. Without him, I *was* cruel.

Without Jack. I was already thinking about him in past tense. I might have sobbed, but my tourniquet was holding fast. Yet my mind suffered, making odd connections.

The whirlpool I'd been trapped in just days ago, spinning like a roulette wheel . . . *roulette* meant *little wheel* . . .

Tess reversing time as though on a backward-spinning carousel . . . *carousel* meant *little battle* . . .

Tourniquet came from the French word *tourner*, to turn or rotate . . .

Everything was turning; *I* was turning. I'd entered Fort Arcana one way; after finding Tess, I was changed forever. I no longer believed with certainty that I was in charge of my own destiny.

In the middle of a clearing, Sol stopped. "Empress, you're lost."

I faced him. "I'm *not* lost." I was completely lost. I never thought I'd miss the voices. I still hadn't heard any. I was relying on my own sense of direction—which sucked.

Even if I could navigate using the sun or stars, neither were visible. Dawn never came, and clouds concealed the night sky. Endless nights.

Now that I assumed Aric was alive, I'd started hailing every puddle for Circe, hoping she would help me, but she never did. I'd imagined I heard her whispers from every raindrop—until I thought I'd go crazy. Eventually, I would.

I just needed to hold off until I'd completed my missions.

Find Aric.

Annihilate Richter.

Sol rolled his head on his neck. "Please tell me where we're going. *Por favor.*"

"I told you. I'm taking you to Death." Would Aric be immune to the Sun's powers? Would his armor protect him?

"What will he do to me?"

"Unless he knows something about you that I don't, he'll keep you cuffed, your movements limited." Aric had once kept me prisoner; I knew the drill. "I'll ask that your Baggers be put somewhere safe." Inside the castle's huge menagerie, Lark's animals now roamed free, their enclosures no longer needed since she'd come into her powers. I could borrow one of the cages. "You'll eat well and have a warm bed to sleep in."

In a quiet voice, Sol pointed out, "I don't get cold, and I was already eating well before—"

"Wait." I froze. A muted cry had sounded from somewhere. "Did you hear that?"

He shook his head.

Another cry, closer. An animal! A bird? I swept my gaze across the sky, spotting a falcon, one wearing a little leather helmet. "Lark! I'm here!" I jumped up and down and waved my arms. "Hey! Over here!"

The falcon banked, hovered, then dove for me.

"Thank God." It was flying in fast, straight for me. "Lark, you're coming in hot. Watch it!"

In a flutter of feathers, the bird leapt onto my shoulder, talons digging in.

"Enough! That freaking hurts." It swooped its wings, seeming to urge me in one direction. "Okay, okay, I'm coming!"

Behind me, Sol said, "It didn't have to be like this, Evie."

I frowned, turning. "How did you know my name—"

His arm was swinging toward me, a large rock in his hand.

Pain.

The falcon's screech.

Blackness.

13

I woke to a creepy sound. A slurping sound.

I managed to crack open my eyes, and almost lost what was left of my mind.

Four new Bagmen ... *drank me.*

They'd bitten me. Had slashed at my clothes to get to my skin. They were greedily sucking my blood, jostling my limp body.

I strained to get away, to summon power... *too weak.* Couldn't move my limbs. Couldn't scream. Sol must've cracked my skull. Blood loss weakened me more.

The falcon tore at the Baggers' faces, its beak plucking at their eyes.

Another nightmare? Real? *Unreal?* This couldn't be happening. I wasn't supposed to go out like this!

Sol looked on with his two favored Baggers, their thorn collars gone. He'd called my bluff. The Sun wasn't gloating, didn't look pleased or displeased. But he was still doing this to me.

Killing me.

I choked out a word: "Why?" Though I hadn't trusted him, I hadn't expected this.

"Already in an alliance." He fiddled with that watch on his wrist. Then he raised his face to the night sky, and light flared from his eyes. Twin spotlights. A signal. He blinked, and the beams flickered in a rhythm.

To signal what?

I gasped, "Then just . . . kill me." The falcon still fought, but the Bagmen barely seemed aware of it.

"That's not the plan. I had them bite you because their mutation neutralizes an Arcana's powers." He intended to keep me alive? "At least, it did on the last player who attacked me."

Who? Sol had been in the game for a while.

He was right, though. I wasn't able to call forth a vine. Even my regeneration stopped working.

A Bagger above me released his bite, but only to sink his teeth into unbroken skin at my waist. I cried out, powerless to stop it. The falcon went crazy.

Would I join Jack and my mom and Mel on some other plane? Or would I become a Bagman myself, cursed to walk the earth? "You'll keep me around . . . like Bea and Joe?"

Had Sol flinched?

Despite the risk of turning, I should be glad of even the chance to join my loved ones. But I couldn't stop imagining Death's reaction to my horrific murder.

Had Aric believed me when I'd told him I loved him too?

Over the falcon's furious cries, I heard another sound: *swoop swoop swoop.* Familiar, but so unexpected; I needed a few moments to place it. A . . . helicopter?

Hadn't I heard one the night of the massacre? That's how Richter had escaped Circe!

Did the Emperor approach now? The Sun must have been working with him all along!

Spotlights flared as a copter came into view. The lettering read COAST GUARD RESCUE. It circled overhead, a metal buzzard. If Richter was in there, I needed to bring it to the ground!

But I was helpless, Baggers continuing to drain me. My body would soon be a husk like Tess's.

The copter landed in the field not twenty feet away, kicking up ash. The wind gusts sent the falcon tumbling away from my attackers.

I turned my gaze toward Sol. He mouthed something to me. I couldn't be sure what.

The four Bagmen abruptly stopped drinking. They stood and moved back, their lips coated with my blood.

The rotors slowed. Not Richter—a *girl* climbed from the pilot's seat and stepped down. Long, jet-black hair curled from her helmet. Behind her mic, her lips were bright red. She wore a green jumpsuit and gloves, and had a pistol holstered to one thigh and a long blade strapped to her other. To take my head?

She strode over to us, yanking off her helmet. Her eyes were vivid hazel, her expression livid. A tableau flickered over her. I saw a wheel spinning in a night sky with a sphinx running on top of it and a winged dragon dancing along the bottom. Ancient clay dice rained down.

The Fortune Card!

Was Lark seeing this? The falcon had taken to the air, circling overhead.

"Que porra é essa?" Fortune snapped at Sol.

"Good to see you too, Zara," he grated. "And one more time: I don't understand your Portuguese." They *had* known each other all along—Sol and *Zara*. "*Dios mío*, that accent!"

"What the fuck?" she said. "Why'd you summon a horde of Bagman freaks?"

Huh? There were only four besides Sol's pets.

He shrugged. "I can't help that they're attracted to me."

My head was splitting, my stomach churned, and those bites burned like acid. But I wanted answers. Why had Sol played along with me? He'd known who I was the instant my tableau had appeared in Olympus, maybe even sooner, if he could see through his Bagmen.

Sol asked her, "Where is Richter?"

"Kicked back, recharging for the big finale," she said. "He doesn't come out for B-team bullshit like her. Did you find out where Death's lair is?"

Sol had used me to locate Aric's? For the *big finale*.

How badly I needed to live, to warn Aric and Lark. But I'd lost so much blood, and the mutation weakened me even more.

Because I was already turning?

"The Empress seemed confident his place is somewhere around here," Sol said. "Since we're in the area, we should do a flyover."

Zara shook her head. "Can't. I'm on fuel reserves just to pick you up. My whirlybird's stripped down."

Sol rubbed the back of his neck. "We need to get airborne." He pointed up at the falcon. "That's one of Fauna's scouts. She allies with the Empress."

The falcon screeched and dove yet again. Zara snatched her pistol from her holster, trained her aim on the moving target, then fired. The falcon plummeted in a lifeless heap.

My eyes stung, but I reminded myself that the bird would regenerate.

"There. No more scouts." Zara asked Sol, "Do your Baggers like poultry?"

"Bitch," I sneered—or tried to. Only a wheeze crossed my lips.

Zara kicked my leg, asking Sol, "Is she contained?"

I couldn't scream. Couldn't die. I struggled to keep my eyes open.

"She's been bitten enough." Again, Sol didn't sound proud or regretful. "She has tried to muster her powers, but can't."

Zara aimed her gun at my chest. "Just in case." She fired.

Once. Twice. Three times.

Three shots—to the *heart*? I laughed at her, choking on blood. Bullets couldn't hurt something that had already been destroyed.

"What a freak." Zara holstered her weapon, shaking her head at me. "I can't believe *you* have icons. The great Empress? You're just a weak little girl." She knelt beside me, pulling off one glove. "And you're about to become a very unlucky one." She reached for my face—

A wolf howled not far away, then another. Lark!

Zara shot to her feet, her gaze darting. "Fauna again?" She brandished her pistol once more, aiming it in all directions.

Sol nodded. "Makes sense."

"Get the Empress and let's go." She hurried to the copter. "Come on, Sun, *anda logo*!"

When Sol waved his hand, one of the Bagmen grabbed my ankle and dragged me over the ground to the copter.

The Sun and Fortune were taking me to the Emperor.

14

As Sol strapped my limp body into a helicopter seat, he yelled to Zara, "We have to GO!" With another wave of his hand, he directed his pet Baggers into two more seats.

In the cockpit, Zara flipped switches and twisted dials. The engines roared louder. Wind swept through the open side door.

"Now, Zara!"

She answered with a spiel about "overtorque" and "max RPM" and "collective pitch," ending with "asshole."

She sounded like she knew what she was doing, and she certainly had Sol's number. So this helicopter was a weapon for her. Part of Fortune's Arcana arsenal.

Sol had just belted in Joe when she snapped, "Fuck it!" and pulled on some lever between her knees. We lurched into the air.

I slumped against my seat belt. Sol lunged to close the side door, but slipped over the metal-plated floor before he reached it. My blood and Bagger slime had slickened it.

He grabbed a handle for balance. Then his eyes went wide. "Oh, *estoy jodido*! Death's riding for us!"

Aric? He was alive! With effort, I turned my lolling head. Death charged into the clearing on Thanatos. The warhorse had survived as well. I shouldn't have been surprised. Thanatos bench-pressed three-eighty and swished his tail at floods.

Aric rode in with both swords raised, and my bullet-riddled heart wanted to beat for him.

But I'd led our enemies straight to him! I needed to warn him. Which meant escaping. *Stay awake. Stay alert.*

"Where's the mounted gun?" Sol yelled to Zara, panic in his voice.

If a knight in black armor on a red-eyed steed charged for me, I'd be panicked too. In fact, I had been *terrified* when in his sights.

Now I was proud. Lark's giant wolves sped forward to flank Aric.

"I told you," Zara snapped. "The copter's stripped!" Since the helicopter was Fortune's weapon this game, she should've conserved her fuel.

The first law of an Arcana's arsenal, Zara? Conserve, conserve, conserve.

She yelled, "Flare your rays!"

His eyes emitted light, a spotlight on Aric. I choked out: *"Don't."*

We seemed to hover in place for several moments. *"Nada.* Death's still coming!" Sol's beams faded. "I don't think it works on him."

"You've got Baggers nearby," Zara said. *"Use* them."

"On it."

Damn it, I had to get off this helicopter. I could jump from the open door, if I could muster the strength to move my legs.

I summoned a single claw, nearly blacking out from the effort. When my vision cleared, Aric looked so far away on the ground. How high were we? I blinked—then again.

Behind him . . . *thousands* of Bagmen swarmed the field, sprinting after him.

Scarface charged ahead of Aric. With a spine-chilling growl, the wolf sprang for the copter . . . we were too high . . .

Caught us! We pitched sharply to the side. Another growl sounded from so close.

Zara screamed, *"Porra!"*

"The wolf's latched onto the skids!" Sol was barely hanging on by that handle.

I clawed my seatbelt free. My body crumpled to the slimy floor. As the copter rolled sideways, I slid toward the open doorway, my head at the edge.

"*No, pequeña!*" Sol reached for me, struggling to keep his footing. "*Estúpida!*"

Scarface was just below me. I met gazes with him—and with Lark through her familiar. "Kill . . . them," I choked out. "They're coming . . . for you."

The wolf thrashed its massive head, shaking the copter like a chew toy. Bea, never belted in, almost fell out of her seat. Sol scrambled for balance.

Lark had once explained why wolves thrashed their prey: to snap a creature's neck instantly. Scarface was about to take this metal buzzard *out.*

If Death didn't do it first; with a bellow, he hurled one of his swords right at me.

My lips curled.

The sword struck the helicopter. Sparks rained. Grinding sounded, like a giant lawn mower hitting a steel pipe. The engines whined. Alarms blared.

BEEEEEEEPPPPPPPPP. BEEEEEEEPPPP PPPPP. BEEEEEEEPPPPPPPPPP.

We spun like Fortune's wheel. Dizziness and nausea surged.

"Fucker took out the tail rotor!" Zara fought that lever. "We're going DOWN!"

BEEEEEEEPPPPPPPPP. BEEEEEEEPPPP PPPPP. BEEEEEEEPPPPPPPPPP.

Sol crawled toward me, just as Scarface thrashed again. Bea and Sol slammed into each other. I slid out farther and vomited blood; it spattered onto the snarling wolf's muzzle.

Spinning, spinning. Like a whirlpool in a flood.

To my left: Scarface. To my right, Bea scrabbled at the edge.

Sol had a grip on one of my ankles and one of hers. But he was slipping over the slick floor. He had to make a choice: save me or Bea.

A last thrash from Scarface—the buzzard's deathblow.

Sol chose.

I tumbled through the sky, weightless.

I glimpsed the copter diving into a nearby canyon, about to crash like me; the wolf released its hold at the last second.

Then—

Impact. I landed in a standing position. The ground pulverized my legs.

15

"I have you," Aric grated. "Hold on, *sievā!*"

Consciousness wavered. I wanted to warn Aric, but speech felt impossible. So I tried to reach him mentally. *The Emperor is coming. He's recharging.*

Aric clutched me with one arm. With his other, he wielded a sword, cleaving his way through Bagmen.

So many. Thousands. Their wails were deafening.

Aric needed both hands, or he'd never get through this swarm alive. I would probably turn into a Bagger anyway. I was handicapping him. *Leave me.*

If Aric heard me, he didn't react, just continued to fight. As he swung and slashed, I saw flashes from the canyon: a blast, then billowing smoke. The helicopter had exploded! Would Aric get Sol and Zara's icons? Or would Lark?

The giant fireball from the crash lit our way.

Two howls sounded over the wails. Scarface and Maneater leapt in front of Thanatos, clearing a path through Baggers like a snowplow.

Aric murmured, "Good show, Fauna."

I was about to black out. "D-Dying. Sorry . . ."

He spurred Thanatos. "You are *not* dying!" We galloped faster. "Empress?"

All my reserves of strength were gone. I couldn't even answer him.

"*Sievā?*" The last thing I heard was his agonized bellow. . . .

When I roused again, I heard thundering hooves. Aric's ragged breaths. Steady rain.

I cracked open my eyes. Had we escaped the Bagmen? I whispered, "Aric?" I'd never been so cold; my body shuddered.

"Ah, gods, you're awake." He raised his helmet visor. "Don't talk. We're almost home." He looked exhausted. Rain pelted his armor and dripped down his proud face. If he'd been burned from the searing flood, his enhanced healing had already mended his skin.

When his eyes went starry as he gazed down at me, I released the tourniquet on my heart and started to bleed out, was dying anyway. "My powerful knight." I peered up at him with all the love I felt for him. "Knew you . . . couldn't be dead." I reached for his face, but my arm collapsed halfway.

"Save your strength, *sievā*."

"Baggers bit me . . . a lot. You'll . . . kill me . . . before I turn. Right?"

"It will not come to that," he said, his voice a rasp. "I will get you well from this."

Mist swirled around us as we rode at a breakneck pace. How was he still going? "Will you take care . . . of Gran?"

"You will not die! I will not allow it."

I tried to shake my head. Mistake. Neck broken? "Emperor will find your home . . . destroy you. Big finale."

"You led the Sun in the exact wrong direction, love."

I had? Naturally. "Will you kill . . . Richter for me?"

"Do not talk! If you save your strength, you will regenerate."

"Sol said the bites . . . neutralize Arcana powers. Healing myself . . . is a power." Something was very wrong inside me. Sickness had me by the throat, wouldn't let go.

Like a wolf *slowly* breaking my neck.

After the tiniest hesitation, Aric said, "Doesn't matter. This will be different."

I disagreed. Which meant I needed to talk to him. "Have to . . . tell you things." All the things I might have regretted. I began murmuring the thoughts in my head, not really aware of what I was saying.

I trusted Aric to pick what was important from my ramblings. I spoke until I was on the verge of unconsciousness again.

Whatever I'd said affected him. He yanked off his helmet so he could press his lips to my forehead as he clutched me close. . . .

I must have blacked out again; I jolted back to awareness when Aric yelled, "Circe, let us pass!"

The sound of waves, and then water receding. Was the Priestess nearby?

Thanatos galloped upward, upward, the air growing even colder. Just when I was about to drift off again, Aric told me, "We're home."

I was back at the castle of lost time? I opened my eyes, squinting. We rode through the giant gate and into the courtyard. Hooves clattered on the brick. Gas lights stung my eyes.

"I'm getting you help. Just hold on." Aric cradled me against his chest as he dropped from Thanatos and rushed inside, spurs ringing. "Lark, get the EMT!"

Lark . . . I'd missed her over the last few weeks. She'd led Aric to me. They'd both fought to save me.

"We're prepped and ready to go in the nursery, boss," she answered. "Under the sunlamps, just like you said."

Sunlamps. Clever Aric. They had strengthened me before. But I sensed I was beyond help. He hurried down the many steps to the underground nursery, telling me, "Stay with me. You must stay with me."

He laid me on a bed. I squeezed my eyes closed against the blazing overhead light. I heard shears as my clothes were cut away.

Lark sucked in a breath. "She's one big wound. I've seen roadkill in better shape."

"Enough!" Aric snapped.

A man said, "She's been bitten multiple times. Those are *bullet* wounds in her chest. The EMT? Wasn't his name Paul? He'd patched up Lark after Ogen's attack. "Her legs are . . . done. What do you expect me to do for her?"

His tone murderous, Aric grated, "Unless you want to die by my sword, I suggest you—*save*—her." I knew how menacing his face would look right now. I'd been on the receiving end of his threats enough.

"I-I'll try to clean these wounds, sir," Paul said, his voice scaling higher. "And start a drip. Lark, can you help me? She's lost a lot of blood."

"Shouldn't Eves have started healing?" Lark asked. "When I sliced off her cilice down here, she was regenerating in seconds."

"Give her time," Aric said. "The injuries are significant." He brushed damp hair off my forehead. "Feel the light, *sievā*. You will heal. You always heal."

I *could* feel the warm lamps, but I didn't sense even a twitch of regeneration—

A woman's scream. "E-Evie!" Was that . . . my grandmother?

I tried to say, "Gran." Blood came out of my mouth. For so long, I'd fought to reach her. She was with me at last, but I couldn't speak a word.

"The Sun did this to her," Gran said. "Did you kill him, knight?" I sensed her and Paul on one side of me, Aric and Lark on the other.

"No. I believe they survived the helicopter crash." They had?

"Then why don't you leave my granddaughter's care to us? While you go *finish the job*?" She sounded as murderous as Aric had.

"I won't leave until she's healed."

"You should have found her sooner! How could you not find her before this happened?" Why was my grandmother baiting him? "You've located her so many times before."

I knew she considered him a villain, but couldn't she see that he cared for me? He'd rescued her from North Carolina, bringing her back to this castle—for me. He'd taken on two Arcana and a Bagger army to save my life.

To *try* to save me.

I still might turn.

Sounding like he was about to strangle her, Aric said, "The Fool has silenced our calls." No wonder I'd heard nothing. What was Matthew up to? "After following every mile of the flood's path, every fork, every twist and turn, I scoured the countryside for the Empress—from here to

Fort Arcana. For some reason, she went in the opposite direction of this castle. I wisely had Lark dispatch sentries in *all* directions."

"*Wisely?* Evie's dying! Or worse."

"She can hear you. Govern your tongue—or leave."

"I am her grandmother!"

"Even *my* eternal patience has limits, Tarasova."

"You're threatening . . . threatening . . ." Her words trailed off.

I heard a strangled cry. What was going on? Why couldn't I see?

Aric bit out a curse in Latvian.

Lark said, "Uh, what's happening to the old lady?"

A scuffling sound. A moan.

"Jesus," Lark muttered. "Eves, you're having the shittiest two weeks in history."

16

"I'm here, *sievā*." Aric brushed a cool cloth over my forehead.

Death's vigil. How long had he been caring for me? I was suspended in some kind of twilight; I didn't die—yet I hadn't healed.

I thought I'd understood physical pain. A few months ago, I'd amputated my own thumb to get free of cuffs so I could fight Death. When I'd drowned not long after that, I'd felt as if my lungs would burst. Then an ogre had choked me, snapping my neck. Lately? I'd lost an arm, been tossed around in a flood, and been bitten and drained by ravenous Baggers.

Yet *real* pain and I had never been introduced before now.

The Bagmen's mutation ripped through me. Whatever Empress power I still possessed battled it. A war had erupted inside my body.

"Fight this. *Fight*," Aric urged me. He sat next to me on the bed, taking me into his arms. "You must return to me."

I tried to speak, to tell him I loved him and to ask about Gran, but no words passed my lips.

"I know why dying might seem tempting"—because I could follow Jack?—"but *I* need you. Come back to me."

Another wave of agony hit. I heard a scream.

Mine?

Voice thick, he said, "I wish to the gods I could take this pain for you." He rocked me. "You're too strong to die, and too stubborn to turn. Your only path is to come back to me."

How could he be so good to me when I'd hurt him so deeply? I remembered his blood-curdling roar when I'd ridden away from him—to be with Jack. . . .

As hours—days? weeks?—passed, Aric remained with me. At times, I could tell he was biting back sounds of grief.

Other times, he talked to me. He told me about my grandmother: "The sight of you gave her a . . . shock. But she will recover. Just as you will."

He told me about the other Arcana: "Lark sent a scout back to that clearing to collect her falcon and my sword. There were no bodies at the crash site. As I suspected, Fortune and the Sun survived."

One time I heard a wolfish whimper, and a slobbery tongue licked my hand. "You have a visitor," Aric said. "Your favorite." Cyclops? He'd made it! "I've always appreciated the *potential* of the wolves, but I never thought we would owe our lives to them."

Now another wave of agony hit. My screams echoed. I didn't want to scare anyone, but I couldn't choke them back.

"I need to help you." He sounded so gutted, as if his pain mirrored mine. "How can I help you?"

I didn't think anything could be done. And so, I had two new missions.

To make sure Aric killed me if I began to turn. And to extract a promise of bloody revenge against the Emperor. As soon as I could speak.

Aric tensed against me. "She returns."

Footsteps neared. "Is there . . . any change?" my grandmother asked in a weak voice. Were her words slurred?

She was maddeningly close. If only I could communicate with her. Did she know that Haven was ash? That her daughter had died?

Aric answered, "The Empress will rally."

"Sir . . ." Paul was down here as well? He did pretty much everything around the castle, from cooking all meals to stitches. I didn't envy Paul his job at Castle Death.

The man was brave enough to say, "She might be starting to turn. If you wait too long, she could bite another."

The idea of harming someone else sickened me even more. I whispered, *"Kill me,"* but no one seemed to have heard me.

"I will do nothing," Aric said, "until—or unless—she craves blood."

I shuddered.

"Leave her with me," Gran said. "You shouldn't be in this bed with her, holding her like that. She's a girl of seventeen."

"She's a millennia-old Empress."

"*I* should take care of her," Gran insisted.

"You forget that this is my home, Tarasova. I will do as I please."

I wondered why he hadn't told her we were married. Aric hadn't been shy in announcing that fact to Jack.

But that had been before I'd rejected Aric and his claim on me. Before I'd broken this man's heart. . . .

17

My eyes darted behind my lids as I hovered between sleep and wakefulness. I was in a bed. I sensed plants all around me.

When the pain had finally dwindled to a manageable level, I cracked open my eyes. Could only make out a white blank.

Ah, God, why couldn't I see? Would my sight return? I blinked over and over. Maybe I was turning, my eyes gone filmy?

No, some kind of brightness blazed down. Oh. The sunlamps. I was in the nursery.

Blurry images began to take shape. Why was there a bed down here? Vines and rose stalks traipsed over my body and the footboard.

Beneath the mass of green, I shifted my limbs, flexing my muscles. My arms and legs were weak and sore as hell, but healing.

I eased my head back. Aric sat up against the headboard, his eyes closed. Vines and rose stalks covered him as well.

In sleep, his brow furrowed, his lips thinned. He had golden stubble over his lean cheeks and dark circles under his eyes, looking older and more exhausted than I had ever seen him. He wore black pants and a thin dark sweater, but I could tell he'd lost weight.

How long had he been here with me? After our history, I was surprised he could tolerate the plants overrunning him.

Memory fragments from my recovery surfaced: his soothing words, his care, his updates about life around the castle. He'd challenged me to heal and stayed with me the entire time.

All around us, plants—even trees—merged to make walls. He'd chosen to remain inside my deadly green lair. I stretched my arm over him, savoring his warmth and strength.

His amber eyes blinked open. He found me staring at him, and his lips curved. "*Sievā*." Pinpoints of light radiated from his spellbinding gaze.

"You're okay with these plants?" I murmured, my throat scratchy.

His smile widened. "I'm thankful to them. They comforted you more than I could have."

I didn't know about that. "How long was I out?"

"For weeks."

My jaw slackened. "That can't be right."

"Those Bagmen bit you more than a dozen times. Your legs were badly injured and you'd been shot. Your regeneration ability had much to contend with."

I did remember landing feet first. "Will I . . . turn?"

"I do not believe that. You would have already." Aric would never lie to me.

I relaxed somewhat. With a wave of my hand, I moved the vines off the bed, off him.

He appeared to relax a touch as well. "If someone had said a few of months ago that I would nod off while surrounded by the Empress's vines, I'd have called him mad." He reached for a glass of water on a tray. He helped me sit up and brought the cup to my lips. "Easy."

I drank enough to quench the worst of my thirst. "The Emperor is planning to attack the castle. Soon."

"I know. You told me. Happily, you led the Sun in the opposite direction of our home."

Our home. "I did?" Totally meant to do that.

In a strange tone, he said, "Do you not remember *any* of the things we talked about on the journey here? Any of the things you told me?"

I cast my mind back. The whole time was a blur.

His gaze flicked over my face, reading my confusion. For some reason, he seemed to be closing down right in front of me. He straightened his shoulders, his demeanor growing distant and formal. "You must have many questions."

A thousand. "Why weren't we able to communicate with each other?" I vaguely remembered Aric touching on this, but not what he'd said. "I called and called for you."

"The Fool disconnected everyone. I don't know why. Perhaps to conceal some players from others. Or perhaps because he'd been weakened."

In the days before abandoning me, Matthew had suffered nosebleeds and increased disorientation. Normally, I hated to think of him in pain. But after his betrayal, I relished the idea.

"Empress?"

I blinked. "What happened to you after Circe's tidal wave?"

"I began searching for you as soon as I broke free from the flood. I feared you couldn't survive without . . . your arm. You must forgive me for that."

"There's nothing to forgive."

"How *did* you survive?"

I recalled being caught in that whirlpool with Bagmen, terrified I'd get bitten. Apparently that had always been my fate. "I latched onto a cell-phone tower. I climbed up and waited out the waters."

"Climbed with one arm?"

"I didn't say I climbed *well.* Circe's an ally, isn't she?"

Nod.

"Will she help us kill Richter?"

He scrubbed a palm down his weary face. "When the time comes."

"The time? As soon as I recover." Then I remembered—my grandmother was here! I reached for him. "I need to see Gran. I thought I heard . . . is she okay?"

He took my offered hand, then stared at our clasped fingers. *Still so unused to touch.* He cleared his throat. "She was weak when I found her, and her health hasn't improved. But she's stable."

"She's been down here though."

His thumb rubbed my skin. "After the first day or so, the many steps to this level proved challenging."

"Will you move me closer to her?"

Firm shake of his head. "You're not ready."

"I could take a sunlamp and a couple of houseplants. *Please?*" I squeezed his hand.

He exhaled. "And still, I can deny you nothing." He lifted me in his arms, and carried me toward the stairs. "You can stay in the guest room next to hers. I'll have all your things moved from the tower."

Because I wasn't a prisoner anymore. "Maybe just some of my clothes. I like my room up there." I'd painted the walls and made myself at home.

As he settled me into bed in my new room, my nightgown shifted, and I winced at the bruises on my legs, my skin mottled black and blue. Then I clung to his hand, not wanting to let him out of my sight.

He frowned and pulled away. "I'll be right back." He drew his gloves from his pants pocket, donning them as he crossed to the door.

Lark sidled past him into the room. "Evie!" she cried. The last time I'd seen her, she'd been wearing two casts, one on her arm and one on her ankle, but now she was all healed up. "The unclean one is back! I thought you were unclean *before* you got Bagger funk all in your veins. You missed me, didn't you?"

"I did. Thank you for helping to save my life."

"Yeah, well, you owe me." Her smile faded. "I don't suppose you saw Finn anywhere?"

I shook my head. "I'm sorry. I thought he'd be at Fort Arcana, but the place was abandoned. I saw ... part of Cyclops." Hadn't the wolf come to see me? Or had I dreamed that? "What happened at the fort?"

"After the big attack, Fortune flew over it with Richter. She was just carting him around, like they were on a fun date or something. He must've been outta Emperor juice, 'cause he started gunning up the place."

As long as I was alive, Richter's days were numbered. *I'm coming for you, Richter.* I would replace his laughter with screams.

Lark continued, "Finn couldn't run with his bum leg, barely got to an outbound truck. I leapt up to fang the chopper to buy time."

So strange to hear her talk like this, as if she'd been there. Which she kind of had been. In the form of Cyclops. *Red of tooth and claw.* And later she'd attacked Fortune through Scarface—saving me.

"Those choppers drive me—I mean, my wolves—batty. Anyway, Richter shot up Cyclops until I couldn't hold on. I dropped right in the middle of the freaking minefield. And *ouch.* Needless to say, I couldn't keep up with Finn's truck." Her eyes flickered animal red as she said, "When we take care of Richter, save Fortune for me. That bitch and I have a date."

"Noted. Did your falcon survive?"

"Yeah. She's one of the scouts I've got searching for Finn." Lark shuffled her feet. "Death told me you'd been riding out to meet Jack, to leave with him."

And yet Aric had come for me and saved my life.

"Eves, I'm really sorry about the Cajun."

I swallowed past the lump in my throat. My recovery seemed to have loosened my tourniquet. *Tighten it!*

A sudden thought occurred. "Lark, where are the clothes I was wearing?"

"Dunno. Paul probably burned them. They looked like you got dunked in Ragu or something—"

"There was a ribbon in my pocket." My last physical tie to Jack. "Please find it! Please!"

"I'll try." Cocking her head, she muttered, "I hear your grandmother coming. Gotta scram. I'll check back in later."

I had so many more questions, but Lark slipped out.

Aric entered with Gran, helping her along with his gloved hands.

She looked so different from the last time I'd seen her. Her face was worn, and her hair had grayed even more. She'd lost a lot of weight, and her dark brown eyes no longer twinkled.

"Evie!" she cried, limping to my bed. She wrapped her thin arms around me.

I returned her hug. "Gran." Her scent cast my mind back to my childhood, bringing on a rush of memories: Her pushing me on the swing at Haven.... Gran and Mom laughing when a duckling chased me.... Gran teaching me how to tend her beloved rose garden; the soil had been so warm....

I'd waited through nine years and an apocalypse to see her again.

Over her shoulder, I caught Aric's gaze. He stood in the doorway, his bearing tense. Hadn't I heard strained exchanges between them? I couldn't remember. I mouthed *Thank you* to him.

Curt nod.

Gran drew back and sat on the bed. "Look at you! You're all grown up. And so beautiful." Her words *did* sound slurred. "I was so worried when I first saw you." Was one corner of her lips turned down?

"Are you okay, Gran?"

"I'll be fine. We need to focus on you. We have so much to catch up on."

When I thought of all the things we needed to talk about—Mom's death, the destruction of Haven, my relationship with Death—exhaustion swept over me.

I looked to Aric for support, but he was gone.

"Lord, you can barely keep your eyes open." She clucked her tongue and tucked the blanket around me. "I'm here, watching over you. We'll figure everything out. For now, you've got to regain your strength. Get some sleep, Evie."

I needed to be doing so many things other than sleeping. Such as plotting the Emperor's grisly death.

Still, my lids slid closed. "Just for a minute...."

18

Gran sat on the edge of the bed, brushing my hair. She chattered about the food here and the worsening weather—any topic except those we needed to speak about.

When I'd awakened around dinnertime, she had been beside me—not Aric. But, as promised, he'd filled the room with plants and sunlamps, and moved my clothes to the closet.

Gran had brought me a tray with soup, then she'd helped me take a bath and get dressed. She'd murmured, "Such pretty clothes Death has provided for you." But she hadn't sounded approving.

Now she laid aside the brush with a labored breath. "I'm plumb wore out."

I turned to face her. "Tell me what's wrong."

She smoothed her gray hair, the length caught up in a careless bun. "Worry's kept me from sleeping. But you're on the mend now."

Slowly. "And you?"

"I'll be right as rain soon enough." Had she averted her eyes?

"Gran, how did you survive the Flash?"

"My facility was old, so there was an actual bomb shelter. I sensed something coming and headed down. I was the only one to make it, which meant I had food and supplies aplenty."

Everyone had told me she would never survive this long, but I'd believed. "I tried to reach you."

"I knew you would, which is why I stayed put," she said. "I figured the one thing stronger than my desire to return to Haven would be Karen's strength of will to reunite with me—once she realized I'd been right." Gran's dark eyes glinted. "Death told me she ... died a few months ago."

Gran already knew; she wouldn't have rested until she'd found out Mom's fate. "She regretted not believing you. It tore at her."

"I hate that she was hurting from it."

I took her hand. Her grip felt weak, her bones brittle. "About Haven ..."

"Was the house hurt on Day Zero? I thought for sure the oaks would protect it."

"They did." Those twelve mighty oaks had given their lives. "Months after the Flash, the Lovers closed in with an army. I didn't want them to have our home. So we, uh ... we burned it down."

"H-Haven's ... gone?"

"I'm so sorry."

She shook her head. "No. Don't be. From what I've heard, the Lovers were as evil as they'd ever been. I'd rather you destroy our home than let them have it." She frowned. "You said *we* burned it."

"Jack and I." Just saying his name tested my tourniquet. "He was a bayou boy I met in school. He saved me from the Lovers, and about a dozen other times."

Her perceptive gaze flicked over my face. "You're in love with him?"

I nodded. "But he ... died in the Emperor's attack."

"I heard Death and Fauna talking about a massacre." Gran tucked a curl behind my ear. "Jack was a human? A regular man?"

Regular? Not in any way. "He was an extraordinary non-Arcana." I found myself recounting a fraction of the brave, incredible things he'd done. Through the stories, Gran learned about the past several months of my life and some of my encounters with other Arcana.

I left out the part when Aric had abducted me, mentally and physically torturing me.

She gave me another hug, saying, "I'm so sorry Jack has passed on. I would've liked to see you with a boy from the Basin." She'd had friends there, visiting all the time. She drew back. "Did you speak Cajun French with him?"

Twist, tighten, constrict. "He loved that I could. Thank you for teaching me."

"Ah, Evie, you lost your love young, didn't you? Just like your mother."

When my dad had gone missing in the Basin, Mom had searched more than a million acres of swamp trying to recover him. I'd tried to reverse time to recover Jack.

In the end, Mom had been forced to just... *accept* her loss. I understood bravery in battle and dying; I now understood true pain. But I couldn't wrap my mind around... enduring.

Acceptance seemed out of the realm of my abilities. "The Emperor took Jack from me forever. I need to kill Richter. It's all I can think about." I'd had more nightmares about Jack burning. My mind seemed to be filled with fog, but I clearly recalled those dreams. They bubbled up like lava.

"You will have your vengeance in time," she assured me. "But the most important thing is the overarching game. You've done a great job setting this one up." She finally smiled. "We can't ruin all your work by acting rashly."

"Pardon?"

"Death walks around without his armor—because you have disarmed him. Well done, sweetheart. He's already defeated."

The dinner I'd managed to get down now threatened to come back up.

She patted my hand. "Look at those icons. You've already made two kills, and you've teed up two more. And if I'm not mistaken, the Priestess lingers nearby. Soon she'll be within reach. You always lure her out of her murky hiding places."

I had feared my grandmother would be hardcore about the game, about killing all Arcana. But to see and hear her... "I don't look at the people here as enemies. I will never hurt any of them," I said firmly. Aric had brought her to me; shouldn't gratitude or decency have softened her stance? At least in regard to him?

She winked at me and whispered, "You don't have to act. They're down at dinner. They can't hear us."

Oh, God. No wonder Aric hadn't trusted me for so long. Aside from my history of stabbing him in the back, he'd believed I would think like Gran.

And I might have—if Mom hadn't sent her away.

How could I tell my grandmother that I hadn't turned out as she'd hoped? Would the shock hurt her worse? I needed to know what was going on with her health before I dropped this bombshell on her.

My body vine budded, as if to comfort me.

She looked delighted by the tiny show of my powers. "We'll bring this game to an end sooner than I thought. My Empress is a bold killer—and a sly manipulator. Victory will be yours."

Don't get sick, don't get sick. "Aric has saved my life repeatedly, risking his own. So has Lark. I'm alive right now because she directed him how to find me."

"I know! It's astonishing how you've got them working for you." Totally missed the point. "Oh, listen to me. There's plenty of time for us to strategize. For now, you need to get back to full strength."

"I *am* tired." Eventually I would change Gran's mind and make her see things my way, but in the meantime, I planned to sneak down and meet with my allies.

"Rest up. I'll see you first thing in the morning." She patted my hand again. "I couldn't be prouder of you, Evie," she said, but she wasn't looking at my face; she was tracing those icons.

19

"You can never turn your back on my grandmother," I told Aric and Lark as soon as his study door closed behind us. Just getting from one wing of the castle to another had made my legs sing with pain.

Aric sat behind his desk, Lark and I settling into the chairs in front of it. She had a sleeping ferret wrapped around her neck, a living stole. With keen eyes, Lark surveyed the area; had she never been here?

Probably not. This was Death's private space. He was particular about his sanctuaries and boundaries, and I was the only one he'd allowed inside.

What would Lark think of his personal study? Behind his desk was a row of soaring Gothic windows. On one wall, he had a collection of ancient swords displayed. Bookshelves that stretched from floor to ceiling contained his library of priceless editions.

Over centuries, he'd protected those treasured books—because he'd had nothing else to treasure.

This was where I'd first started falling in love with him. We'd sat together on the couch in front of the fire, and as I'd read his favorite books, he'd gazed over at me with satisfaction brimming in his expression.

Now I couldn't tell what he was thinking or feeling.

He steepled his fingers. As usual he wore all dark clothing, and his *power-over-everything-I-survey* vibe was firmly in place. "What do you think the Tarasova is capable of?"

"She expects me to kill both of you. I want to explain to her my feelings about this game—unfiltered—but I'm worried her health will get worse."

"Paul thinks she suffered a stroke," Aric said. "When I found her, she wasn't well. She was on the last of her stores and weakened overall."

"Thank you for rescuing her." I'd bet he regretted that gesture now. "Do you think I could hurt her more when I give her the news?"

Lark said, "It's A.F., Eves. We're all gonna eat it soon enough. But let's say she lives another thirty years; are you gonna listen to her talking about murder the whole time?"

Good point. And what if Gran discovered the way I truly felt, then took matters into her own hands? "I will have to change her mind about everything, but until then, I can't promise what she would and wouldn't do. I won't risk either of you. Stay on your guard."

Aric gave me a tight nod. What was going on in that brilliant mind of his?

During my recovery, he must've gotten me used to his nearness and warmth; my gaze dipped to his chest, and I imagined resting my head there, my ear over his heart. His strong arms would clasp me against him.

I dragged my eyes away, turning to Lark.

"I'll be on guard, surrounding myself with fur." She petted the ferret. The creature woke, yawned, then conked out again. "So now that the Empress is back in the office, you got any grand plans on how to take out Richter and his alliance?"

"The Sun Card *was* my big plan. He empowered me." Hadn't I heard that both Sol and Zara had survived the crash? They must have; neither Lark or Death wore new icons. "I figured if we all joined forces, we could challenge the Emperor. But then Sol sicced his Bagmen on me." The memory of that made my head start to ache.

"Why did you trust him?" Aric asked.

Lark said, "Didn't you learn your lesson when *I* dicked you over?"

I narrowed my eyes at them. "I did learn—and I *didn't* trust him." I told them about Sol's attachment to those two Baggers and how I'd threatened them. I ended with: "He called my bluff."

Aric no longer steepled his fingers. I'd wager that under the desk he was clenching his fists. His tell. Though his face was often emotionless, his hands said a lot. "I will bring you his head, Empress."

"I . . . Sol's not like Fortune," I rushed to say. There must be something good in a guy who'd loved as deeply as he had. But then, Vincent had also considered himself in love with his sister, an absorbed twin. Still, I tried to reason with Aric and Lark. "He's not vicious like Zara is."

Aric raised a brow. "He had contagious zombies dine on your blood."

Lark added, "Hey, what's vicious about that?"

"I told Sol I was immune. And I could argue that he saved my life through that attack." A stretch, but . . . "Zara could easily have taken my head; she didn't because I was contained. In any case, why *wouldn't* Sol have attacked me? I took him prisoner, threatening the 'lives' of his loved ones. I behaved like a lunatic and gave no sign that I'd be his ally. I told him I was taking him to Death and outlined his imprisonment here." *It didn't have to be this way . . .* Sol's words to me just before he'd taken me down. "Naturally, he fought back. And he used the tools he had at hand."

Lark rolled her eyes. "She wants to be friends with another one!"

"It's not that! I'm just saying I gave him no reason to choose our alliance over his own. In his mind, I'm probably as bad as Richter."

Looking back, I could tell Sol had been shocked by my description of the Emperor's massacre—and then by the *evidence* when he'd followed me into the mountains outside Fort Arcana. But he'd already been in deep with the Emperor and Fortune. Maybe the Sun believed it was too late to do anything about his alliance.

Or I could be projecting my instincts and feelings onto him.

"I repeat: he had zombies dine on you." Aric's arm muscles flexed under his thin sweater. Yep. Clenched fists. "Perhaps those bites have affected your thinking?"

Lark snorted. "You can't be *this* big of a dumbass."

I was confused on a number of things. I was half-crazy. But these two had a lot of nerve giving me flack about this. "Of the last four Arcana who have abducted me, each one gave me a reason for his actions. Arthur wanted to experiment on me. Guthrie tried to turn me into a cannibal. Vincent planned to sever parts of my body and watch them grow back. *Death* wanted to cut off my head for vengeance, threatening the 'creature' every day that he would do so."

Aric's brow furrowed.

I gazed from him to Lark. "When I asked Sol why he was hurting me, do you know what he said? 'Already in an alliance.'" I rubbed my temples. My head was now pounding. "For no other reason, we should keep him alive because he juiced my abilities like nothing before."

In a measured tone, Aric said, "That is something to consider."

"Yeah. Sure, Eves."

I hadn't changed their minds whatsoever. So I changed the subject. "How did Sol and Zara live through that crash anyway?"

Aric rose, heading to his bar service for a bottle of vodka and a shot glass. "Fortune possesses the divine power of luck." He poured a shot, then decided to bring it and the bottle back to his desk. "When fully empowered, she can overcome insurmountable odds."

He didn't offer me a glass? We'd also shot vodka in this study, talking into the night.

Lark said, "Like she'll always get a lucky bounce?"

He took his seat again. "In that crash, any number of scenarios might have played out. She could've been thrown from the helicopter, landing perfectly on the remains of a tree, cradled between two limbs. Or she could've plummeted into a pond deep enough to break her fall. All I know is that she walked out of that canyon, likely unscathed."

Lark frowned. "I thought she was associated with fate. Her Arcana name's Our Lady of Fate."

"As she desired it to be," he said. "But it's a very liberal translation."

I'd thought these Arcana things were set in stone. Now the goalposts were moving.

He downed that shot, then poured another. "She *appears* to control fate, but she doesn't have any influence over what happens to her. Her power is passive. She doesn't read the future and consciously affect it—not like the Fool does." Aric's gaze grew distant. "Ages ago, Fortune was known more accurately as Lady Luck. The Fool was known as the Hand of Fate. She despised him for that and envied his power."

I'd once called Matthew the hand of fate. He could see a thousand years into the future, but he'd also been able to guide me through a hail of bullets. "But how would *Sol* have survived?"

"Fortune's allies often benefit from her luck—unless she takes it from them. She's also a luck thief. That's her active power."

I murmured, "She can steal it through touch." As Death stole life. She'd been about to touch me before she'd been interrupted. "When Matthew said fate had marked me, he meant *destiny* in general? Not Zara?"

"I would believe so."

Adjusting the creature around her nape, Lark tugged a folded-up piece of paper out of her jeans pocket. "I'll update my new list of Arcana." She stood, then flattened the page on Aric's desk.

I crossed my legs, leaning down to massage one aching calf. "I thought you kept a laminated one on the fridge."

She snagged one of Aric's pens, making some notes. "I don't flaunt the list anymore. Not after a decent Arcana died. I might not have gelled with Selena, but I respected her."

Selena and I had just gotten to be good friends. I recalled the Moon raising her beautiful face to the drizzle as she'd talked about my ceasefire plan for the game: "Jesus, Evie, what if it catches on? What if we could all live in peace? Use these powers for good?"

What if fate had marked me because I'd been trying to foil the game? Had I lost Jack as punishment?

Matthew had once told me: *Fate demands her due.* In other words, the game demanded blood. . . .

Lark made a last note. "Think I've got it. You two wanna look over?"

Shaking myself from my thoughts, I rose and hopped up on the edge of Aric's desk, daring him to say something. The three of us began to read the list:

The Cursed Twenty-Two

0. The Fool, Gamekeeper of Old (Matthew)

I. The Magician, Master of Illusions (Finneas)

II. The High Priestess, Ruler of the Deep (Circe)

Aric tapped the page beside Circe's name. "Just *the Priestess*. Also known as the Water Witch."

Lark wrote "Hand of Fate" next to Matthew's, then edited Circe's. "Considering Poseida of the deep, or *whatever*, has been parked outside the castle for weeks, I think we should discuss this witch. What're her weaknesses, boss?"

I added, "If she remains in the abyss, how could she ever be defeated?"

Aric looked amused. "Give up my ally's vulnerabilities?"

My? I drew my head back. So did Lark.

I said, "If we are your allies and she's one too, doesn't that make all of us allies?"

His tone was flat as he answered, "No, it does not."

I parted my lips to argue, but I didn't trust my muddled mind yet. I bit my tongue, and we read on.

III. The Empress, Our Lady of Thorns (Evie)

IV. The Emperor, Stone Overlord (Richter)

"How did you defeat the Emperor two games ago?" I asked Aric.

"His rage is his strength, but also his weakness. He expends his power too readily and too extremely. I used another card to bait him— until the Emperor was depleted. After that, he was a mere mortal."

So how to bait him? *Coming for you, Richter . . .*

V. The Hierophant, He of the Dark Rites (Guthrie)

VI. The Lovers, Duke & Duchess Most Perverse (Vincent & Violet)

VII. The Chariot, Wicked Champion (Kentarch)

I glanced up. "Who's Kentarch?"

Aric said, "My other ancient ally."

And I was Death's ancient *enemy*. "What's his power?"

"Teleportation and intangibility." To Lark, he said, "In games past, he was better known as the Centurion."

She scribbled again.

"Why isn't he here?" I asked. "Will he help us?"

Aric shrugged. "He searches for his wife. I doubt he will do much of anything else until he locates her."

But we could use him! "You can't talk him into fighting for you? Call on your friendship?"

"He and I aren't friends." Aric seemed to grow more distant by the second. "Our interests have been aligned."

I bit back my frustration, planning to keep working this angle.

> *VIII. Strength, Mistress of Fauna (Lark)*
> ~~*IX. The Hermit, Master of Alchemy (Arthur)*~~
> *X. Fortune, Lady ~~of Fate~~ Luck (Zara)*
> ~~*XI. Justice, She Who Harrows (Spite)*~~
> *XII. The Hanged Man, Our Lord Uncanny (??)*

"The Justice Card was known as the Fury," Aric said. "Her title, She Who Harrows, is the same."

Lark updated the list. "What were Spite's powers?"

"She was a fanged demoness with batlike wings and the ability to spit acid. Strangely, her acid wouldn't rise when we faced off."

"A Bagman might have bitten her," I said. "Sol talked about a card whose powers were neutralized."

"By the way, boss"—Lark's eyes grew tinged with animal red—"I officially called Fortune's kill. Zara and her stupid choppers are mine."

He raised his brows. "Good luck with that. You'll need all the luck you can get."

"What are the Hanged Man's powers?" I tried to remember more about that player.

"I don't know," Aric admitted. "I've never faced him, nor seen him mentioned in any chronicles I've read. The Star had his icon in the last game. But did the Arcane Navigator take it himself, or harvest it from another?" Aric rotated his shot glass on his desk blotter. "The Hanged Man remains a mystery. That is why he's called uncanny. In this game, all have been accounted for, but for him."

"Then he's the inactivated card?" One Arcana was dormant—until he or she killed another player. "Matthew told me to beware of that player but wouldn't reveal an identity." He'd just said, *Don't ask, if you ever want to know.* Merely thinking of Matthew made my anger churn. "Of course, the Fool's a cowardly liar, so I'm not banking on anything he said."

Both Aric and Lark looked surprised by my tone.

How could they be? Seething, I turned my attention back to the page.

> *XIII. Death, the Endless Knight (Aric)*
> ~~*XIV. Temperance, Collectress of Sins (Calanthe)*~~
> ~~*XV. The Devil, Foul Desecrator (Ogen)*~~
> *XVI. The Tower, Lord of Lightning (Joules)*
> ~~*XVII. The Star, Arcane Navigator*~~
> ~~*XVIII. The Moon, Bringer of Doubt (Selena)*~~

Just as I'd reduced Selena and Jack to epitaphs, Lark had reduced the Moon to a scratched-out name. Because of Richter, Selena had been banished to history.

> *XIX. The Sun, Hail the Glorious Illuminator (Sol)*
> *XX. Judgment, the Archangel (Gabriel)*
> *XXI. The World, This Unearthly One (Tess)*

Oh, God, they hadn't heard.

"I had a scout on Tess for a while," Lark said. "She's possibly the nicest person I've ever stalked."

"Her powers will suffer this game, becoming unstable," Aric said. "She needs mass amounts of calories to wield her abilities, and there's little food out in the wastelands."

Voice thick, I said, "The World is . . . gone."

"You mean *dead*?" Lark's lips parted. "Did Richter get her icon? Figures it'd be him!"

I shook my head. "Her death was an accident. Joules or Gabriel must have her icon." In the case of an Arcana's accidental death, the closest player would receive it.

"What happened?" Aric asked, with what might have been sympathy in his eyes.

"I believe Tess reversed time, and her power got away from her." At Lark's frown, I explained, "Each minute she went back in time drained her. Her corpse was wasted, the way it looked when she reversed time before. She loved to help so much. . . ."

Lark folded up her list and pocketed it. "You saw her body? Gabe and Joules just left her to rot?"

"Someone had buried her in Fort Arcana."

"What'd you do, Eves, go grave-digging?"

Aric had once told Jack, *If you can't speak your deeds, then don't do them.* "I . . . did. I had to know if it was Tess's grave—if reversing time was an option or not." Yet more evidence of my love for Jack.

I glanced at Aric. His eyes had turned cold as ash.

Lark made a sound of disbelief. "Damn, girl, you went to the mat, huh?"

It hadn't mattered. I hadn't been able to change fate. Did that mean I *never* would be able to alter the course of my life? Would I always fail—because I had zero control over my own destiny?

I was learning a lesson, painfully: maybe fate *couldn't* be changed.

And we were all fated to fight. Or die.

When Aric and I just stared at each other, Lark muttered a curse. "I forgot you two have . . . unresolved issues."

My need for revenge overshadowed everything. The Emperor was all I could think about now. I felt as if I hadn't taken a real breath since the massacre, hadn't truly slept between nightmares. All-business, I asked Aric, "What do you think Richter will do next?"

Aric's demeanor was equally emotionless. "In time, he and his alliance will locate us. If Fortune finds another helicopter, she could fly the Emperor here when he is at full power. If she acquires a *military* helicopter, she could fire on us herself, even deploying missiles. But Fauna's creatures will be our sentries, alerting us to any attack in advance."

Lark lifted her chin. "Damn straight."

Her animals would be our PEWS, a perimeter early warning system. Jack had taught me about that the day my mother had died. The day we'd burned down Haven and escaped together.

To keep from reacting, I imagined how Richter would look when I injected him with poison—the first time.

"But we'll be blind whenever she sleeps," Aric said. "So the Priestess keeps watch through her rivers. She has surrounded this area with water and controls the only road to the castle."

I somewhat recalled him yelling for Circe to let him pass. "Did she spare me because of you?"

He knocked back a shot. "Ask her."

I intended to. I'd been talking to puddles all this time; why stop now?

Then understanding dawned on me. "Whoa, whoa, it sounds like we're preparing for . . . a *defense.* I need the Emperor dead."

Aric's gaze fell on one of his shelves. "I forfeited the one weapon that could have defeated him from afar." The lightning javelin? He'd stolen it from Joules and safeguarded it for millennia. To save Selena from the Lovers—and gain my favor—he'd used the weapon intended for Richter.

In order to win me. Another decision he must regret.

Selena had died anyway. I'd chosen another man, and Aric had missed an opportunity to take Richter out the night of the massacre.

Can't change fate. "Then *I* will kill him. You promised that you and my grandmother would teach me how." In a past game, I'd taken down galleons, cracking them open like eggs. If I could tap into my full potential . . .

"The Tarasova will have more information about your abilities," he said. "I can help you train. But even if we felt confident of a victory, how will we find the Emperor without the Arcana calls?"

The idea of waiting to get vengeance nauseated me. I couldn't continue like this for much longer. It felt an awful lot like *enduring*—which was a slippery slope toward *acceptance*. "Lark and Circe will find him."

Lark's eyes flashed. "I've already got my scouts combing the area for Finn—and Richter. I'll merge with my animals as much as possible. On that note, I'm gonna make like a stray and get lost." She rose with her ferret. "Oh, here," she said, reaching into her pocket. She handed me the red ribbon, then slipped out of the room.

Feeling Aric's gaze on me, I fought not to react. He would suspect it had something to do with Jack—

"A token from the mortal, no doubt." Of course Aric would know. "You're taking this better than I'd expected."

He should've seen me at the gravestone. I clenched the ribbon and remained mute.

"Outwardly at least. Are we not to talk about Jack?"

His name was like a sudden gunshot about to free an avalanche. "No, we're not. I can't." Not yet.

"This is consuming you, but I'm not to be privy to your thoughts? Then you've turned your back on me again."

"Don't think of it like that, please." If Jack had been the love of my life, Aric was my soul mate. I loved this man, I regretted his lonely existence, and I appreciated everything he'd ever done for me. But I felt as if I'd lost Jack mere days ago.

The weeks I'd spent unconscious hadn't blunted my grief. When I'd had the hope of going back in time, I hadn't allowed myself to grieve. After that, I'd been too busy trying to reach Aric. "I'm hanging on by a thread here." As Jack had once told me.

"Then let me help you." Aric seemed to be saying so much with his eyes, yet I understood so little. I got the sense that he wanted me to remember something—but my mind wasn't up to speed.

I shook my aching head, struggling not to bleed out. *Not quite yet.*

He raked his fingers through his hair. "If you won't let me help, then what am I to you?"

Now, on the spot, I was supposed to label our relationship? We loved each other, but we weren't together romantically. If I believed that the game demanded blood and that fate couldn't be changed, then we never *should* be.

I didn't want to say the wrong thing, so I settled on the safest: "I . . . don't know?"

"Then Fauna is mistaken." His tone was like ice. "There is nothing unresolved on my part."

"What does that mean?" Where was the man who'd urged me to live, who'd cared for me?

"You are welcome in my home. We are allies, of a sort. That will be the extent of our relationship."

Of a sort? "I see." What were *my* eyes telling *him*?

I love you, but I have nothing left inside me. I'm a drained husk like Tess. My head's not right and won't be till Richter begs me to kill him.

Does the game demand *blood?*

I stood to go. "For what it's worth, thank you for the last two times you've saved me."

Voice gone low, he asked, "You're glad you didn't follow Deveaux into the flames?"

"No, you were right. I need to avenge him."

I didn't realize until later how unintentionally cruel my parting words to Aric had been. As if I had nothing else in my life?

Where's your head at, Evie?

20

I woke to my own cries, out of breath from another nightmare about Jack. Tears flowed down my cheeks like crimson seeping from a tourniquet.

"Twist, tighten, constrict," I muttered, gazing around with confusion. Where was I?

My glyphs lit my new suite. I frowned to find Cyclops taking up half of the bed. He must've nosed his way in here.

He blinked his eye at me. *Whatcha gonna do?*

I lay on his neck and scratched his scarred ears until the roosters began to crow (whenever they thought it should be dawn). Then I rose and took a shower.

Under the steaming water, I struggled to clear the fog in my mind and decide my path going forward.

Now that I'd warned Aric and Lark about Gran, I would take more time with her, chipping away at her beliefs day by day—while gleaning as much information as possible about the other cards. I might not agree with her about my allies, but she and I would be on the exact same page about my enemies.

Dressed in a sweater and jeans, I let Cyclops out, then knocked on Gran's door. No answer. Figuring she must still be asleep, I headed to the tower. The stairs were a misery on my still healing legs, but I made it to the top.

From the panoramic windows, I gazed out past the castle's slate roof into the drizzly darkness. The river at the base of the mountain coursed like a moat, looking small from this height.

I turned back to the room, surveying the sunny landscapes I'd painted on the walls. This tower was a time capsule in itself.

I sat on the bed and fired up the laptop—one present among the many Aric had given me. I'd stored my zip-drive's worth of family photos on it. Some part of me must have always known I would return to the castle of lost time.

From the bed, I could see my ballet slippers hanging on the back of the door. Aric had found them for me. Dancing for him had been pure pleasure, and each day I'd fallen for him more. I'd dreamed about him in this bed. And hated myself for missing Jack. . . .

Forcing my gaze from those slippers, I scrolled through pictures on my laptop. Gran might like to look at them. God, everything had been so shockingly green. This was how Jack had envisioned Acadiana. I patted my jeans pocket, where I kept the ribbon—

My eyes went wide. I didn't have a single picture of him. I scrambled for one of my blank drawing journals and a pencil set. I hadn't sketched much while here. Nothing had moved me to.

With my pencil flying over the paper, I drew Jack as he'd looked after taking command of the Azey South army. He'd ridden into Fort Arcana with his expression so heartbreakingly proud. He'd liked being a leader, and he'd been good at it. I would've said he'd been born for it, but his life had been cut too short.

On another page, I tried to capture the look in his eyes as he'd gazed down at me in Selena's pool, just before our first kiss. Next I would draw him within the cypress stand he'd described to me, when he'd told me a story about our dream day together: *We decided it was our place. No one else's. Because that was where we became Evie and Jack.*

As my pencil moved, I repeatedly whispered, "Twist, tighten, constrict—"

"Your grandmother is looking for you," Aric intoned from the doorway. I'd never heard his spurs. "She can't climb these stairs, so she bade me to come get you."

I clasped my sketchbook against my chest. "I tried her earlier, but she was asleep." How strange that I could be so numb inside, but I still felt love for Aric. My blood-starved heart had leapt at the sight of him.

"I'm sure you're keen to catch up with her about old times." Sarcasm?

"Will she and I talk about the past? I hope so." In time. "But I'm also mindful that Richter could be heading our way. I need to learn everything she can teach me."

He leaned one of his broad shoulders against the doorframe. "And she will be delighted to instruct you, I assure you."

I narrowed my eyes. "You brought her here. You told me you wanted me to learn."

"After I saved your life and reunited the two of you, I didn't think her first lesson would be to eliminate *me*. At best, it's flawed game strategy, since I am motivated to protect you."

"I can pick and choose what I decide to believe," I assured him. "To *use*."

"Take care that she doesn't poison your mind."

"Didn't you hear? I'm immune to poison."

Aric parted his lips to say something, then seemed to think better of it. As he strode away, the sound of his spurs rang in my ears.

I glanced back at my sketch. When had I drawn a frame of flames around Jack?

21

THE HUNTER
SOMEWHERE FAR IN THE WEST

"Goan to die in this hellhole," I muttered. "Down here in the dark."

I hadn't choked down anything but hardtack in weeks, would be damned before eating the "meat." My bones were jutting, but I wouldn't last long enough to starve.

Fever would take me soon.

I shook, sweating against the freezing ground. Breaths wheezing. Dirt and salt caked my damp skin, all along the whip marks on my bare back. Stung like fire.

The slavers gave prisoners four hours a night to sleep, but I refused to pass out. I couldn't stand the nightmares, the *ghosts*. They were coming for me—'cause I was about to walk among them.

I squeezed my eyes closed. Yet that made the sounds of the ghosts even louder.

Maman's liquor bottle clinking against a glass. Her rosary beads whispering as I took them from her neck. Clotile's soft-spoken French. The sharp pop of gunfire when she shot herself.

I heard the folks in my Azey army. Just before Richter attacked, there'd been laughter and music. Everyone had been happy. Hopeful.

Over and over, I heard Selena's scream of fury: *"Emperor!"* She'd sensed Richter a split-second before he'd struck.

I replayed her fierce look as she'd shoved me off a moving horse into an abandoned mine. I'd crashed through rotted planks down into that deep shaft just as the blast had hit.

Radio busted ... lava chasing me underground ... a rushing flood carrying me through the mountain and out the other side ... miles ... pain ... darkness ... waking in shackles ...

Slavers had sold me west. Now I was trapped in yet another mine.

Evangeline haunted me more than all of them. Was she among the living or the dead? I'd led her right to the Emperor. Had she been far enough away from the explosion? Sometimes I thought yes, sometimes no, tormenting myself, going back and forth.

Death hadn't been far. He might've sensed the Emperor's approach like Selena had. Domīnija could've used his unnatural speed to rescue Evie.

I would give anything to know she was okay. Would sell my soul to see her eyes one last time. Whenever she got excited, they shimmered. I'd imagined them all lit up when she'd talked to me on the radio about snow. She'd laughed, and my heart had soared. She'd chosen *me.*

Right before the blast—

My eyes flashed open in the dim mine. Had I heard *whispering* along with the ghosts? I couldn't make out the words.

I darted my gaze. After my last fight with the slavers, I was still seeing double—which was how I'd gotten this fever in the first place. Desperate to escape, squinting in the dark, I'd swung my pickax at the lock on one of my ankle cuffs.

Fucking missed.

I'd gouged out a good chunk of flesh. At best, half of my leg would be lost to infection. What use would the overseers have for a slave who couldn't mine salt? None. They'd slit my throat and feed me to the rest.

Probably why the other prisoners avoided me.

'Cause I was already dead.

The whisper returned: *"Hunter."*

The hallucinations were getting worse. Losing my mind right along with my leg.

"Hunter, Hunter, Hunter."

Sounded so real. I wanted to yell, "I ain't the hunter!" The hunter was the idiot who got all those people killed. The idiot who might've gotten Evie killed.

"Hunterrrrrr."

"Va t'en! Laisse-moi tranquille!" Go away! Leave me alone!

"HUNTERRRRRR!"

I shot upright from the dirt. Damn near blacked out. Was that . . . the Fool's voice?

22

THE EMPRESS

Cold rain fell outside, but Gran and I were warm in her lavish sitting room in front of the roaring fire.

If the flames reminded me of Jack, I gave no outward sign, numb again after this morning. I'd furiously filled half a notebook with sketches of him.

Gran sipped from her teacup. Though I sensed a nervous energy in her, she looked more exhausted than yesterday.

She nodded toward the fancy tea tray, with its cheese and fruit selections. "Despite all of Death's faults, he does provide some perks."

"He's definitely equipped to ride out an apocalypse in style." The inside of the castle was as luxurious as the outside was spooky.

The Flash had charred its gray stone walls with black streaks. Fog seemed trapped on the grounds. Flickering gas lamps lit the courtyard, the training yard, and the long winding drive.

I remember thinking this castle was haunted by Death. By his loneliness. I told Gran, "You could call him Aric, you know. His name is Aric Domīnija."

She shrugged. "I know. Death introduced himself when he picked me up."

So much for my little attempt at humanizing him.

"When I first got here, I snooped around," she said. "And I asked Paul questions. We talked a lot." She sounded as if she liked the guy. Paul was about twenty-six or so, with buzz-cut black hair. His blue eyes were widely spaced, and he had a toothy grin that made him approachable. "He told me Death calls this place Lethe, named after one of the five rivers in Hades, the river of forgetfulness. Do you know why?"

I'd called this place the castle of lost time, which hadn't been too far off the mark. "It is close to *lethal*. But I don't know for certain." Aric was such a stickler for meanings and details, I could be sure he'd picked the name for a reason.

In the past, he'd told me he never wanted to forget my previous betrayals. But in the agonizing centuries between games, he'd smoked opium, had probably *yearned* to forget.

"The knight prepared this place for just about every catastrophe," Gran said. "It's out of the flood zone, and away from nuclear fallout sectors. There are thick metal shutters to cover every window. I even found copper plating in the walls to shield against electrical storms."

With no sun and the temperatures dropping, this castle was a self-sustaining oasis. I pictured it as a spaceship on a barren moon, with the only life support around: crops and livestock, clean water, sunlamps, filtered air, and tankers of fuel.

Too bad it couldn't withstand a helicopter missile attack. Or a volcano.

Gran reached for the teapot to top off her cup. "We're not close to active magma, so if the Emperor attacks, he will have to spill blood to generate his own lava."

Richter created it with his blood? "The way I generate plants when none are around?" The way the Lovers had created their carnates.

Circe had told me the Emperor's hands bled lava. I hadn't made the connection. No wonder he was recuperating.

Gran nodded. "Which drains your power." She set down the pot, looking fatigued just from lifting it. "There's another way to grow. I'll show you—" She coughed, the movements racking her frail frame.

I leapt up to rub her back. "Did you sleep at all?"

When the fit eased, she smoothed her hair. "For ten hours. Woke up more tired, though. Stress must be catching up with me."

I took my seat again. "Gran, what if you had a stroke?"

"Did *Death* tell you that?" The sudden venom in her tone startled me. "Next he'll tell you that I'm losing my wits. He means to drive a wedge between us." Her teacup shook when she raised it to her lips.

"Aric wouldn't do that. He doesn't lie. He could have a hundred times to further his own agenda, but he refuses to." What had he told me and Jack? *Lies are curses you place on yourself.*

She set her cup down hard. "*All* Arcana lie. And feign emotion and betray. It's the nature of the beast."

In the past, I'd tried to seduce Aric, faking affection. Finn had disguised himself as Jack to seduce Selena. She'd lied to me, Lark too. Matthew most of all: *Empress is my friend.*

My denial died on my lips. Still, I didn't believe Aric would. "He told me that you would know a great many things about the game, and that you might have foresight."

She allowed the change of subject. "Nothing like the Fool's precognition. But I get feelings about the future. They guide me, directing my movements. Right now I'm feeling you won't be ready for the next stage of the game."

"Why not?" I asked, revenge ever on my mind.

"Your powers aren't mature. If they had been, you could've fought off those Bagman bites instantly. You need to practice, from your basic skills on up." She dug in her pocket, retrieved three seeds, and set them on the tray. "Do you feel a connection to them?"

"I sense their potential." And I could tell their species: pomegranate, climbing ivy, and wisteria.

"Now try to bring forth a bud without blood. Imagine them sprouting. Casting off their shells."

Shells. Husks. A withered corpse planted in the dirt. Tess's body was like a forever-dead seed. "I-I'll try."

"Once you master this, you'll be able to sense buried seeds out in the Ash. Your arsenal will be anywhere on earth."

I concentrated on the ones before me and pictured them growing. I sucked in a breath when they began to vibrate. No bloodletting necessary. A tiny sprout was budding from one seed, had gained only about a millimeter. I focused, beginning to sweat.

"You're doing great. Look at you!" Her words reminded me of my childhood. I recalled how she'd praised me for finding colored eggs one Easter. I'd proudly held up my basket, and someone had snapped a photo of me, Mom, and Gran. Mom had held that picture as she'd passed away with Jack by her side.

She'd died because of Bagmen. We'd burned her body because of the Lovers. Jack had died without grace because of the Emperor.

Jack's eulogy had been Richter's laughter. Rage welled in me, as powerful as Circe's tidal wave. *Replace the Emperor's laughter with screams—*

The seeds cracked open; plants exploded outward to crawl and fork across the ceiling and walls.

"Good Lord, Evie!" Gran looked at me ... with awe. "I think you could be the most dangerous Empress ever to live." She surveyed the new growths.

Regardless of the seed species, all had become vines with daggerlike thorns. I slumped back in my seat. "As long as that means the Emperor dies."

"You're one step closer to truly becoming the Empress."

I swiped at my forehead and reached for a glass of water. "I'm not now? What will change?"

"When you fully give in to the heat of battle, your hair will turn red permanently and your skin markings will always show. You'll be more powerful than you can imagine."

All I had to do was give myself over to the red witch forever. Would I take that risk to kill Richter?

One problem: the red witch might not stop with him. *Evie is a sliver of ME!*

Gran frowned. "I was actually surprised your hair is still blond. But no matter. We'll keep working. You mastered that so quickly, I think there's something else you should work on. Close your eyes and cover your ears."

I did. I sensed movement, a scrape of metal. One of my vines shifted, so I opened my eyes.

Gran stood in front of me with a sharp paring knife inches above my head—and that vine gripping her wrist.

I waved a hand to release her. "You really were going to, uh, stab me?"

She set the knife back on the tray. "Yes." Rubbing her wrist, she sat again. "You would heal, and the attack needed to be real for your vines to react."

My soldiers had had a mind of their own. And I'd seemed to sense through them.

At the Lovers' lair, I'd set vines free, commanding them to kill Bagmen, even perceiving destruction through them. But I'd never felt them working on autopilot before, with no conscious thought from me. "I wouldn't even have to look behind me to aim?"

She nodded. "Your vines have an awareness. Even when you sleep, they keep watch. Unfortunately, they're not foolproof. Some players, like Death, are too quick. He's slipped past your sentries before. Other players—like the Tower—strike from too far away for your plants to detect them."

"What else can I do?" I asked, eager to learn.

"You can become a talented healer. You have an innate knowledge of medicinal plants, and I'll teach you more. You can also manipulate wood. Past Empresses crafted priceless jewelry pieces, giving them as signs of favor. And with a wave of her hand, one Empress constructed bridges and shrines, building an entire civilization, easily garrisoning her army of men."

Aric had told me I'd commanded an army in the past, one that had clashed against the Emperor's.

"Another Empress could spy on foes through any plant on earth. She could even meld her body with a tree, transporting herself from one trunk to another."

"No way!" Could I meld into a tree? Hadn't I once had the urge to put my fingers in the soil and take root?

"Not that there are any trees left to travel through." Gran sighed. "I'll show you more after you've rested. You're still recovering."

"I'm fine. I can do this." But *she* looked as if my exercise had weakened her.

"In time. For now, why don't you tell me about your interactions with Death? He was the *last* person I expected to show up at my door."

"What made you go with him?"

"I had a feeling that was my path, and I was on borrowed time anyway. Plus he knew things about you. Your art. Your ballet. The name of your horse. He said that you'd spent months trying to reach me, and he planned to give you whatever you desired. Could've knocked me over with a feather."

Despite knowing everything about me, even my malicious past, Aric still loved me. I didn't want to hurt him anymore. But every time I contemplated my life, all I saw was my past—Jack—and my future—Richter.

"Death is very protective of you," she said. "He can't help it. He's cursed to desire you each game."

Ouch. "Gran, it's more than just desire."

She sighed. "He's got you believing he loves you, doesn't he? He's killed you two out of the last three games. He *beheaded* you." As I'd pointed out to him last night. "He's a villain, Evie."

Time to explain the new program to Gran. "Aric would give his life for mine. I trust him."

"I admit he did go to great lengths to rescue you. But only because he can touch you. He's a red-blooded male, and you're the sole woman he can be with. What wouldn't he do to preserve your life?"

Again, ouch. "Then why would he return you to me?"

"As a courtship gift, to sway your favor. He's notoriously calculating, does everything for a reason."

She was right about the courtship. Aric had admitted as much. He'd intended to use my grandmother to coerce me, but in the end, he hadn't gone through with it. He'd wanted me to choose him—but only if I loved him more than Jack.

How could I explain that to Gran? She would never believe it anyway.

"We will use this to our advantage," she said. "He'll continue to protect you, so you should keep him alive to the very end." Aric would be happy to know her game strategy was no longer flawed. "Your victory is so close."

I shuddered at the idea of *winning*. "Can the game be stopped?" Could fate be changed?

"I don't follow." She blinked at me, as if I'd just asked, "Hey, can I borrow your credit card and pop over to the mall?"

"I know others have tried to stop it before."

"Some players united, making a big show of peace. But in the end, all those alliances failed. Arcana are born to kill. They only delayed the inevitable."

"Why is it inevitable?"

"The gods decreed this game," she said. "They set these events into motion eons ago. Someone has to win. No matter what, someone *will* win. Say the last two cards allied for a couple of decades: they would both age. Once one died, the other would walk the earth—older, weaker. Disadvantaged in the next game."

When he'd sought a future with me, clever Aric had already come up with a solution to this problem. He and I would live our lives together, with Lark tagging along. We would somehow predecease her (that part had been vague), and she would endure for centuries, forced to play the next game against Arcana young enough to be her grandkids. Yet she'd volunteered for it!

Being with Aric had seemed so complicated, so loaded with intrigues.

When I'd chosen Jack, I'd also been choosing the future he represented: building Acadiana, far from the game, repurposing my abilities to help others.

Gran said, "Not that the Minor Arcana would allow such a union anyway."

My eyes widened. "They exist?" In a Tarot deck, there were fifty-six

Minor Arcana cards, divided into four suits: cups, pentacles or rings, wands, and swords.

Such as the eerie *ten of swords* card. I couldn't imagine that one as a person.

Gran's gray brows drew together. "Of course," she said, as if she was telling me something I should already know. "They can be as dangerous as Major Arcana. Especially the court cards."

"Where are they?" Did they converge too? "How do you find them?"

"You *don't*," she said. "Best avoid them. Let's hope the Knight of Swords perished in the Flash. The Queen of Cups too. Truly, a good dozen of them are walking nightmares."

"Aric said he sees evidence of them everywhere in some games; other games, no sign at all. He also said that some believe Tarasovas are Minors."

Gran crossed her arms over her chest. "Bull manure. I'm no Minor. They have their own functions—to hide evidence of the Major Arcana, to hasten the game, and then to rebuild the civilization afterward. *My* function is to make sure you win."

Why hadn't Matthew told me about them? Or had he? The last time I'd seen him, he'd said there were now five obstacles to beware: Bagmen, slavers, militia, cannibals, and . . . Minors. "The Fool told me the Minors watch us, plotting against us. I thought he was talking about *miners*, with an *e*." How many times had I misunderstood his decoder-ring talk? Sometimes I could have sworn he'd confused me on purpose. "Why would they plot?"

"They'll want the earth righted as soon as possible. Minors like to see *dead* Majors—because catastrophes end with the close of the game."

I'd made promises over my mother's body to find Gran and see if we could fix all that the apocalypse had broken. Was *dying* the most helpful thing I could do to further that end?

"Once you've collected all the icons, the earth should come back," Gran said. "The sun as well."

"*Should* come back?"

"There's never been a disaster like this. I can't say for certain." She rubbed her temples, like I did whenever my head was hurting. "When you were a girl, I knew you would be important to the future of humanity, but I didn't know how. Maybe you're supposed to reseed the planet."

Yet I couldn't do that permanently until the game ended and daylight came back—if I even won. For that to happen, I'd have to lose Aric, Lark, Circe, Finn, Joules, and Gabriel. In other words, I'd be insane.

Now Gran had just confirmed a new threat—to all of them. I'd have to think about the Minors later. *Put 'em on the list.* "When the Empress won before, what did she do until the next game?"

Aric had revealed how he'd spent his solitary centuries: "I wander the earth and see men age before my eyes. I read any book or paper I can get my hands on. I watch the stars in the sky; over my lifetime some dim, some brighten. I sleep for weeks at a time and chase the dragon."

When he'd made that confession, I'd thanked God I hadn't been cursed to that. *His horse looks sick, and he has no friends.* Why would he have made friends? Just to watch them die, over and over?

Gran frowned. "What did the Empress *do*? She was immortal."

"But how did she spend her time? What was her life like?" *My life.*

"I don't know," she said, clearly stumped. "Chroniclers only document the games. She probably ruled over men as a goddess. And relived her most glorious victories."

So the Empress had spent centuries gazing at the twenty-one icons on the backs of her hands. *I'll pass.* The more I thought about the game, the more I saw my battle against Richter as a one-way ticket. I didn't expect to walk away unscathed from a murderer who leveled mountains and bled lava.

And I'd never stop until he was dead. "Gran, would you rather that I live happily for a few months or be miserable for hundreds of years?"

"We don't have time for silly questions," she said, exasperated. "Your immortal life will be a tribute to the gods. You will be the winner. You must be." She waved at the vines seeming to pulsate all around us. "And why *shouldn't* you win? You've already made brilliant plays. Your alliance is well-picked for the most part. Though Circe can be tricky." A sudden gust of wind spattered rain against the window. Gran's eyes darted toward the glass. "The Flash must have weakened her. Circe's attack on the Emperor would have too. But she regains her strength with every single drop." Gran met my gaze again. "At least that little Fauna will be easy to remove."

My claws sharpened at even the imagined threat to Lark. The vines on the ceiling skittered. Enough. "I need you to understand some things. I didn't turn out like you hoped. Given the choice, I would never fight or play this game. These icons on my hand disgust me—I have them only because I fought for my own life. I'll help take out the Emperor and his allies, but I could never hurt my friends."

Her eyes went wild. "Friends? *Friends?* They will betray you at the first opportunity!" Spittle dotted her lips. "The only reason Death might not is because his lust is stronger than his age-old need to kill." She leaned in aggressively. "Do you think they care about you?"

I squared my shoulders. "Yes, I do."

"You won't for long," she promised me. "Not after you've read our chronicles from front to back."

"What are you talking about? We don't have written chronicles."

"You *know* we do."

Mouth gone dry, I shook my head hard. "You would've ... you would've shown them to me."

"Evie," she said in a measured tone, "I *did*."

23

THE HUNTER

"Coo-yôn?"

A light neared, getting brighter. A lantern? Shadows wavered over the rock walls. I raised a hand to my forehead, shielding my eyes. Hadn't seen this much light in weeks.

I squinted. Blinked. Blinked again. The image remained.

Before me was two of . . . Matthew. "Hunter!"

"You a ghost? You goan to take me to hell?"

He frowned. "Do you know the way?"

Sounded like something he'd say! Could this truly be *coo-yôn?* My heart got to pounding—made my leg throb like the devil. "You real?"

In a too-loud voice, he said, "We're leaving."

"Shhh! You *are* real." I choked out words: "Did Evie . . . d-did my girl . . . live?" I held my breath, waiting for his answer. The next few seconds would decide whether I hoped for a future—or accepted the end of a life that already felt too long.

Every moment of my existence seemed to lead up to this strange kid's next words. All the pain. All the confusion. And then that sweet, sweet time when Evangeline Greene was all mine . . .

"Empress lived. Her smile died."

"Ah, God, my girl's alive." Relief made me even more lightheaded. *"Alive."* I shuddered, and my eyes grew damp. Couldn't control my emotions, me. "How? I thought I got her killed like the rest."

"Tredici saved her."

"Tre-what?" Was he talking about Domīnija? I'd figured as much.

"Death!"

"Quiet, *coo-yôn*." I slept apart from the other captives, but somebody would hear him before long. "I gotta get to Evie." I tried to scramble up on my good leg. Only busted my ass.

Waves of dizziness hit. I had to gnash my teeth to keep from blacking out. "How'd you sneak past the guards?" Shackled slaves could move around down here at the terminus, but two armed guards kept anyone from getting near the mine elevator.

Coo-yôn shrugged. "Mad skillz."

"Who's with you? They comin' in guns blazing?" I was going to get free of this hellhole! I'd get back to my girl.

He lowered his lantern. "I'm *rogue*."

I tried sitting up again, slowly. "What's that mean? Is Evie close?" *God, let her be.*

"I'm alone."

The fuck? "No other Arcana with you? Then I'm trapped here. And soon you will be too if you doan go." I sank back against the stone wall. "Tell her I love her. Tell her... tell her I'll see her again. Somewhere, someway. Now leave!"

He shook his head and covered his lips with a forefinger. He was shushing me? After he'd been so loud? "Time for you to go."

Started to ask him if he was crazy. Already knew the answer to that, me. "You must mean I'm about to die. You here to see me out?"

"To see you *up*."

"You talking topside?" I squinted again. Was that blood on the backs of his hands?

Blood on his hands. Just like I had blood on mine. An army's worth. "Why didn't you warn me about Richter?" Jaw clenched, I grabbed the hem of his coat. "We lost Selena to that *fils de pute*. We lost an army."

"I see far."

"Goddamn it, *why*. Tell me you had a reason to let everyone die."

"I had a reason."

"More important than the future of mankind? 'Cause that's what we were dealing with." Maybe that attack had kept Richter from targeting even more people. Maybe the entire army would've gotten bonebreak fever and died in agony. "How can I trust you again?"

"Attempt escape, Hunter. Or be cut up for meat."

Trusting him would be like playing Russian roulette with more than one bullet in the chamber.

He slanted his head. "It's time for you to go. I thought you'd want to see her."

"Of course I want to! Desperate to. But unless you got a hacksaw . . ." My blurry eyes tried to follow his movements.

From a backpack, *coo-yôn* produced a goddamned hacksaw! The Fool was saving my ass? The rescuer being rescued?

Dizziness had the mine spinning. I gave my head a hard shake. "Might pass out, *coo-yôn*. You got a plan to get us out of here?"

He knelt to saw. "No plan."

Merde! "You ready to fight your way out of here, boy?" I asked, though he'd never lifted a finger to fight in the past. "If we doan win, they're goan to catch us and lock you down here."

When he peered up at me again, my blurred vision failed to place him for a second, almost as if I were seeing another face. Or a . . . mask. He didn't look like the boy I'd spent months working beside.

Then he gave me his usual blank grin, back to the Fool again. He truly *didn't* have a plan.

All the sudden *I* could read the future. By tonight, he would be in chains, and I'd be butchered. . . .

24

THE EMPRESS

Creepy book in hand, I sat beside the fire in Gran's room.

Sure enough, the Empress's line had chronicles.

Either I was going crazy, had gone crazy, or my grandmother was lying. Had she truly shown the book to me half my life ago? How could my memories have gotten so scrambled?

Both Matthew and Selena had said my line chronicled, but I'd thought the knowledge had been passed down verbally or something.

After Gran's revelation, she'd dug an ancient-looking book out of her bag, having trouble lifting the weighty thing. The battered leather of the cover looked like the skin of a Bagman.

She'd been stunned by my lack of recognition, sinking down on her bed, looking ten years older. "No wonder you hesitate to kill them," she'd said, as if explaining the worst tragedy. . . .

Now she watched me like a hawk. "Nothing?" I shook my head. "How could you not remember?"

"I was only eight when you went away, and I was forbidden to talk about anything you taught me." Young as I was, I'd been old enough to know that Mom had banished my grandmother for her beliefs. Why wouldn't I have pushed Arcana stuff from my mind to avoid a similar fate? "When I got older and I had visions of the apocalypse, Mom blamed you, so she sent me to a head-shrink place, like the one you went to. I got . . . deprogrammed."

They'd pumped me full of drugs, then asked, *Do you understand why you must reject your grandmother's teachings?* Those mental ward docs had done a number on my head, but I'd thought I'd shaken off most of their "therapy."

Yet I'd failed to recall vital events from the past. No, the situation was worse than that: I hadn't even realized the memories were missing in the first place. "I have ... gaps in my memory." My brain felt like Swiss cheese at this point. Apparently, the gaps even predated the deprogramming.

If Gran was telling the truth about all this ...

So why did I sense she was lying to me—about *something?* "I remember the day you were arrested. You talked to me about the cards."

"I'd been talking to you about them all your life, always telling you stories." Almost to herself, she said, "I knew Karen hated my beliefs. Didn't know how much though."

"Maybe reading will trigger some recollection." Would I recognize these pages from my childhood? Why would she ever lie about this?

But I hesitated to open the book. It gave me chills. Even Gran gave me chills. "This was passed down?"

"From my mother, and then her mother before her."

Mom had told me the whole line was disturbed. I supposed I was merely the latest in a long line. "How far back do these chronicles go?"

"There are detailed entries from the last two games, but the games before that are summarized." She waved me on. "Open it, then."

If this book was the gateway to transforming permanently into the red witch, would I be tempting fate just to read it?

With a shaking hand, I cracked open the weathered leather. The scent of old parchment swirled up. An orderly script filled the page. It began: *What followeth is the trew and sworne chronikles of Our Lady of Thorns, the Emperice of all Arcana, chosen to represent Demeter and Aphrodite, embody'g life, all its cycles, and the myst'ries of love. . . .*

"Who was the chronicler here?" I asked. "Who wrote these words?"

"They've been translated by chroniclers over the generations, transcribed and retranscribed. But they were first recorded by the Empress's mother."

"*My* mother, in that other life. Was Mom reincarnated too? Were you?"

Gran shrugged. "Maybe. We can't know for certain."

"Was this chronicler a Tarasova?"

"Probably. We've been fortunate in our line. Our chroniclers are usually gifted with second sight."

I took a deep breath, bracing myself to read. . . .

At the beginning of the oldest entries, the Empress's mother— possibly Mom in another life—had summarized what they'd gathered about the previous games, all the way to the first one.

In the inaugural game, my allies had been the Fool, Fauna, and the Priestess. My kills: the Star, the Hierophant, and the Hermit.

Though I'd been brimming with power, it hadn't saved me. My death had been at the hand of a trusted friend, the ultimate winner—

The Fool.

My jaw slackened. My stomach roiled. He'd murdered her.

Me.

Matthew, my former best friend, had beheaded me. His ally.

Gran's tone was smug as she said, "Still feel the same way about your *friends?*"

No. No, I did not. I'd barely cracked open the book before I'd almost puked.

Matthew had won the entire game. And he remembered the past! He *knew* about his betrayal. My nausea worsened as I gazed at the back of my hand, at my icons.

Did the Fool stare at his hands so much because he missed seeing his own sick icons? *The markings must be earned. . . .*

25

THE HUNTER

The second metal cuff finally fell away, revealing my lower leg. I winced. Infected to high hell and back. I told *coo-yôn*, "If you doan have a plan—or an army—to get us out of here, then we need weapons."

Say we could somehow make it topside. I knew of only two ways in or out: one for people, and one for trucks. The first was insanely guarded, the second *impossibly* guarded.

"No weapons." He stretched my arm over his shoulders, lifting me with surprising ease. But then, I'd lost weight and he'd gained muscle. He'd grown taller too, was my height now.

He started down the mine shaft. Too bad we'd never get *to* the elevator, much less *up*.

We passed coughing, bedded-down slaves. Everyone down here seemed to have sickness in the lungs, myself included.

The other men didn't holler to be freed or to join us. 'Cause they all knew this escape attempt was hopeless. I heard some of them muttering: "Dumbasses." "Where do they think they're going?" "We'll be dining on them all week."

Matthew and I neared the elevator. "*Coo-yôn*, I can't see shit. But I know the guards have automatic weapons."

"Yes."

Again, what choice did I have but to trust this boy? When we arrived at the elevator, I frowned. No guards?

Damn my heart for pounding. All it did was make my head swirl and my leg throb some more. And it wasn't like we would get past the dozen or so slavers above anyway.

Matthew shoved the elevator gate aside, helping me in. It took me three tries to push the right switch. We started upward. "If they ain't waiting for us, then get ready to run for the door."

We were about to reach topside! Never thought I'd live to see it again.

The elevator clanged to a stop. He dragged back the door with a screech, and I tensed to fight. . . .

No one. "I'll be damned." We lurched out into the overseers' quarters, a large area with corrugated metal walls. Low fluorescent lights dangled from the rock ceiling. Beds and chairs were scattered throughout. "Where is everybody?" Maybe the Fool had timed this rescue while the men were away.

"Think," *coo-yôn* said. "Safety starts with you." Huh? He pointed to an old workplace sign that I could barely make out.

"*Ouais.* Thanks for reading that for me." Below the sign was a weapons cage. I squinted and made out a padlock. "Need inside that cage, me."

He helped me head toward it, rounding some map tables. "Why ain't there a soul . . . ?" I trailed off when something squelched under my bare feet.

Blood? It had congealed in the dirt.

I gazed past the tables. My vision couldn't be right, 'cause I saw hacked-up and bullet-riddled bodies.

Glassy eyes. Jutting tongues. A nearly severed head. Spatter painted the walls.

Who'd done this bloodbath? "You . . . you gotta be working with Gabe? Joules?"

Though Matthew had never locked gazes with me before, he stared me down. In a spine-chilling tone, he said, "Hunts. And campaigns."

"*You* did this?" He'd never once set out to hurt anyone before. Never even raised his voice, except with fear.

"They did it to themselves. Knives and guns."

Two dead overseers had bloody machetes in hand. Others held rifles. I'd been so far down in the mine I hadn't heard gunshots. "But you somehow *made* them do it."

"I hunted and campaigned."

Again, I felt like I was with a stranger.

A man's voice sounded from the entrance: "Where the hell is everybody?"

"*Putain!*" I bit out under my breath. "The next shift must be here. A dozen more men'll be between us and the exit. You got any bright ideas?"

In the space of a heartbeat, he was back to being a nonchalant seventeen-year-old. "Didn't get farther than this. My power ran out."

"Go snatch a gun off the dead!"

Blank look.

"All right, take *me* to a weapon."

He guided me to a fallen overseer, then helped me dip to grab an automatic rifle. I straightened—

A bullet whizzed past my head.

"Go, go!" I fired blindly over my shoulder. A yell told me I'd hit somebody.

As Matthew started away, more bullets peppered the metal wall beside us.

He was all but carrying me as I hobbled along on one leg, slowing him down. Fucking hated being dead weight! I blindly fired again. *Click. Click.* Out of ammo!

The slavers stopped shooting their precious bullets, probably 'cause we were headed *into* the mine. We'd be trapped. The only other way out was the impossible exit: the vehicle bay.

Coo-yôn led me deeper into a maze of corridors. We turned right. Then left. Right again. Unless some allies were back here waiting for us, we were just running toward our doom.

The corridor opened up to a wider area. He dragged me along, then propped me up against something. A six-foot-tall truck wheel? He'd stopped at one of those monster-size haulers.

"Here, Hunter!" He waved toward something.

A set of blurry steps jogged in front of my eyes. Must be ten feet up to the hauler's cab. "Leave me. I can't make those—"

Matthew swooped me up in a fireman's carry and bounded up the stairs. Just like I'd done with him in his flooded basement—the first time I'd saved his ass.

Coo-yôn was loading *me?* Up was down. He dumped me on the floor behind the pilot seat. The world spun. *Stay conscious or die.* "You doan know how to operate this thing!" I had only a general idea. Back when I'd plotted my escape, I'd studied the drivers and how they handled these loaders down on the slave level. "You've never even driven a car, *non?* I gotta get behind the wheel, me. Is it automatic?" No way I could use this leg for the clutch.

"Not automatic."

Damn it! "You got any idea how to drive a stick?"

"In theory!"

If I could somehow talk him through this, we might—*might*—have a shot at breaking out through the vehicle bay. "Battery switches... outside in a box. Flip every one." *Please doan let the box be locked.*

He set off. A minute later, lights in the cab blazed on.

More shouts, still in the distance. They didn't know where we were. For now.

When Matthew climbed behind the wheel, I said, "I'm goan to help you drive this thing." I tried to sit up. Bad move. Definitely about to black out. I collapsed back. But this meant I couldn't see anything above the dash. "Look for an engine ignition."

Coo-yôn started pushing every button and yanking every lever. The heavy-duty hauler bed groaned as it chugged higher and lower. Belts hummed. Blinking lights flashed.

"Damn it, you just let 'em know where we're at. You didn't see that coming?"

"Told you. Power. Empty."

"Find the ignition, and lay off the buttons!"

Too late; bullets riddled the truck door. Men yelled for backup.

"Ignition?" Matthew asked. The engine rumbled to life.

My eyes went wide. "Hell yeah, now take off the brake!" Between gulps of air, I coached him how to work the pedals, how to work the gearshift to one.

Grinding. Metal on metal. Cogs sounded like they were about to buckle. Then . . .

We were moving!

Backward?

BOOM!

We'd collided with a giant pillar. A *support* pillar. "Work the gearshift opposite of *R*!" I heard rock cracking. "Fast, fast!"

Grinding again. We were moving . . . forward. "That's it, boy!" We had to be headed toward the vehicle bay! By now the slavers would be lining up trucks to block us in.

As we picked up speed, we bounced off the mine walls like a pinball, *coo-yôn* overadjusting the steering wheel.

"Try *NOT* to hit the sides!"

He craned his head back and cast me a grin.

"Eyes forward!" We scraped another wall. "Doan try to shift. Keep it this speed."

The lights grew brighter in the mine. Shouts got louder. More gunshots. We had to be getting close.

"They parked a line of trucks," he said. "Blocking the bay doors."

"Is there a load in the back of this hauler?"

He glanced over his shoulder. "Yes."

"Get up some more speed!" Maybe with the size of this truck and the weight of a full bed, we could bust through. "Aim for the space between the two smallest trucks, but hit it head on. Doan angle it, and do not let off that gas—you hear me?" I braced my good leg against the side of the cab. "Faster! Redline this engine!"

"Hold on!" He laid on the horn—

BOOM!

We rammed the blockade. I barely kept myself from slamming into the back of Matthew's seat.

His head snapped forward, face smacking the steering wheel. Had he let up on the gas? "We're stuck between trucks, Hunter."

Bullets pinged the door. Shattered the windshield. The hauler heaved, made like it'd stall. "Drop the hammer! More gas!" Metal shrieked. The engine strained. The cab vibrated till my teeth felt like they'd rattle out of my head. "Pedal down!" More straining. More bullets. Engine about to blow.

I heard a couple of men yelling, latching on to the hauler, climbing to the cab. "*Coo-yôn*, find the lever that raised the bed!"

He reached forward. "This one?"

The hydraulics engaged. "Rev that one too!" Shafts spun. Pistons pumped. The bed rose faster, dumping salt.

Then... the resistance gave way! We were grinding forward between trucks, scraping off men and spewing tons of salt.

"Hunter, hold on. We're about to hit the—"

CRASH!

"—doors."

Fighting off more dizziness, I said, "Try for the next gear."

Grind, grind. The transmission shifted, and the hauler rumbled along, still dragging something that screeched.

"The salt buried their trucks on our way out!" *Coo-yôn* peered back at me again. "All clear." Blood welled from his forehead, coursing down his face, a crimson mask.

Again my blurred vision made out another face. Matthew was like a *sosie*, an evil double.

"All clear," he repeated, but I didn't feel that way at all.

My head grew light, consciousness fading. "You goan to get me to Evie?" My life was in the hands of somebody I didn't recognize. "Tell her I'm coming."

"If you make it. Fifty-fifty."

I couldn't fight off the blackness anymore.

26

THE EMPRESS

I banged on the door to Aric's study. After rereading the Fool's betrayal for what must've been the hundredth time, I'd realized something.

This murder might be the secret Aric had kept for Matthew.

I'd slammed the book shut and announced that I was heading down to talk to Death. As I'd limped out of the room, Gran had called, "Remember not to kill him yet!"

Now Aric muttered from inside his study, "Leave me in peace."

"Open it, Reaper." As I'd hobbled down here, the lingering pain in my legs and head had ratcheted up my irritation. "Or I'll use a claw to jimmy the lock."

After a while, he opened the door.

I sidled past him and took my customary seat.

He didn't offer me a shot of vodka, but he poured himself a glass—from the bottle already on his desk. His hair was disheveled, his amber eyes bleary.

Despite everything, concern for him welled, muting some of my anger. I felt as much tenderness toward him as ever. Maybe more. "Aric, why are you drinking so much?"

He scowled at me.

When he'd searched for me and watched over my recovery, had he buried his feelings about my choice? Maybe he'd been too numb to react. Until now. I didn't want him to hurt, but I didn't know what to do to ease this pain.

Then I recalled Matthew's deal, and my irritation rekindled. "Why stop with vodka? You could smoke opium again."

Smirk. "The thought has occurred."

I sliced my thumb and grew a poppy plant straight into his desk.

He exhaled. "I liked this desk."

"Then you should smoke it, Reaper."

His smirk deepened. "And to what do I owe this pique?"

"Why didn't you tell me the Fool killed me?"

"That happened quite a while ago." He shot his glass and poured another. "Ah, I'll wager your cunning grandmother has chronicles, hasn't she? I'd wondered why she wouldn't relinquish her bag. I'd suspected she carried a pistol to use against me. Perhaps your chronicles will prove more dangerous?"

"Answer the question."

"Keeping that secret was the price I had to pay to hear your thoughts and see your life."

I knew it! Matthew had said, *I'm in Death's pocket, so he's in my eyes.* "So to prevent me from finding out his murderous past, Matthew gave you access to my mind?"

Aric hiked his shoulders. "I warned you not to underestimate him."

"You're just as much at fault! You made that deal with him. Like the deal you made with Lark? To make her win the entire game?"

"Yes," he said, honest as ever—which made it difficult to stay mad at him. "Obviously both were ill-advised."

"How could the Fool have decapitated me? I'd been powerful in that game."

At the rim of his glass, Aric muttered, "You must not remember how he fights." He knocked back his drink.

"Matthew doesn't have a violent bone in his body." Or I'd *thought* he didn't.

"I told you he was the most intelligent Arcana ever to play, but you continued to see him as a bumbling schoolboy."

No longer.

Aric poured another shot. "On the subject of secrets, you didn't tell me your line had chronicles."

"I didn't know."

"Why would the Tarasova not tell you?"

I rubbed my forehead. When would the headaches end? "I was young when we were separated. Things in my mind got . . . confused." At best. At worst, my grandmother was playing her own game.

For all Aric's power plays—and despite our history—he was the only one on earth that I could truly trust. Which, again, made it hard to stay pissed at him.

His eyes flicked over me, assessing. "You didn't *remember*. I suppose I should be glad of that." After a hesitation, he said, "You have the answer to your question, so begone."

"You're kicking me out?" Now that I'd reined in my temper, I thought we could talk.

He sank back in his seat. "You might be back here, but things will never be the same as they were."

In the weeks before I'd fled the castle, I'd been happy with him, falling for him more each day. "I know that. But I can still miss the way we were."

Tension stole over him, his fists clenching. "Do you miss those nights?" He wasn't asking only about the nights when we'd read and drank and talked in this study. *My last night at the castle. And that night on the way to the Lovers.* "Do you ever think about how we were then?"

Aric never lied to me; I wouldn't to him. "Yes."

"And yet . . ." He exhaled. "Not only did you choose another man, you sought to reverse time for him."

"Not just for him. For all those people, and for Selena, and for *you*."

"Why for me?"

"We couldn't communicate, so I feared you were injured." I swallowed. "Or . . . drowned. You were wearing armor—in a flood! I imagined awful stuff happening to you. When I thought I'd lost both you and Jack, I nearly lost my mind." The love of my life *and* my soul mate.

Aric looked like he wanted to believe me, but didn't quite. Because Arcana lied. "Leave me, Empress."

Though his dismissal stung, I stayed. Even if our relationship had been broken by my choice, we still had an enemy to defeat. "What are you working on?" Papers and books were strewn everywhere. "What happened to the Lovers' chronicles? Is there anything about the Emperor?"

"I'm still translating them."

"As usual, you know more than you're telling me."

He shot his glass, then slammed it down on his desk. "I've been too preoccupied to translate—because I've been living in the goddamned nursery for weeks while urging you to live."

He was right. I parted my lips to apologize, but he said, "Your grandmother is already sowing her seeds of discord. Perhaps I should be on my guard against you once more. Tell me, Empress, was our truce only temporary?"

Ugh! "You *know* I would never hurt you. I had the chance to inject poison into your neck, but I didn't. I could have killed you with my kiss, but instead I made sure you were protected. At the first sign of trouble with my grandmother, I came to warn you. So why say things like that? To punish me for my choice? That shouldn't have undone the trust we established."

Staring into his empty glass, he said, "Maybe I am punishing you."

As if he hadn't done that enough in this life? "Then you should break out your favorite torture tool: the cilice." I'd never forget the pain of that barbed cuff and the frustration of having no powers. Then cutting the thing off . . . "I'll bet it still has pieces of my skin on it."

He raised his face, an unsettling resentment in his eyes. "Perhaps I've made a *choice* to be cruel to you. If you don't like it, you should stay away from me."

I rose and turned to go. Over my shoulder, I said, "Go to hell, Aric."

"Already here, *wife*."

27

I lay in bed replaying my entire weird day, but especially my interaction with Aric. After leaving his study, I'd curled up under the covers, hating that he was in pain. I hated that we'd fought.

Most women and men who shared a romantic history had difficulties to contend with. Sometimes an ugly breakup. Possibly lies. Maybe a betrayal.

He and I had millennia of bad blood—and murder.

Even if I didn't dance on the razor's edge over Jack's death, I didn't see how Aric and I could overcome so much to mend the connection we'd once shared.

Or that we even should. *The game demands blood.* Would I get him killed as well?

Uneasy and alone, I finally drifted off to sleep … into a dream so vivid, I knew it was a memory from a previous life. I was the Empress known as Phyta.

"Are you certain the Empress is asleep?" the Magician asks Fauna.

The two Arcana are meeting again, beneath the moonlight—in my garden. Fauna believes she has nothing to fear from me.

She tells the boy, "Phyta sleeps."

Not so. I regard them from my balcony. As I have for the last three nights.

He whips his head around at a noise. "What was that?" His eyes dart.

"The Empress moves her vines as she dreams."

In a wry tone, he says, "I believe that is the most disturbing thing I've ever heard."

I also move my vines on purpose, so an Arcana like Fauna will ignore any sounds I might make up here. Her hearing is remarkable, as is her sense of smell.

Fauna would surely scent my presence—if she and the Magician didn't meet among my flowers.

She smiles at the boy. "And do my creatures also disturb you? Or my fangs?"

He casts her a mischievous grin. "Why would I be disturbed? I adore your fangs. And all of your creatures adore me."

The boy has shown a surprising lack of fear of her lions. The great beasts laze among my plants, their muzzles still stained with blood from an earlier kill. They'd taken out a band of the Hierophant's demented followers.

Fauna shyly says, "I adore your illusions."

The Magician conjures a ball of light above them, then shapes it into an infinity symbol: an unbroken line that stretches through eternity—and back on itself.

Fauna is duly impressed. The light reflects in her eyes.

He turns to her and brushes his fingers over her cheek.

Are they in love? How does one know? If love has moved them to be so careless, it seems a dangerous emotion.

He leans in, catching her gaze, just before he presses his lips to hers.

I tilt my head, running the pad of my forefinger over my lips. What does kissing feel like? By the sound of her sighs and his groans, it must be heavenly.

For some reason, my last meeting with the Reaper dances in my thoughts. He continues to trail me through this game. Observing, watching, lying in wait, no doubt. Why is his attention so fixed upon me? Because he is Death and I am life?

What would it be like to kiss him? I shiver, and my heart starts racing, which shames me. He is my worst enemy, can kill with his very *skin. Despite his godlike looks, he's a monster who proudly wields his Touch of Death. . . .*

Even if he could kiss me, it wouldn't last long—for I would expel poison through my lips to end him.

Fauna draws back, then she and the Magician sit forehead to forehead, catching their breath.

He says, "I want you to run away with me."

I roll my eyes. This has gone on long enough. I shall have to kill Fauna and her admirer sooner than I'd anticipated. . . .

I woke with a cry, my eyes darting.

Cyclops was in the bed again. He glanced up, but I couldn't meet the wolf's gaze.

Oh, just remembering how I planned to kill your mistress. No big deal. How casual I'd been when deciding to murder a young couple.

They'd had no idea that some evil force plotted to punish them because they'd dared to fall in love—and to want out of the game.

As I lay in the dark centuries later, I couldn't help drawing parallels to my own life—and to any future I might imagine with Aric.

28

I'd buried myself in the chronicles, uncovering one secret after another. Shocking, gut-wrenching secrets.

Each day over the past week, I'd headed to Gran's room to read. Naturally, she wouldn't allow me to take the book anywhere else. But to guard it when I wasn't around, she actually . . . slept with it in her bed.

Now I gazed over at her. She'd nodded off again after dinner. She was sleeping more and more, but eating less. While all my injuries had healed, she continued to deteriorate. Yet no matter how much I'd pleaded, she wouldn't let Paul examine her, insisting she would rally.

Though I no longer believed her, I refused to think about her dying. . . .

When she and I weren't discussing the book—everything from the section on Minor Arcana to the pros/cons of my last alliances—I read on my own.

I knew more than I'd thought about the players just from my own encounters with them, but the book held so many surprises.

With each one, I would muse, *Jack will think this is cool.* Then I would remember. He'd been murdered.

Jack and I had marveled at the snow.

The temperature continued to drop. Soon the rain would turn to snow again. I thought I'd lose it then. The tourniquet would snap, my heart would swell, and I'd bleed out in the white.

For now, I would strangle the pain and keep studying my chronicles.

I'd also begun editing and updating the book. I'd added details from my vision-dreams and recorded battles from this game. I'd even illustrated certain plants. The process was slow going, but I didn't have anything else to do.

Aric avoided me, seeming as if he could barely stand to look at me. We hadn't spoken since our fight, and I hated how we'd left things.

Did he miss me at all?

I missed *him*, had begun to dream about him more and more. I missed simply visiting with him—discussing books and playing cards, sharing meals together. When things had been good between us, I'd loved every second with him, panicking whenever he'd ventured out into the dangerous world.

I hadn't spoken to Lark either. She hunted for Finn—and Richter—with the single-minded focus her card was named for, running Scarface, the falcon, and a team of other creatures ragged out in the Ash. She kept Cyclops on the property as her weapon (though he slept with me), and Maneater remained—because the she-wolf was pregnant.

A lot of creatures were. Lark's animals were breeding like crazy. . . .

I'd headed down to the river a few times seeking Circe, but she hadn't answered. Was she avoiding me as well? Too busy replaying my betrayals?

I knew I'd been evil; the chronicles told me I was in good company.

Two games ago, the Emperor had captured me and tortured me for months. He'd burned away my limbs with his lava hands, keeping me weakened until he'd finally taken my head.

Had Sol been about to deliver me to a similar fate?

In another game, Ogen had dunked me in a river, toying with me, robbing me of air. Though I lasted longer than most, I *could* drown to death. Before he finished me, Circe had pulled him down to the deep.

In this game, Ogen had been afraid of water. Maybe he'd retained some animal memory of Circe's reach.

In a battle against Joules and Gabriel (allies even then), the Lord of Lightning had blasted my oaks to splinters, then speared me in the heart with one of his javelins. While I'd been stunned, Gabriel had taken to the air, dropping burning oil on me and my plants.

I'd been seconds from dying when Fauna's lions had dragged me from the flames.

Joules and Gabriel hadn't yet known that I—and my trees—could regenerate. In the end, my oaks and my thorn tornado had defeated those two. Unless something had been skewed in translation—*let's hope*—I was pretty sure I'd desecrated their corpses.

And I might have hung Gabriel's silken black wings over my hearth.

I was like the movie monster that never died, returning for more jump scares. Beheading was the only way to be sure.

Regeneration was a handy ability to have, but others' powers were just as enviable.

The Fury possessed batlike wings that changed color like a chameleon's skin, camouflaging her. An Arcana could be walking along, unaware that she stalked him—until a shower of acid rained down.

The Emperor could travel via his lava—riding it like a wave.

When the teleporting Centurion became intangible, no offensive strike would work against him for as long as his powers held out. I'd managed to kill him once before, by stumbling upon a battle already in progress. Just as his reserves hit empty, I'd launched my thorn tornado, scouring his body down to the bones.

Fauna had the ability to revive all animals, and not merely her connected familiars. In the same way that my blood seeded plants, her blood could reanimate a creature, bringing a bird back from a feather or a bull from a fragment of horn.

Did Lark know about her animal resurrection power? Did Aric know? When was I going to tell them?

The book, with its constant tales of treachery, was making me nearly as paranoid as Gran. Aric's distance wasn't helping. I understood why he avoided me, but I didn't want this rift between us to widen—for more than one reason.

An ominous feeling had descended over the castle of lost time. I got the sense that something *big* was coming down the pipeline. Something in addition to the Richter threat or Gran's failing health. But what??

If we weren't a united front . . .

The Fool had told me that things would happen beyond my wildest imaginings. I no longer thought they'd be *positive* things.

Biting my lip, I returned my attention to the book. The next section was titled "Setting Moon." Sometimes as I read, I would look up from the page in a trance, *remembering* a certain battle or day. Now I recalled Circe and me relaxing in the middle of my fortress of plants—my "green killers," as she'd called them. A river had circled us protectively. We'd been laughing about something. . . .

An arrow sped through my vines, hitting the tree inches from Circe's head.

She and I leapt up and whirled around.

Atop a distant hill stood a girl with silvery hair, a bow, and a quiver. Her tableau revealed her to be the Moon. She called out, "I could have killed the Priestess." Indeed. Somehow the Moon's arrow had perfectly threaded my vines. "I did not, because I want to be a part of your alliance."

Circe and I met gazes, smiling at each other.

"She is bold," I said. My vines slithered like snakes.

Circe's river thrummed with power, gathering to strike. "Normally we might reward such daring . . ."

". . . but not today," I finished for her.

We'd killed the Moon. Circe had gotten her icon.

No wonder Selena hadn't trusted me! No wonder she'd been shocked when I'd faced off against the Lovers, hell-bent on rescuing her.

I'd never known how much she'd overcome to be my friend. I narrowed my eyes, my glyphs glowing. Matthew could have told me. Circe could have. She treated me like I was some vicious backstabber; she'd been just as bad.

Whenever she finally deigned to talk to me, I was going to give her a piece of my mind! Not that I had much left to give—

"*This* is what I've wanted to see," Gran said from her bed. She rubbed her eyes, shaking off sleep.

"What?" I closed the book and set it away.

"Your anger." With difficulty, she sat up against the headboard, and I hurried over to help her. "Did you read about a double cross?"

"Not exactly." I sank down on the edge of the bed.

"Do you dream about past games?" At my nod, she said, "So the Fool transferred your memories."

"Yes. But they come slowly." I frowned. "Why would he have done that?"

"Not as a kindness to you, I promise. The Fool must believe knowledge of the past will somehow render you more careless or weaken your alliances." She reached for a glass of water on the nightstand, and I rushed to hand it to her. "Whenever you see the past, look for symbols. In the present as well. Tarot cards are filled with symbols, because *life* is."

"What do they mean? What's the purpose?"

"To remind you to mark some detail or remember some moment. Symbols are waypoints on your journey." She took a sip of water. "Learn this: as with life, so with the cards."

Was that why so many things had begun to feel connected? "Gabriel sees symbols from up on high, things he says can't be random. He told me he has the senses of both animal and angel—and he recognizes the gods' return."

"Ah, the Archangel, the errand spirit." I'd read that he sometimes acted as a messenger between allies. Like a herald or courier. "He is an *uneasy* hybrid of angel and animal, both halves at war inside him. His animal senses are as keen as Fauna's, and he has claw-tipped fingers like her." His claws were actually more like talons. "Yet he also possesses angelic wings. Those are his strength—and his weakness."

"Is he right about the gods' return? Will they hear prayers now?"

"Perhaps they have returned. He would recognize such a thing. If they have, they will hear us. Prayers fuel them, the way food fuels us." Her lips thinned. "But they won't hear prayers asking to end their game, if that's what you're wondering. There's only one possible way to right the earth: by finishing this."

At my expression, she sighed, as if I'd just exhausted her. Again. She no longer hid her disappointment. "You read the origin of the Arcana?"

"I'd already heard the story from Aric." He'd told me and Jack on the way to the Lovers. The three of us had shared a bottle of whiskey while sitting around a fire. When I'd passed out, Jack and Aric had finished it together. In a different time and place, they might have been friends.

"How strange that Death has been teaching you," she said. "I would expect him to be a miser with his knowledge."

"Oh, in general, he's still tightfisted with it." Yes, my recovery had distracted him from translating the Lovers' chronicles, but he'd already gotten a start on them. He could've divulged *some* tidbit from those pages.

"Did he tell you about Tar Ro?"

I nodded. "It was a sacred realm as big as a thousand kingdoms. In the first game, twenty-two players were sent there to fight."

"Think of Tar Ro as an arena"—like Sol's Olympus?—"with deities in the stands. Why do you think the gods would end their amusement? Would you stop the Super Bowl because one athlete didn't want to play?"

The gods sounded like dicks—not exactly the types to care if their "amusement" caused an apocalypse. Except... "If they consume prayers, how many people are feeding them right now? Does Demeter receive prayers for a good crop? There are no crops. What about Aphrodite? Few people are thinking about love after the Flash. A death deity? Who prays over the dead anymore? Most survivors leave their fallen on the side of the road."

If I'd gone to a funeral for every friend or loved one who'd died since the night of the Flash, I would have attended more than a dozen.

"This is not for you to question," Gran said, steel in her tone. "Your purpose is to follow the rules of the gods. Anything else is blasphemy."

Aric had said, "I was twice a blasphemer." I was one as well. And I'd been punished. "I plan to follow the rules with Richter. Tell me how to defeat him."

"Death has killed him before. Your best play is to seduce your protector into bringing you the Emperor's head. We can hope both will fall in the clash."

My fists balled. Inside, I primal-screamed. "That's it?" I was getting nowhere with her.

"Until you fully embrace your viciousness, you have no chance against the Emperor. I can't teach you to develop powers you don't yet possess."

Not the first time she'd told me that. Another impasse.

Maybe I should dig for information about my parents. She was my last link to Mom, and even to my dad. "Gran, what was Mom like as a girl?"

"Stubborn. Refusing to believe what was right before her eyes! Like *you*."

I was proud to be like my mother. "What about my dad? Mom used to talk about him a lot, but over time I heard less and less."

"David Greene was kind, and he had a sense of humor. He made your mother laugh."

That was all Gran could muster up? "Did you not like him?"

"He wasn't a big believer in Tarot. Humor aside, he was a very practical man. From *New England*," she added, as if that explained everything. "I'd been wearing Karen down about the Arcana—until she met him. Before I knew it, your mother was pregnant. Even then, I sensed you were *the* Empress."

"He didn't want us to live up north?"

"David planned to move there." Her gaze went distant. "To move *you*—the great Empress—away from her Haven." That must have gone over well. "In the end, I convinced them not to go."

My dad had disappeared in the Basin just two years after I was born. If he'd insisted on moving north, would he still be alive? Or would he have been—at least until the Flash? I might have grown up with a father. "He died so young." Twenty-nine.

She nodded. "That man only adored one thing as much as Karen: you."

Mom had told me he'd doted on me—

My head snapped up. I sensed something outside: energy, a faint thrumming. Circe was here—just down the mountain. Had she come to visit her ally Death? Were they together right now? If so, I would *drop in* on their members-only meeting. "I'll be back." I rose and headed toward the door.

"Where are you going?"

I paused in the doorway. "To visit the river."

Gran blinked at me. "Why are you so sure you're coming back?"

29

With a lantern in hand, I made my way toward the water. My breaths were puffs of smoke in the chilly, dark night. The storm had waned, rain drizzling on and off.

I pulled my poncho hood over my hair—

Aric emerged from the mist, his tall frame outlined by a flickering gas lamp. He wore all black, his tailored garments highlighting his powerful body. His pale hair was tousled and longer than he usually kept it.

I stutter-stepped at the mere sight of him.

He was heading from the river back to the castle. As he neared, I noticed he looked weary, his gaze filled with shadows.

With pain.

Which called to mind my dreams of him. Over this week, my nightmares had come less frequently, making way for dream-memories of the last game, when I'd been known as Phyta. Aric had pursued me then, had eventually revealed that I'd married—then betrayed—him in a past life. Realizing how badly he'd ached for a companion, I'd begun to seduce him, all the while planning to kill him. . . .

Each morning here I would wake, shamed by my behavior—and rocked by his loneliness. Rocked by his fragile hope of a future with me.

Never slowing his pace, he intoned, "Empress."

"Hey. What were you doing down there?"

"Visiting my ally." As I'd suspected.

I frowned when he passed right by me. To his back, I asked, "You've been talking to Circe?"

Without turning, he said, "As I often do."

When I hurried ahead to block his path, he exhaled an impatient breath. "What do you want?"

This close, I caught a thread of his addictive scent. Hints of sandalwood and pine, two trees, made my lids grow heavy. In the lamplight, his face was hypnotically gorgeous.

But my attraction to him was more than physical. Endless epochs seemed to tie me to him. A bone-deep connection that endured.

If past Empresses hadn't been raised from birth to hate him, they would have fallen for him. *I* would have fallen for him. "How long will we go on like this, Aric?"

Finally, interest lit his amber eyes. "What is the alternative? Tell me what has changed."

I didn't know! I glanced down as I tried to string words together and noticed his gloved hands were clenched. Words left my lips: "You want to touch me." He'd once told me it was a luxury he'd always savor. I gazed up. Unable to help myself, I reached for his proud face.

But he caught my wrist in his strong hand, his eyes growing cold as the night. "And since when has it mattered what *I* want?" Releasing me, he strode away.

I stared after him long after he'd disappeared in the mist. Miserable and confused, I trudged down to the river.

Was the water level even higher than the last time I was here? A blanket of fog covered the calm surface. At the bank, I raised my lantern. "Circe?" I called. "Where are you?"

Water in the shape of a hand waved, then collapsed in a splash. She couldn't even hold that small form?

My earlier anger toward her faded. She might not have been avoiding me; she could've been too weak for a long chat. Especially if she'd been talking to Aric a lot.

"You can hear me?" I asked.

A slight ripple. Then a murmured: "I hear. Hail Tar Ro."

"Hail Tar Ro to you." I tried out one of my new powers—sensing seeds latent in the dirt—but found none, so I slashed my thumb with a claw and grew some grass along the bank. I set the lantern down and pulled my poncho under me to sit. "Thank you for saving my life."

"You assume I did, Evie Greene?"

"Okay. Then thank you for not killing me outright. Maybe you did it for Death? You two seem tight."

"Hmm."

"He was just here, huh?" No answer. Anyway . . . "Your tidal wave was mind-blowing."

"An afterthought. Soon I will show the game a *reckoning*." Softening her tone, she said, "I regret that I couldn't save all those mortals. Your mortal. The Fortune Card avoided flying over rivers on her approach. By the time she and Richter crossed over water, I was too late."

The tourniquet twisted, and I barely showed a reaction at all.

"I wonder how they knew of my powers," Circe said. "Their lines don't chronicle."

"Would the Sun know?"

"Possibly. He learns much from his Bagmen. I heard about your run-in with them. Becoming food must have been . . . unpleasant."

Unpleasant? Would I ever get over those slurping sounds, those grueling bites? That was one memory I wish I could forget. I told myself I shouldn't fear them now that I'd seen their worst. I'd survived an attack—without any long-term effects.

Possibly.

Circe asked, "Still think we can stop the game?"

I shrugged. Every now and then, I would feel a silly glimmer of hope, but mostly I didn't. The game demanded blood. I would give it the Emperor's.

And then? And then? And then?

"I told you we needed to kill Richter."

I was taking my lumps with her and with Aric. "I'm listening now. Do you have a plan?"

"Enemies almighty must replenish." She'd called us that before. "Unless you intend to take your grandmother's advice to send the Endless Knight after him." At my raised brows, Circe added, "I told you, whispers flow down to me like water." Had she heard Gran's hate-filled murmurs as well? "Your grandmother sounds ... intense."

Yep. "And paranoid." I sprouted a few dandelions among the blades of grass.

"Can you blame her? Your chronicles tell her to be. History does as well—your line is notorious for its aggressive Tarasovas and chroniclers." In a wry tone, she said, "Turning budding young Empresses into serial killers since time immemorial."

Arcana humor? In my present state, I almost had the urge to laugh. "I'd thought she might help me stop the game, or save the earth, or get rid of my powers. Stupid, huh?"

"Necessary. She was your grail. We all seek things that attract us to a particular hunting ground."

What was it Matthew had told me? *We follow MacGuffins.*

"Often the grail is love," she said. "The Magician and Fauna run headlong for each other, or try to. The Moon became the Archangel's grail for a time, and she followed your mortal."

Right to the very end. I wondered if Circe had heard *my* frantic mutterings.

"Kentarch searches for his beloved wife."

"You know the Centurion?" I asked. "Where is he?"

She sighed, and mist rose from the river's surface. "I don't think the Centurion—my ally over many games—would want the Empress to know."

Fair enough. "Why do you never ally with the Fool?" *Empress is my friend.*

"Can't you answer that question as well as I, Evie Greene?"

"Because he's more untrustworthy than most."

"Do you know the word *fathomable*? It means *measurable*, in the sense of *depth*. *Fathomable* is an ancient word because man has been trying in vain to know the depths of my ocean domain for thousands of years." She paused, then said, "The Fool's powers are *un*fathomable even to me."

I felt as if I'd just received a warning. "Death said Matthew can fight."

She repeated in a whisper, *"Unfathomable."*

I swallowed. "Do you know where he is?"

"Not near a body of water at present."

Thanks for narrowing it down. "What's your grail?"

"It's secret. But know that it won't lure me to land. *You* won't."

At her words, a memory from one game arose:

"Why would you ever surface?" I asked her. "You are invincible in the sea."

"You seduced me here, sister almighty."

"I did?"

"Like you, I'm a sociable creature. It is my weakness. Yet my abyss is unutterably lonely and echoing. From a distance, I watch exciting events unfold, but I am held apart. I see the ways of men and women, but don't experience love. I hear mortals sharing laughter. But I share nothing. I'm drawn to you because we are kindred. Together we experience life."

I couldn't comprehend the Priestess's reasoning. "But the vulnerabilities . . ."

"I am cursed. To truly live, I must make myself vulnerable and trust. Death isn't the only one who risks everything just to feel. . . ."

"I'm not trying to get you on land," I said firmly. "You need to stay put."

"Hmm."

Starting to hate it when she said *hmm.* "What's the Emperor's grail?"

"We all are. He wants to defeat 'worthy' opponents, with as much carnage as possible. He also enjoys the occasional cataclysm, just because it feels good to him."

"What happens if he wins?"

The river grew choppy, the fog dissipating. "Hell on earth. His reign would mark the end of mankind. All the cards must sense this."

Surely that was the root of my ominous feeling, my sense that something big was coming down the pipeline. So why did my unease feel removed from Richter? "We can't let him win. If you hang tight in the abyss, you can simply outlast him, right?"

"Oh, are we back to playing? I thought the innocent Empress wanted no part of the game. Except when an Arcana irritates her or steps out of line in any way."

How could water convey such snark? "You're still pissed about whatever I might have done to you in the past." Though I'd found evidence of her cold-bloodedness, I still hadn't read how I'd betrayed her. "I get it. But we were both evil. Admit it: you would've double-crossed me if I hadn't done it to you first."

Eddies twirled.

Irritating eddies. "Ugh! That's your way of ignoring me, isn't it?" As if she'd covered her ears and sang, "La la la." I snatched up a stone and threw it at the water. "I remembered the day we killed the Moon. *You* took her icon."

The eddies subsided. "I might have worn it *best*, Evie Greene, but you wore it *next*."

In other words, the icon had transferred to me when I'd killed Circe.

"Empress, *you* are the only one protesting your innocence in this game. I've made no such promises."

"I'm not innocent. I don't know what I am. But I know I have zero interest in winning." I plucked the flowers I'd grown. "You said Arcana sometimes *ask* you to take them to the abyss—that it's the only place they can see to go. I didn't understand before, but now I do."

I braided dandelion stems to make a wreath. The prospect of my death didn't bother me—my one-way ticket loomed—but the idea of Aric dying made my glyphs burn.

"What are you thinking about that upsets you so?" she asked.

I shrugged and tossed my wreath into the river. Water rose beneath the circlet in the shape of a head, and I almost smiled. "When I relive our interactions, I remember how close we were."

Another sigh. "Apparently, not close enough." A wave gulped down the wreath.

That time, I'd definitely received a warning.

30

THE HUNTER

Closer to her . . .

"How long till I see her?" I muttered from the backseat of our most recent ride. I dimly remembered Matthew getting yet another vehicle and helping me in.

I was still laid out. Never been sick a day in my life, but I couldn't shake this, no. My bones ached so bad I was certain I'd caught bonebreak fever. Delirium was setting in.

I slept most hours, barely remembering the ones when I was awake. My breaths whistled as if a weight pressed on my chest, and the skin on my bum leg felt red hot, itching like something was crawling all over it. Or *in* it.

But Matthew had given me a fifty-fifty shot of pulling through. *Had worse odds, me.* "Want to see my girl."

As usual, *coo-yôn* didn't answer me.

We remained far in the west, as far as I could tell. Most roads had been blocked, and gas proved as scarce as ever. I didn't know where Domīnija's place was, just knew it could be reached within a week on horseback from Fort Arcana. At our present pace, it would take the Fool and me *months* to reach even the area.

But I had to assume he would eventually get me to Evie.

In a rough voice, I said, "Woan answer me? Then tell me this, *sosie*. If you can fight . . . why didn't you ever before?" I thought of all those times

I'd needed help out of a tight spot, when he could've changed the tide.

In the salt mine, that boy had taken out a dozen men—without a weapon. I supposed if I could see every move an opponent would make ahead of time, I could defeat just about anybody.

Pointing at his temple, he said, "If I do that, I don't do *this*."

My head pounded too hard to pursue the subject. "Can't say I've missed these little talks of ours."

"Empress made you a gravestone."

Of course, she would've figured I'd died with the rest. The odds of me surviving that blast were a million to one. Then the lava, and *then* the flood, which Matthew had blamed on Circe. I hated that Evie had grieved for even a second. "What'd she say when you told her I lived?"

Silence from *coo-yôn*.

"You *did* tell her?" No answer. My eyes shot wide. I wheezed, sucking in a breath. "Damn it, boy!" I'd never imagined this possibility. Because I'd thought he cared about Evie in his own way. "She . . . she doan know I'm coming?"

"Nope."

Putain! And I wasn't strong enough to sit up, much less choke the spit out of him. If she thought I was gone, had she already accepted Domīnija? "Is Evie with Death? They together?" *Say no, say no.*

After she'd chosen me, I'd felt like hell for Domīnija. Actually had sympathy for the bastard, 'cause I knew how it felt to lose her.

When she'd wanted to stay with him back after he'd abducted her . . . I'd lost my goddamned mind.

Matthew said, "Not yet."

My eyes slid closed with relief. But it was short-lived. Not *yet.* "Tell my girl I'm coming for her! Tell her it'll always be Evie and Jack."

No reply.

"At least answer me this: Do I got a chance with her?" Without her as the light at the end of this tunnel, I didn't know how I could keep going. Grief over the army threatened to do me in. I'd gotten all those people killed. By using Arcana players to establish order, I'd lured in that monster.

Folks close to me had a habit of getting dead. Clotile blew out her brains to save me. Selena burned. I remembered Maman on Day Zero and shuddered.

"Yes. A chance. *Chance* means *luck.*" Matthew glanced at me in the rearview mirror. "Empress despises me for letting you die."

"Then tell her I'm alive!" I yelled, bringing on a new bout of dizziness. Couldn't catch my breath. Sweat broke out over my skin, even as I felt freezing. "You've let her . . . believe I've died—twice. You trying to drive . . . her insane, you *sosie*? Or manipulate her?"

"I don't manipulate the Empress. Alone. I manipulate much."

"Give me a reason . . . you're making her suffer."

He tapped his temple. "Switchboard on. Emperor hears."

So *coo-yôn* had turned off the calls to keep her out of Richter's reach. *Merde*, I couldn't fault his reasoning. Still: "Could he track her from a quick call . . . If she doan know I'm alive. . . she's goan to be with Domīnija." The thought made my heart thunder.

My fever was spiking again, getting worse by the second. Pain wrenched a groan from my wheezing lungs.

Hell, Matthew's odds for me might've been generous.

"You want me to risk the call to her, Hunter?"

When black dots swarmed my vision again, I rasped, *"Non."* Not yet. "'Cause I'll probably be dead anyway. . . ."

31

THE EMPRESS
DAY 437 A.F.

"What are you doing in this wing?" I asked Aric. He'd just come from my grandmother's room.

This was the first time I'd spoken to him since our run-in down by the river. His training had ramped up again, and he spent hours each day practicing with his swords. Otherwise, he kept to his study and his black-walled bedroom.

Just like before, the atmosphere around the castle felt like a powder keg—except now we had outside threats to worry about. I'd considered demanding a talk with him, but what could I offer? Nothing had changed between us.

His eyes went starry at the sight of me before he shuttered his gaze. With his tone neither warm nor cold, he said, "I sought the wisdom of a Tarasova, so I went hat in hand."

"What did you want to know?"

He hiked his broad shoulders. "Alas, I . . . upset her," he said, not answering my question.

"Upset." I could only imagine. Her hatred bubbled up more and more, keeping pace with her rapidly declining physical and mental health.

She'd gotten so paranoid she wouldn't allow me to turn on the electric lights anymore—because of "the Tower." Only the fire lit her room. Shadows crept over the walls, over my vines, the flames a constant reminder of loss.

When her mouth grew slack on one side, she'd finally allowed Paul to examine her. His diagnosis: a stroke and continuing ministrokes—which she'd refused to believe. She'd slurred, "I wouldn't be surprised if Death is making me sick. He needs me out of the picture."

Paul had given her a prescription from his stockpiled medical supplies, but the pills hadn't helped. My grandmother was dying, and there was nothing we could do for her.

Now I sidled even closer to Aric, craving comfort, companionship, *anything*. I continued seeing him in most of my dreams, making me miss him even more. "Please tell me what you wanted to know from her."

He ignored my question. "You look exhausted, Empress." Was that a flare of pity in his eyes?

My own line's Tarasova was beating me down—because I was desperately clinging to my trust in my allies, and to myself as a person.

Yesterday Gran had murmured, "All you have to do is surrender . . . draw on your hatred and pain. Become her: the Empress you were meant to be." My grandmother was trying to "program" me again, to undo the work of shrinks and psych meds. To undo everything Mom had taught me about being decent.

My mind felt like a bloody battlefield. I dreaded going to see Gran, which made me sick with guilt.

Aric said, "Paul could help out with her more."

"He's already with her so much." Whereas I seemed only to frustrate her, he could get her to calm down and even to eat. But he'd also told me she couldn't hold on much longer. "I keep thinking each day will be her . . . last." Couldn't Aric sense impending death? I wondered what he'd say if I asked him for a heads-up.

I also wondered why I wasn't sadder about Gran. Yes, she was being hateful, but she hadn't been during my childhood. At least, as far as I could trust my memories.

Maybe I'd grown so numb to grief that nothing could affect me. What if I'd strangled my heart until it was permanently damaged?

I gazed at Aric and knew the answer to that question. I was grieving for him as much as for Jack, even though Aric was *right here* in front of me.

I'd lost the love of my life. But the man I considered my soul mate was waiting for me. How much longer could I claw my way through an apocalypse alone?

Studying my face, Aric said, "The Tarasova will no doubt tell you I've harmed her. For the record, I would never hurt her."

"And I would never believe you could."

With a curt nod, he strode past me. "Empress."

I followed him. "If you won't call me *sievā*, then use my name: *Evie.*"

"I've told you: your ever-changing names don't matter. Empress remains the same."

"E-V. Evangeline, if you must." I trailed him back to his study. "How long are you going to avoid me? You said you'd train me."

He took a bottle and glass to his desk, sinking into his chair. "At present, your grandmother is seeing to your ... education."

"You'll be happy to hear that Paul doesn't give her long."

"That doesn't make me happy. It doesn't make me anything."

"Because you and I are merely allies. *Of a sort.*"

Shrug.

"So we'll go long stretches at a time without seeing each other?" Sadness washed over me.

"You had planned *never* to see me again, Empress." His expression grew so enraged that I almost took a step back. "You rode away with that full intention."

"Do you think that was easy for me?"

He hissed, "*Effortless.*" Then he inhaled to get a rein on his temper. "I offered you everything. And you spurned me for another. What's so bad is that I can't fault you."

"What do you mean?"

"Deveaux fought with bravery. He was intelligent. He had cunning and was a born leader. If I was going to lose you to anyone, I would want it to be him."

"I told you I don't want to talk about him."

As if I hadn't spoken, Aric continued, "I hated him at first, was seething with jealousy when the two of you were together. But through your memories, I learned a lot about him. I saw what he'd struggled against as a boy. I comprehended his frustrations and his dreams." Aric shot his glass, and poured another. "I needed to continue hating Deveaux, but ultimately I *liked* him. Which made everything more confusing."

I took my usual seat. "The night you two got drunk together, something changed."

Nod. "And when we fought together. Plus he was the only man on earth who understood the way I had felt about you, the only other man who dreaded your coming decision."

Had felt about me. Past tense. Was Aric moving on? From the one woman he could touch?

He gave a humorless laugh.

"What?"

"I know this will be difficult for you to understand, but Jack was the closest thing I've had to a friend since my father died."

A pang twisted in my chest. "I had that thought. In a different time or circumstance, you two would have been fast friends."

"At the fort, I shared more whiskey with him, and we talked for hours. Toward the end of the night, I explained all the things I could offer you. He agreed to march without you—in order to make it easier for you to leave with me. But he told me a very real truth."

"Which was?"

"He said, 'If Evangeline Greene wants something, she's going to get it. If she sets her sights on me, it'll happen, whether I want better for her or not.'"

"I've set my sights on things right now, but I'm not getting them."

Aric tilted his head. "Such as?"

"Revenge against Richter."

He released a breath. "Leave me, Empress."

I didn't move. "I want us to read together and talk into the night. I want to be friends again."

"Spend time with you as a friend? Impossible."

"*Why?*"

His eyes flashed. "Because I don't want merely a friend. I want my wife!"

"Can't we just . . . see how things go?"

"We are *wed*. Yet it seems I am the only one who cares about that detail."

I almost pointed out that he hadn't seemed to care about that detail when he'd tortured me.

Aric raised his full glass, peering into the clear liquid. "I am disgusted with myself for continuing to desire you like this." Appearing lost in thought, he absently said, "In a moment of weakness, will I beg?" He glanced at me, seeming shocked by what he'd admitted. He abruptly stood. "I might not fault you for your decision. But it still gutted me. When I told you something died in me that day, I meant it." He started toward the study door.

I blocked his path.

"Move out of the way. Damn you, I won't be a stand-in substitute. Cease tormenting me."

"You do still love me."

He squared his shoulders. "*I* didn't say it lightly."

"You think I did?"

"Perhaps once you told me of your love, you should not have told me good-bye directly after."

I winced. "What do you want from me?"

"What I can never have: for you to have chosen me!" His fists clenched. Even now he was fighting not to touch me. "When you rode away, you looked back at me, and for a second I thought you were going to turn around."

"So did I."

His lips parted. "It was that close?"

"When I faced Vincent, he searched my heart and saw it was divided. He said that I loved two men equally."

"You told me as much on the way here after you were bitten by the Bagmen."

And then I'd forgotten what I'd said.

Aric's eyes glittered; I could feel his yearning. He wanted to believe so badly. "What do *you* expect from *me*?"

"Closeness and trust," I told him. "I expect you not to treat me like an enemy. Or a stranger." I laid my hand on his arm, and his muscles flexed to my fingers. "With our lives on the line"—*Richter, I'm coming for you*—"we shouldn't be divided like this."

"Imminent peril is your reason for seeking more time with me?" He drew my hand from him. "Armor or no, I've got your dagger in my chest. You love to twist it."

I was saying all the wrong things. "That's not what I meant! I regretted so much with Jack, so many things I wished I'd done or said. When I couldn't find you, I felt those same regrets. Then ... then you were there. Alive. When I die, will you regret not spending this time with me?"

"I vow to you, Empress, you will *never* die before me," he said, turning to stride away.

But he tensed when I whispered, "That's what I'm afraid of."

32

"You look like utter hell," Circe told me.

"I wish you'd stop sugar-coating things, Water Witch."

Over a month had passed since I'd first heard my grandmother's voice in the nursery. For so long, I'd dreamed of our reunion. I'd had such great intentions, and yet everything had gone to hell.

Each day I watched her deteriorate. Sometimes she would rail at me with so much venom, Paul would have to rush inside the room to calm her. Other times, she rambled, barely lucid.

As much as she'd been talking, she hadn't answered any of my questions. For instance, I still didn't know why Aric had approached her.

Despite my grandmother's anger, I wanted to be with her at the end—as I hadn't been with Mom. So I returned to Gran's room, day after day.

Circe said, "You are drained because you fight her at every second."

Between my grandmother, my confusion about Aric, and my dread . . .

I glanced back at the castle. That ominous feeling of mine remained firmly in place. *Something* unexpected was approaching. Were we on a countdown clock?

Tick-tock.

Changing the subject, I said, "I don't think it's fair that you can comment on my looks and my mental health, but I can't even see your expressions when we talk."

"Trying to get me on land again?"

I rolled my eyes. "No. But you could make that girl water-form again." She'd once manipulated water into her likeness. "Or you could do that window thingy."

A small wave rose before me. The water morphed until an oval shape emerged, like a wall mirror—only this was a window.

Into the abyss.

Circe appeared, seated upon the coral throne in her underwater temple. With her flowing black hair and luminous eyes, she was drop-dead gorgeous.

The Priestess inclined her head regally. In her temple's firelight, the dazzling blue scales on her forearms and the backs of her hands shimmered, almost the same blue as the fins jutting from her elbows.

Talk about presentation, Sol.

When skittering sounded around her throne, I cocked my head. Possibly a tentacle? I'd never seen below her knees, so the jury was still out. And how did one go about asking that? I was also curious how she made clothes out of sea-foam, but I didn't want to come across as juvenile.

"When are you going to meet the other member of our alliance?" I asked. "I think you'll like Lark." I'd been trying to set up a meeting.

"You presume much." Circe adjusted the golden trident over her lap. "I'm not in an alliance with you and Fauna. I ally only with Death and Kentarch. Besides, Fauna has her hands full." With her search—and with animal breeding. "Even your grandmother has noticed."

Gran had murmured, "The animal calls ring out in the night! Every new beast is a weapon. I hear predators prowling around this castle. Their claws skitter over the floor. They'll eat your entrails while you watch!"

The last time I'd visited Lark, her room had been an overflowing ark. I'd stopped by to confess my behavior in past games, and to talk about her deal with Death to win this one.

As usual, her eyes had pulsed red. Her hair was growing out into a wild mane, and her fangs and claws were getting even longer. The more time she spent mingling her senses with her creatures', the more animalistic she grew. She'd been in no mood to talk. "Make it snappy."

Once her eyes had returned to normal, I'd said, "You were in love with Finn in at least one other life. In that game, I betrayed the two of you. I kind of . . . killed you guys."

"Yeah, Eves, the boss already told me that part, pretty much on Day Zero." She'd once said that her family chronicled, a lie to conceal where she'd really gotten her information. "He told me lots." Her eyes had turned red again, but as I'd exited, she'd called, "Don't let any animals out! Boss said the castle's off-limits to anything but Cyclops."

Had Aric made that exception for me because that wolf was my favorite . . . ?

Now Circe pointed out, "Of course, your grandmother also warns against me."

Gran had told me that she heard waves right outside her window, and that my lungs would explode and my eyeballs burst from my skull. Oh, and that Circe would take me down to her murky hiding places where I'd never see the light again.

Circe chuckled. "Considering her feelings on the subject, I doubt 'Gran' would approve of our visits."

I raised a brow. I did come down most nights. Sometimes the Priestess and I discussed past games. Other times, I could sense her presence as we sat in companionable silence.

Each visit I had to create a new patch of grass—because her river truly was rising. Water covered the bridge to the castle and continued to climb up the mountain.

While Fauna increased the number of her "weapons" and Circe's floodwaters gained momentum, I'd managed a few more vines in my room.

For some reason, my powers seemed to be . . . weakening.

"You haven't spoken with Death?" Circe asked.

I shook my head. How easily he could go without talking to me.

"He is hurting. He knows the only reason you might choose him is because there's no choice. I wonder if he wasn't born to suffer."

Cursed to want me. "He visits *you* a lot." They talked "often." Though my memories of him were sporadic, Aric and the beautiful Circe remembered each other over all these ages. They might not be able to touch, but what if they felt ... affection?

"Look at your eyes go green with jealousy." Jack had said the same thing.

I wasn't merely jealous of Circe. I was jealous—of myself. My dreamed memories of Aric and Phyta together made me crazed—like the night she'd planned to poison him with her kiss: *By the time I release my poison, I will have him so far gone in the throes, he'll wonder if it's not worth it.*

I wanted to touch him. *I* wanted to send him *into the throes.* Not to hurt him, but because I loved him.

He'd told Phyta, "Empress, you were born for me, and I for you. One day I will convince you of this."

What if he already had?

Circe laughed. "Your glyphs are glowing again, Evie Greene."

"Do you have feelings for him?" I demanded.

"My heart belongs to someone else," she said. "I will never love another."

"Really?"

Her eyes were filled with sorrow. "Do you think you're the only one who's lost someone? My wedding was supposed to have been on ... Day Zero." The river grew choppy.

"Oh, God, Circe, I didn't know." That day had been fateful for several Arcana in more ways than one.

My birthday. Sol's anniversary. Circe's wedding.

Her gaze grew distant. "After the Flash evaporated the seas, I was trapped inside an aquifer beneath the ocean floor, unable to reach my island home, unable to reach my fiancé, my entire family. It took months for me to get free. Once I found what remained of them, I was so dried out and thirsty I couldn't manage two tears of grief."

"What did you do?" Petals appeared on the surface of the river. Without thought, I'd grown roses for her pain, scattering them.

"I ... I ..." She trailed off, going quiet for tense moments, before finally saying, "Enough of that." She airily waved her hand, and water swayed in the river. "We're talking about you and Death now. You have the potential to harm him much more than in games past."

I let her change the subject. "How?"

"He is two millennia in age. He has spent all of those years one way. Now, for this short span—really only a blink of an eye over his lifetime—a nobleman knight from a different age finds himself in love. You've been with him for a heartbeat's time, but he is *reeling*."

As though with an affliction. Like the Lovers had said.

"Death craves knowledge," Circe said. "How frustrating that some mysteries must go unsolved even after thousands of years. He now comprehends what it means to love another—but not to be loved in return."

"I do love him."

She arched a brow. "Clearly."

What could I say? Why convince her?

"Death told me the Fool showed you a vision with ten swords in your back."

I nodded. "The ten of swords card indicates that a devastating catastrophe is headed one's way and will strike without warning. Bingo, Matthew."

"Hmm."

"Hmm, *what*?"

"That card is also about letting go and accepting one's current circumstances."

Accepting that you can't change fate. As my mom had done with my dad. "Should I let go of Jack? Like *you* let go of the man you lost?"

She lifted one slim shoulder. "You'd already fallen for another."

"I swore revenge on Richter. How can I think of surrendering that need?" *Richter, I'm ... not coming for you?* "Do you know what I fear more than marching off to die fighting him? That I might have to live with what he did."

"No one's suggesting you give up your revenge. But what if we can't find him for half a year? Two years? Will you cease living till then? Will you force Death to stop as well? He yearns to be a normal man. Even if just for a day. Will you not give that to him?"

"I made the point to him about our limited time," I said, still cringing at my clumsiness. "All I did was insult him."

"He wanted a wife. Not a buddy."

Was she listening to *everything* in the castle? "I don't want to hurt him, but I don't know what to do."

She pinned my gaze with her own. "Therein lies the lesson of the card, Evie Greene. The lesson of *life*. When you can't change your situation, you must change yourself. You must rise and walk—*despite* the ten swords in your back."

What was harder than dying? Living a nightmare.

Mom had learned to live without Dad. I had learned to live without Mom. Could I go on without Jack? "I shouldn't even be thinking about Aric. I disobeyed the dictates of the game, and I got Jack killed. What if I do the same to Aric?"

Circe made a sound of amusement. "You always did think highly of yourself. Do you believe *you* had something to do with that massacre? Think logically. Richter could have reversed the order of his attacks—targeting Fort Arcana earlier, vaporizing the Magician, one of Fauna's wolves, and the stronghold of his enemies. He could have shot at the army by helicopter afterward. Instead he targeted mortals and *one* player. The Moon."

My lips parted. "Because she was more of a threat to him."

"She was the only one in the area who could slay him *from a distance*. Richter will target the Tower as well, since Joules shares that ability," she said. "So if we should blame any card for your mortal's death, blame the Moon."

"I'll never blame her."

"Yet you'll blame yourself?" Circe shook her head, and the river swirled. "I say we blame the Emperor." Could it be that easy?

Had Richter always had Selena in his sights? If fate couldn't be changed—then she'd been doomed to die the second we'd saved her from the Lovers.

I swallowed. I'd never forget how hard she'd hugged me that night, shocked that I was truly her loyal friend. *To the end, Selena.*

"The game spools on." Deep in her abyss, Circe spun a finger, and a whirlpool circled here.

Ever since my grandmother had told me to look for symbols, I'd been seeing them everywhere. Infinity symbols. A bow. A jagged fracture of rock like a lightning bolt.

A vortex.

I recalled my dreams: When the Magician had created that infinity symbol for Fauna, there'd already been one in that scene. Behind the two of them, the lions' long tails had curved over each other, making two perfect loops.

Patterns continued to appear before my eyes. Circe's whirlpool was like a helicopter's tailspin on its way down. Or a carousel that would never spin backward again. Like a tourniquet twisting.

"But for how long?" she murmured, and her whirlpool tightened.

"Has any game lasted more than a couple of years?"

"What you really want to know is whether you have any time left to let go. To accept ten swords in your back and still rise. To *live.* Ask the question, and I'll answer."

I had to clear my throat to say, "Do I have any time left?"

"Even if you had a mere hour, you should rise." Her eyes seemed to glow like phosphorescence. "Emotions are like tides. While you wait for your grief to ebb, Death is being carried farther and farther from you. Soon he'll be out of your reach forever."

Panic flared. "I'm the only one he can touch. He *has* to want me." Just as Gran had said.

"Stupid, Empress!" In her temple, Circe clenched her trident.

From the river, a wave rose up in the form of a hand, poised to slap me. I scrambled back. "What?"

The wave dissipated, and her water window dissolved, merging with the surface. "You can always bed him," she whispered, her voice fading. "But with each hour, his heart grows as cold as his sword."

Aric was strangling his heart as well.

Alone, I stared at the river and recalled his words from the night before my decision: "By all the gods, I desire you, but you must know that you have my love. It's given, *sievā*. Wholly entrusted to you. Have a care with it."

Yet I hadn't.

He believed that if we slept together—if we took that step—I'd finally be his. For the last two millennia, he'd taken me to bed again and again, only to have his hopes crushed each time.

And not just in the distant past. A few months ago, we'd been on the verge, but I'd balked because of a lack of protection—and my love for another man. Before I escaped him last, I'd knocked Aric out with a drug from my lips—while in bed with him. He'd thought I'd been trying to murder him once more. With his eyes devastated, he'd said, "You'd kill me before you ever accepted me."

Why *wouldn't* he turn his heart from me? If I went to him with another empty promise, I *would* lose him.

A life with him had seemed so complicated, so loaded with intrigues. But now the idea of us growing old together seemed laughable. Did my concerns about Death's deal with Lark no longer factor?

I had learned my painful lesson: *Some fates* can't *be changed.*

Shouldn't that lesson apply to everything? If I was fated to be with Aric, then maybe Death was inevitable. In every sense.

On my way back up to the castle . . . snow began to fall.

33

THE HUNTER

Closer to her . . .

I was freezing cold, but sweat slicked the truck's vinyl bench. Fever blazing? My mouth was so dry, my head splitting. My lungs rattled. I shook, rocking uncontrollably.

None of that mattered, no, 'cause I could see Evie. Pretty blue eyes and curving lips.

She liked to take care of me, fussing over me. *Ma belle infirmière.* I could see her so clearly that she had to be here with me; I could even smell her honeysuckle scent. "Evie, *bébé . . .* that really you?"

The truck slammed to a stop. Matthew's door opened. Then *my* door opened? He hauled me into a sitting position.

Evie *wasn't* here. *Gutted, me.* I squinted, saw snow coming down.

Did it snow wherever she was? Could she be thinking about me? I would do anything to see her again.

Just once.

"Your future refuses to behave." *Coo-yôn* yanked off the jacket he'd sourced for me. *Up was down.* Then he stepped back. And released me—

I toppled over, falling out of my seat onto the ground. Was the *sosie* dumping me on the side of the road? 'Cause I was about to die? "Now, let's just talk . . . 'bout this, *coo-yôn.*"

He caught hold of my good ankle, then dragged me farther away from the truck. He'd hauled me into . . . a bank of snow.

THE EMPRESS

Jack and I had marveled at the snow. I spun in circles as flakes fell, dizziness overwhelming me.

I'd known this was going to send me spiraling. Gasping for breath, I collapsed, tears streaking down my face.

Lark's animals fell silent. The river's current stilled. The better to hear my sobs. I missed Jack so much; I missed Aric so much. I cried for them both.

The skies opened up with an intense shower of snow, till it'd painted the ground white.

"Isn't it amazing?" I'd told Jack that last day. "Everything looks clean."

What I should have said: "You're about to die, and there's nothing I can do about it. And in a few short weeks, I'll be so messed up that I'll decide to live for more than revenge."

To tighten my tourniquet, even now. To delay a grief that could bury me. To rise and walk.

I'd thought the sight of snow—and all the emotions it brought— would make me less likely to be with Aric.

Just the opposite; because I could see my future so clearly. If he died before I did, some symbol—like snow—would mark the end of his existence. Later I would experience that waypoint (because everything was connected) and wish to God I'd taken a different path.

Death *was* inevitable. Why make him wait any longer? In a perfect world, I would've taken more time to grieve Jack and get my mind straight.

This world was as far from perfect as it could get.

I decided then that I would map my own journey and mark my own waypoints. The snow would symbolize both the end of one story and the beginning of another.

A new slate. But not a blank one. The red ribbon would be a cherished remembrance, but I wouldn't keep it with me at all times.

I lay in the snow and lifted my hand to the sky. Flakes landed on my damp face. Each one was a cool kiss good-bye.

THE HUNTER

Lying in that bank of snow, I gazed up at the falling flakes. They drifted over my face. Soft, soft. Like Evie's lips. With effort, I lifted my scarred hand to the sky. I closed my eyes and pretended my Evangeline was caring for me.

J'ai savouré. I savored each cold kiss....

34

"You still have only two icons?" Gran murmured as I sat beside her bed.

Over the last week, the snow had melted as if it'd never been—while I remained changed. I'd made a decision that affected my future, and then I'd made preparations.

Soon, I would rise.

"Why haven't you taken another marking?" she said, her faint voice slurring. "Because your powers are suffering?"

They continued weakening. I had a theory about that, but I pushed it from my mind. "Hey, I brought some pictures with me." I collected my laptop, then sat beside her on the bed. Though I wanted to learn more from her, I refused to listen when she talked about killing my friends. So I grasped for other subjects.

I opened up the family albums. As I scrolled through them, her eyes appeared dazed, as if she wasn't seeing the images. Yet then she stared at a large picture of my father.

I said, "I wish I could remember him."

"David used to carry you around the farm on his shoulders," she said. "He read to you every night and took you to the river to skip stones. He drove you around to pet every baby animal born in a ten-mile radius. Lambs, kittens, puppies." She drew a labored breath. "He brought you to the crops and the gardens. Even then, you would pet the bark of an oak and kiss a rose bloom. If the cane was sighing that day, you'd fall asleep in his arms."

I imagined it all: the sugarcane, the farm, the majestic oaks, the lazy river that always had fish jumping. My roots were there, but I knew I would never go back. Jack's dream had been to return and rebuild Haven. A dream we'd shared. I would feel like a traitor going home without him. Plus, it'd be too painful. Everything would remind me of the love I'd lost.

"David's death was so needless," she said. "Don't know what he was doing near that cane crusher."

I snapped my gaze to her. "What do you mean? He disappeared on a fishing trip in the Basin."

She frowned at me. "He did. Of course."

Chills crept up my spine. Was she *lying*? Why would she, unless . . .

No, no. I shook my head hard. She had the same kind of mental fog I had, understandable if she'd had strokes.

With all the double crosses of the game, I was paranoid. She'd loved my mom. Mom had loved my dad. Gran would never hurt him.

"Love of her life, gone forever," Gran muttered. "Nearly broke your mother. Now *you* are broken. You're getting weaker. If you don't win this game, then my life has meant nothing. Karen's sacrifice for you will mean nothing. Nothing!" For the hundredth time, she said, "Take out the little Strength Card. The low-hanging fruit."

My well of patience spat up sand, dry as a bone. I slammed my laptop closed and shot to my feet. "I will never agree with you about the other Arcana here. We should avoid discussing them."

I searched for another subject, realizing there were none. Every conversation led back to the murder of Aric and my friends.

As if I hadn't spoken, she said, "Weaker, weaker. Take the icons while you still can. Even Death's. Seduce him out of his armor, then strike. Use your poison kiss!"

I lost it. "I am *not* killing Aric. I will *never* hurt him!"

At last, she seemed to have heard me. Comprehension lit her eyes for the first time in forever. "Dear God . . . you . . . you . . . *love* that monster."

Her face grew red and blotchy. "You don't deny it? You will rue it!" She went into a coughing fit. "I-I spent eight years in an institution, caged, trapped—for you! But you refuse to hear me. To *see*."

I backed away from her. Maybe she'd done even more than those eight years. My grandmother might be a murderer for the Arcana cause. And now her player was refusing to conform.

An angry vein pulsed in her temple. "You want Death so badly, he'll end your life. He will take your head; I swear it. And if you've truly fallen in love with him, then you *deserve* it!"

As I stared at her in disbelief, Paul strode into the room.

In a firm tone, he told me, "Evie, you need to take a break. Now. I will stay with her till morning."

I staggered on my feet. I needed *Aric*. I needed us to be the way we were. Hadn't I always been on this path to him? Our story had been building for two thousand years. I might as well try to hold back the waves of the ocean.

Jack wouldn't begrudge me this, not at the end of the world.

And this time, I wouldn't be going to Aric with nothing new to offer.

I told Gran, "I-I'll be back soon." In a daze, I headed toward Aric's study. Animals tromped past me in the halls—a black tomcat, a rabbit, and a goat. In the living room, a bear cub and a lion cub sparred, shredding the carpet.

Aric's well-ordered sanctuary had been overrun. He was going to be furious.

I opened up his study. Not there. But I felt a pang to see that he'd left the poppy growing in his desk. I gave it a little juice to perk it up, then headed to the training yard. No sign of him. Then to the stable.

Thanatos was gone.

I hurried down to the river. "Circe! Where'd Aric go?"

"Hmm."

"Not now with that shit, Priestess!"

"The last I saw of him," she answered in a snippy tone, "his eyes were alight with anguish."

I sprinted back up the steep drive. I found Lark in her room—which now had wall-to-wall fur, feathers, and scales. I stepped on something's paw and earned a hiss.

As usual, Lark's eyes glowed red as she searched.

"Where's Aric?"

She shook herself out of her trance. "Away."

My glyphs flared. "*What?*" He was out there alone? With the Emperor on the loose? What if Aric never returned? If Richter found him . . .

"Chill, unclean one. The boss has been leaving on and off for the last few weeks. You just never noticed."

Guilt twisted inside me. "Where did he go?"

"Dunno. He always passes outside of my animal network when I'm asleep."

Then he did it on purpose, because he didn't want to be tracked. Still . . . "Lark, I need Cyclops to scent his trail and lead me to him."

"No way, Evie!" She held up her palms, her claws curling. "He'd be freaking furious! That would seriously put me in his crosshairs."

I narrowed my eyes. "What makes you think I won't do worse than he ever could?"

She tilted her head. "Good point."

THE HUNTER
SOMEWHERE EAST OF THE
OLD MISSISSIPPI RIVER
Closer still . . .

Another truck. Another highway.

But Matthew swore we were closing in on our destination.

Barely a week had passed since he'd broken my fever in the snow. Only yesterday I'd felt my first glimmer of hope that I would hang onto my foot and leg after all. I was using a crutch and a crude brace to walk, but I was fast on the mend.

My vision and lungs were clearing, yet my head and my heart still suffered, 'cause I knew I was running out of time to reach my girl. Urgency clawed at me, till I thought I'd go mad.

Did she remember that it'd always be Evie and Jack? That even death—or Death—couldn't keep us apart? Would she remember how perfect it'd been between us?

With her, I'd known true peace for the first time in my life. Hadn't she?

As *coo-yôn* and I covered miles, I'd craved that cellphone—with its pictures of Evie—and her taped recording. When I'd been separated from her before, I'd used her voice like a drug. Now I was a junkie needing a fix, but my pack had been stolen early on. Gone forever.

Matthew had sourced another one for me—*up was down*—but it was empty. Fitting. 'Cause I was starting over with nothing.

From behind the wheel, *coo-yôn* said, "You need her."

"Tell me something I doan know."

He frowned, taking me literally. "You don't know the future. I see *far*. I see an unbroken line that stretches through eternity—and back on itself."

"Uh-huh." *Just hold on, peekôn, I'm coming.*

35

As I followed Cyclops on horseback through the drizzly rain, panic was my constant companion.

I'd been so freaked out at the castle, I'd barely taken time to stuff gear into a pack before galloping down the drive, with Cyclops leading the way.

I had no idea how much time or distance had passed since Circe had opened her floodgates for me. Dark rolled into dark as I ascended mountain trails and traversed canyons.

No signs of life. No Baggers. Just ash.

To keep myself occupied—and to keep from replaying my grandmother's words—I'd tried to sense seeds buried in the earth. Surprisingly many. At one point, I must've crossed an old farm; the ground had been thick with them.

When I crested another rise overlooking a valley, Cyclops grew more animated, craning his huge head back at me more often.

"Are we getting close?" *Talking to a freaking wolf again.*

He snuffled, so I took that as a good sign.

We followed a meandering path that descended gradually, skirting the valley, before opening into a clearing.

I was almost upon a small cabin before I'd realized what I was seeing; the structure looked as if it'd been built right into the side of the mountain. Beside it was a stable under an overhang of rock.

Thanatos! The massive warhorse snorted a warning to me, but didn't really commit to it. I tied my horse beside him, then hurried to the cabin.

The door wasn't locked, understandable with Thanatos as sentry. I ducked my head inside, calling, "Aric?" No answer.

What a weird place. The walls looked like ... copper. Maps of constellations were pinned to corkboards. Some kind of electronic gadgetry covered a large workstation.

Aric's things were in a back room. His *armor!* Why was he outside unprotected? My pulse raced so fast I thought I'd pass out. He could be in danger right now!

He could be dead.

With a cry, I lurched from the cabin. "Take me to him!" I commanded Cyclops. The wolf started off, following a path between boulders. As I tripped after him, the rain grew more intense, drumming down on my head. Lightning flared—

A chunk of ice the size of a soccer ball landed feet from me, and other smaller ones pattered all around. Postapocalyptic hail? Aric wore no helmet! "Let's go, wolf!"

The path veered around an outcropping of rock; I rushed along it to another clearing, then stutter-stepped. A raised plateau stretched before me. Atop it was a gigantic dish, dozens of feet tall.

Was it a telescope? Or some kind of antenna? The Flash had scorched the expanse of metal black in places.

I raised my hand to shield my eyes against the rain. Spotted Aric. He was climbing in the base of the structure, amid the framework. That explained his lack of armor. He wasn't even wearing a shirt as he effortlessly moved from beam to beam.

Why was he here? Uncaring of the hail and lightning, I found a path leading up. As soon as I reached the plateau, he caught sight of me.

He leapt down from what must have been twenty feet, then stalked toward me. His muscles flexed with tension, and the tattooed runes on his torso seemed to come alive.

He'd told me those slashing marks were our story, to remind him never to trust me. I'd told him history didn't have to repeat itself.

"What in the hell are you doing here?" He seemed to grow larger with every step closer, his body thrumming with aggression. In the night, his eyes glittered with fury.

I refused to back down, meeting him halfway. "I came to find you!"

"Some emergency couldn't keep?"

No. Maybe. Yes! "What is this place?"

"It *was* a sanctuary. Since mine has been spoiled." He scowled at the wolf, and Cyclops trotted off, tail between his legs.

"Spoiled?" I cried. Was he so fed up with me that he wanted me to move out?

Ignoring me, he turned away, heading back under the dish.

I struggled to keep up with his long-legged strides as he went deeper into the framework. "Do you want me to leave the castle?" I had to yell as the worsening storm pounded the metal above us.

He twisted around, stabbing his fingers through his soaked hair. "That's not what I meant."

"Then what?" I felt as if I were needling a bear. The storm only ramped up the tension between us.

"I can't sit there and listen to that woman poison your mind! And if I say or do anything, I'll only be proving her mad accusations."

"You assume I'm letting her poison me?"

"If she doesn't, your chronicles will."

"I've read them. I've remembered so much more about you. And here I am."

"Why did you come?" His damp chest grew still. He was holding his breath!

My gaze darted. How to say this? "You . . . you're not safe out here with no one to watch your back!"

His fists clenched, the muscles in his arms bulging. "Get back on your goddamned horse and leave—me—in—peace."

What sounded like an explosion boomed above us. I jumped and glanced to one side as more gigantic hail plummeted from the sky. Facing him again, I promised, "I'm not going *anywhere* without you, Aric."

Confusion. "Why?"

"Because I love you."

His hand shot out. His fingers made a loose cage around my throat. "Never say that to me again!"

I swallowed, knew he could feel the movement against his grip. I whispered, "I love you."

With his other hand, he punched the metal, sending vibrations through the structure. "I told you something died in me the day you chose him! Let it lie."

I shook my head. "I can bring it back to life."

He narrowed his eyes. "Why would you?"

"Centuries ago, you told me that you were born for me, and I for you. You told me you'd convince me of that one day. You *have*." Through his caring. And his patience and generosity. His selfless protection.

"Damn you, Empress!" He was wavering. He moved his hand from my throat to my nape. So steady in battle, his hand now shook.

My missions had changed once more: destroy Richter, and make Aric happy. Time was running out for both. Which meant I would force my mind from the past. From the other half of my heart. "We don't have time for this."

"For what?"

"For not being together."

He dropped his hand, seeming to steel himself against me. "And still your interest arises only because of our circumstances."

I'd told him my feelings; I'd put myself out there. I'd never expected this much hostility. "I came here—despite all the things going on in my head—to offer you my future. And you're refusing to meet me even a tenth of the way? That's the reality of our 'circumstances.'"

He was seething with something that looked a lot like . . . hate. "If Deveaux were here, you would choose him."

"Still punishing me for my choice?" But then his eyes gave away a flicker of another emotion. Insight from my dreams and our past hit me, and for once, clarity sparked in my messed-up head. "That's not the main issue, is it? You could get past that. No, you're pushing me away . . . out of *fear*."

No denial.

"At this moment, you're afraid something will tear us apart yet again. You'd rather have the ongoing dream of a future than risk having your hope crushed once more."

In a rare glimpse of vulnerability, he said, "Each time, right before you struck, I ... *believed*. In the last game, the end of hope nearly destroyed me. Those first moments after your death, when I comprehended I would spend a dozen more lifetimes alone ..." His expression grew stark. "I could not survive it again."

"And I couldn't survive losing you." I pressed my fingertips to my temples. "Maybe we *shouldn't* be together. Part of me still fears I'd be risking your life—because of the game or the gods or whatever—just by loving you."

"I don't believe that. But say it was true. I'd accept any risk to myself if I *knew* I would be your husband in truth. Understand me: if I could trade seven hundred years as the victor for seven months as your husband, I would make the bargain in an instant." He moved a step closer, gazing down at me. "I would trade those centuries for seven days. Seven *hours*."

"Aric ..." I sidled closer, inhaling his heady scent. "What are we going to do?"

"I can't vow that you'll never lose me, and no vow of yours will alleviate my dread." Nothing could convince him that we'd actually— after two thousand years—sleep together.

"Then maybe we should make a promise *about tonight*," I said. "We either consummate our relationship now—or never. If we don't move forward, our worst fears will be realized in a way."

"Tonight?" His voice had roughened.

I nodded up at him, aching to touch him. To trace those runes and make him quake. "Tonight." Lightning crackled overhead, and the hail grew louder. "Before you decide, I need you to know something." I placed my palms on his warm chest. His heart was racing beneath my fingertips. "Aside from everything else ... I want you."

Mesmerizing light radiated from his eyes. "That, you *must* say again."

I wetted my lips. "I want you." Desire sizzled between us. Soon neither of us would be able to fight it.

"For all these lifetimes, I've waited for you to say that and to *mean* it." He had endless centuries of pent-up loneliness—and lust.

I was almost afraid of what we were about to unleash. "I do mean it." I leaned in to press a kiss against one of his runes, my tongue flicking rain from his damp skin.

"My gods." Voice a rasp, he said, "And so I am snared? I won't deny us—because I *can't?*"

I drew back, shucking my pack, gaze drifting to his mouth, to that sexy dip in the center of his bottom lip. "Let's talk after you kiss me."

His arms wrapped around me. "Good idea." He leaned down, his lips descending over mine. At the contact, my eyes slid closed; his pained groan rumbled against my mouth. When his tongue slipped between my lips, I twined my hands around his neck.

He slanted his mouth, his tongue slowly tangling with mine. For someone with so little practice, he was a devastating kisser. He tasted like rain and need.

My toes curled as we shared breaths. At some point he'd begun holding me upright—my legs had given way.

Gripping my ass, he easily lifted me. He groaned with approval when my legs wrapped around his hips.

My hands flew to his shoulders, kneading with delight as his muscles rippled beneath my palms.

But he broke away from our kiss, leaving me panting. His gaze narrowed with intent. With possessiveness. "If we cross this line, there is no returning from it. I will never let you go. You will be my wife in truth."

"I won't let you go either. And you'll be my husband." He. Was. Mine.

"We will be forever. We *are* forever."

I gazed at his noble face, raising my hand to caress it. "Yes."

His eyes slid shut with bliss when I smoothed my fingertips along his jawline, across his strong chin, over a broad cheekbone. *"Sievā."* That one word was laden with yearning.

He wants to be a normal man. I was determined to give him anything he needed from me. *Now.* Amid all of my emotions, *I* dreaded that something would prevent this. The gods, the universe, whatever . . . When I yanked my poncho over my head, his eyes opened and went wide.

"Here?" He swallowed thickly. "I need to get you ready . . . you should have a bed. . . ." His sentence died away when I pulled off my sweater, revealing my glowing glyphs. They reflected in his gaze.

"Here, Aric." I unfastened my bra from the front, shrugging out of it.

He stared with such hunger that my breasts seemed to swell for him, aching for his sword-roughened palms to cover them. I whimpered, arching my back.

At the sight, his jaw slackened. His pupils were blown. Then came more of that starry light. Like a sunrise.

As I pulled his hand to me, the rain and hail intensified. I was glad of the wild storm all around us. *Feels fitting.*

He kneaded me, biting out a choked sound of pleasure. "This will be over before it starts." Had his accent ever been so thick?

My eyes went heavy-lidded. "Don't wait another second."

He shook his head hard. "I didn't plan for this, don't have anything."

"I'm on something." I'd refused to approach him with nothing new to promise, so I'd gone to Paul for contraception the night of the snow. "I'm ready for this, Aric." For his first time. "For you." I surrendered completely to lust and adrenaline and the driving need to experience passion with him. My senses overloaded. My skin was flushed, my nerve-endings hypersensitive.

I smelled the rain, the electricity, his addictive scent. How could he possibly smell so good? His taste lingered on my tongue, making my head swim. "I'm ready *now.*"

My expression must have betrayed my emotions; he looked stunned. *"Sievā?"*

A pulse point beat frantically in his neck, drawing my gaze. I leaned forward to kiss it. With a moan, I sucked on his skin, feeling the strong beat against my tongue.

His head fell back. He bit out something in Latvian that sounded like a curse. In a dazed tone, he said, "This will happen. I . . . I *believe*."

The awe in his voice made me desperate for him. "Now, Aric." Lightning flared almost as bright as day, thunder booming mere instants later. "Before something stops us!"

He raised a knee, pinning me against a metal support to free his hands. "Nothing could take me from you. *Nothing*." He tore open my riding pants, yanking them and my panties to my knees. Unhappy with the barrier between us, he used his strength to rip my clothes in two.

My glyphs swirled wildly.

He sucked in a breath, his rapt gaze following his fingers as they roamed between my thighs. Over me. In me. He groaned at the feel. "You're so perfect."

I rolled my hips to his hand.

"Yes, yes," he murmured as he watched me writhe. "You like my touch." He teased me till I was just on the verge.

"Don't wait!"

Material ripped as he shoved his pants down his narrow hips. Between my legs, his hardness nudged and prodded.

I moaned, my head lolling.

He wrapped my hair around his fist, holding my head up. "Look at me." Our gazes met as he began to press inside. With wonder in his eyes, he rasped, "Gods almighty." His chest muscles flexed against my breasts, his ancient runes kissing them.

Sudden winds howled, and the structure groaned. Aric withstood each gust; he was strong. As I clung to him, my hair whipped in the wind, snaking over him like vines.

Cannonballs of hail pounded the dish. Louder. Louder. *Louder.*

So earsplitting I needed to scream. Vibrations shook the metal at my back. Bolts of lightning struck nearby rocks. Bits of stone were darts against my skin. Thunder boomed so violently, I could feel the percussion in my stomach.

Pouring rain, hail, lightning, winds—as if the universe warned us not to go further. Two opposing forces joining together.

Life and Death.

With his forehead resting against mine, he bit out, "We might be going . . . to hell for this." But that wasn't stopping him; pressure grew as he pushed deeper.

I gasped. "Then we'll rule it together."

His lips parted. *"Es tevi mīlu."* I love you.

For an instant, I saw Jack above me. *A moment of time. . . .*

I blinked, and I was staring into starry amber eyes again. "I love you too."

Aric tilted his hips up and plunged.

My scream and his yell were lost to the roaring winds.

When he was deep inside me, he clenched me close, somehow holding himself still. I felt his heart pounding as he grated words in Latvian.

"English . . . ?"

"You're *mine.*" He withdrew with a shudder. "How long I've waited." The heat of his body seared me when he thrust.

"Oh, God, *yes.*" My hands drifted down to his hips, urging him on.

Between ragged breaths, he said, "Nothing . . . could possibly . . . feel this good. Nothing!" Supporting me with one hand, he used his other to caress me.

"Aric!" The pressure inside me kept mounting.

He gnashed his teeth. "Never want this to end!"

Heat and friction. Electricity. Aric's increasingly desperate groans. The storm. Everything built and built. "So close . . ." Soon I was on the brink, could only moan and move with him.

"I can't hold back!" His pace turned feverish. *"Sievā,* you feel like heaven!"

Sensation overwhelmed me, and I screamed.

I dimly heard him telling me that I was his, that we were forever, that he could feel my pleasure.

That he was helpless not to follow me.

His muscles stiffened. Eyes lost, he bit out: *"Dream?"*

"No, no . . ."

His body arched, head thrown back. His bellows shook the night, over . . . and over. . . .

Afterward, we clung together, our breaths so loud.

He pressed his lips to my forehead. "Mine." He clasped me even tighter, his strong arms locked around me as if he'd never let me go.

The storm ebbed. The winds died down, and the hail ended. The last lightning bolt faded away.

36

We lay in the bed in the cabin, just stripped of our wet, ruined clothes. We'd returned to find Cyclops whimpering at the door, but Aric had simply said, "You are *quite* forgiven. Go home."

Now Aric wedged his hips between my legs and stroked the back of his fingers over my cheek. "I plan to have you all night, love. Do we need to do something more for contraception?" He dipped down to nuzzle my breasts.

Cheeks gone red, I muttered, "I had a shot." Paul had said it'd start working right away, but I'd waited a few days to be on the safe side.

Aric raised his head. "You *premeditated* this?" That seemed to delight him. "I never stood a chance, did I?"

"Just shut up!" I slapped his shoulder.

He grinned, so sexy he robbed me of breath. "You *did* want me, little wife." His arrogance had rebounded with a vengeance. "I couldn't resist you before I loved you; now . . . you hold my heart in your hand once more."

I swept my palm over his tattooed chest. "I'll have a care with it this time."

His eyes went starry again. "I believe that."

"You're not disappointed I took precautions? You wanted a kid." I was ready for a future with Aric—but not with a baby.

Bringing a child into a world without daylight seemed cruel. Would we describe the sun? Maybe we'd say: "Yes, it was millions of miles away, but you could still *feel* its warmth. I guess you had to be there."

"Do I appear disappointed?" he asked in a wry tone. No, he appeared overjoyed with me.

"Such a turnaround from before?"

"I've realized how selfish that was. And things are ... different now. If we never have a child, I will be happy. I want all the time I can get with you."

What little time we had left.

He lowered his head to kiss across one collarbone, his lips hot on me. He scorched a line up my neck ... across my cheek ... the corner of my lips. Then fully on my mouth. Cradling the back of my head, he kissed me thoroughly.

When he broke away, he left me aching, my hips rolling for him.

He rose up on straightened arms, raking his gaze over my face, my body, my bright glyphs and restless hips. "I still think this is a reverie, one of my countless fantasies of you." When he pressed inside, his eyes nearly rolled back in his head. In a strangled voice, he said, "How could *this* ... be real?"

Afterward, we lay on our sides facing each other. I murmured, "I know it couldn't possibly be worth the wait for you, but was it—"

"By all the gods, it was worth the wait." He cupped my face, had to clear his throat before he could say, "Do you understand how precious you are to me? Not because I can touch you—that merely allowed me to recognize you."

I laid my hand over his heart. For two thousand years, it'd been one way. Now it was changed.

His brows drew together, as if he was trying to sort through chaotic thoughts. He opened his mouth to speak, closed it, then tried again: "That wild storm was a tiny fraction of what was going on inside me. I look at you ... and I *soar*. I make love to you, and everything is new; I feel ... *so much*. I'm certain my chest will explode from it.... Gods,

I make no sense, do I?" Color tinged his broad cheekbones. "Tonight has boggled my mind. *You* have boggled my mind." He held my gaze with his own. "*Sievā*, I am a planet off its axis."

I lost myself in his eyes. "I love you too, Aric."

The corner of his lips curled.

He dozed with me tucked against his side. I peeked up and sighed over his spellbinding face, wondering how I could ever have hurt this tender, caring man.

But now we'd rewritten history.

He stirred and opened his eyes, his amber gaze studying my expression. "Regrets?"

We'd had sex four more times over the night. "None." Aric deserved whatever happiness I could give him. Did I think I deserved *him*? No. But I still wanted him for my own. "You?"

He shook his head. "I was dreaming in color."

37

"You want to tell me what you were doing with the dish?" I asked as we readied for the trip back. Morning had arrived far too soon.

He finished lacing his black pants, then dragged on a long-sleeved shirt to wear under his armor. "I've been trying to repair it."

"What does it do?" I picked clothes from my bag. Good thing I'd packed some. I currently wore only one of his T-shirts.

"It picks up radar and radio signals from all over the earth. And in space. Everything from distress beacons to ham radios."

"How'd you find it?"

He sat beside me on the bed and pulled on his boots. "I had it built."

"That must've cost a fortune."

"We're very rich. Not that it matters much anymore." Now he was rich in food, water, and fuel. "In any case, I knew whatever catastrophe the game brought would likely take out widespread communication...." He started talking about wavelengths and parabolas and other stuff I didn't understand.

"In English?"

"It enabled me to listen, to track, and, if needed, to transmit." He stood, stretching his tall frame.

"Why keep the dish away from the castle?" I pulled on panties under the T-shirt.

He watched avidly. "Enemies can use transmissions to triangulate positions."

"Can you track Fortune's next helicopter?" I tugged on my jeans.

He canted his head at my movements, absently saying, "I could have, but the dish will no longer work without certain parts."

"What do you mean?"

"I checked it while you slept. The hail battered it almost beyond salvage."

"You aren't angry?"

He grasped my hand and pressed a kiss to my wrist. "For some reason, I'm in a fantastic mood. The best of my entire life."

My cheeks heated.

Releasing me, he crossed to his things. "We'll have to rely on this." From his saddlebag he produced what looked like a cordless phone with a thick antenna.

"Is that a satellite phone?" Brand's dad had had one for his yacht. *Jack's dad as well. Tighten . . .* "Are satellites still in space anymore?"

"I believe they remain untouched."

"But what about the Flash? The solar flare?"

"After last night's storm, I wonder if the Flash came from outside the planet at all."

"I don't follow."

He sat, pulling me into his lap. "What if the entire earth is Tar Ro, the gods' sacred arena? What if they're controlling everything within? Even down to a storm to warn Death and Life never to unite."

"What will happen now that we have?" *Can't lose him!*

Full arrogance on display, he said, "Nothing. I refuse to give you up. After all we've been through to get to this point, we deserve each other." Seeing my worried expression, he said, "I'll sell my soul if I have to."

I let the subject go for now—the horse was out of the barn on this score—but I decided he would wear his armor whenever he went outside. And that he could never leave the castle without me. "Do you think the gods would purposely ruin their Tar Ro arena with an apocalypse?"

He shrugged. "Perhaps this is the game of all games, with a field of battle to match. Or perhaps they are punishing our abuse of the planet."

Either way, they still sounded like dicks. "Who would you call on that phone, anyway?"

"The Centurion. Kentarch might be the game changer for us."

Like I'd thought Tess would be. But the carousel couldn't be reversed. The game continued. I'd desperately wanted to stop it. Now that felt more impossible than ever.

My three current missions: to make Aric happy, to ensure we had no regrets when we died, and to kill Richter. I vowed I would complete all three. "Circe said he's searching for his wife."

"He was the last time we talked. They got separated."

"How would Kentarch change the game?"

"His powers could help us defeat the Emperor. When the Centurion's intangible, nothing can stop him, not a wall of steel, not a volcanic eruption. Unfortunately, Kentarch hasn't answered the last few times I've called. I thought it might be the signal from the castle, but it's not."

The castle. *Returning to it.* Soon I'd have to see my grandmother again. The thought made me queasy.

Aric noticed. "What's wrong?"

Real life kept intruding on our honeymoon. "I wish we could just stay here, hit the pause button, and forget about the game. Forget about my grandmother. I dread going back to see her, and that fills me with guilt."

"I can't imagine how difficult that must be, but you won't have to endure it alone." Cupping my face, he said, "You're my wife. We are united in all things. Any burden you carry, I carry as well."

I gave him a shaky nod. I'd been longing for someone to trust, to have my back—but I hadn't realized until now how close I'd come to shattering from everything. "Then we should get on the road." I stood to finish dressing.

"Very well." He hesitated, frowning at his armor. Tailored to fit him, it wasn't much thicker than a suit of cloth, the mysterious black metal nearly as lightweight. He moved in it fluidly, and silently. Understandable, since the armor might've been designed by a death deity.

"Why the frown?"

"On our return, I want you to ride with me. And I hate that this metal will be between us."

I shook my head hard. "Uh-uh. I want you protected—for as many hours a day as possible."

My vehemence seemed to take him off guard. He raised his brows. "As my lady wishes."

"I'm serious, Aric."

In a contemplative tone, he said, "This is the first time anyone's ever wanted Death *in* his armor."

38

Aric and I rode back together, with me in front, his arms wrapped around my waist. He'd removed his helmet halfway to the castle, though he kept it close, telling me, "I could don it more quickly than any enemy could strike."

Like the rest of his armor, his black helmet was incredibly lightweight—and intimidating. I'd asked, "Is it such a hardship to wear it?"

"Indeed," he'd answered, then he'd demonstrated why. Throughout the journey, he would kiss me, or inhale the scent of my hair, or simply tuck my head under his chin.

I hadn't wanted to have our first married fight so soon—but I was going to lay down the armor law soon. . . .

Every mile closer to the castle unsettled me more. I'd been away from Gran all day, the longest since she'd gotten here.

At what would have been dusk, we arrived at the river. Circe parted the waters with a sighed, "Death and Life. *Finally.*"

When he and I walked inside the castle hand in hand, a tiny coyote pup chased a gangly heron through the foyer; some kind of half-grown turkey perched on the banister, ruffling its wings as if it wanted to try flying. Cyclops lay with all his legs splayed, looking like a breathing rug. I could *see* him shedding his frizzy fur.

Oh, hell. I glanced up at Aric, but he merely shrugged. "You aren't mad?"

He tucked my hair behind my ear, repeating, "I'm in a fantastic mood."

I went up on my toes to give him a quick kiss, which swiftly turned heated. But I forced myself to draw back. I couldn't put off my visit much longer. "I need to go talk to her."

He exhaled. "You're right." Then he cocked his head. "*Sievā*, her time is ending. Today."

Why didn't his words make me feel ... *more?*

Brows drawn, he asked, "Can I go in with you?"

I bit my lip. "She wouldn't like that."

"Then I will be right outside her room."

Paul met us in the hall. He looked exhausted, must've been up all night with her. Add more guilt to the mountain of it.

He'd spent countless hours taking care of her, cooped up in that room. "I'm glad you're back, Evie. You should go in and say good-bye."

"Thank you for staying with her." What would we do without him?

"Of course." With a respectful nod at Aric, he left.

I knocked on Gran's door and opened it, but I gazed back. Aric had taken a seat in the hall, his eyes promising me, *Not going anywhere.*

Inside, I called, "Gran?"

She was barely holding on, her chest rising and falling with labored breaths. She held the chronicles in her arms, embracing them like a child.

A bout of dizziness hit me, and I was taken right back to that morning at Haven, when I'd first seen Mom after she'd died.

Two tears spilled down my cheeks. I kept waiting for grief to swamp me, but it didn't.

Gran cracked open her eyes. "A rat, Evie," she murmured. "A rat on my table ... gnaws the threads ... the salamander stares at me from the shadows ... the serpent coils around the tree ... and chokes its roots."

How had she gotten so much worse in such a short time? "It's okay, Gran." I pulled up a chair beside her bed.

Her gaze darted. "Spite couldn't spit . . . and the Devil knew his verses. The cups see the future . . . in a chalice of blood." She was rambling more than ever. "Only you can bring us back. You must win . . . the earth depends on it. Cards know it . . . beware the Fool . . . dark dealings. The dark calling, the calling dark."

This was new. When she started on another rant, I touched her arm. "What about the Fool?"

"The wild card! The game keeper." She reached for my hand, digging her yellowed nails into it. "You have to kill Death. He will turn on you—they all will. Death is poisoning me!"

I pulled free of her. "No, Gran, he's not."

"He's murdering your last blood relative. A rat! The agent of Death. A salamander. Noon serpents in the shadow. Midnight takes my life!" She was getting infuriated with me, even now.

I reached for the chronicles, but she hugged the book closer. "I could read them to you, Gran."

She hesitated, then relaxed her grip.

I slid the heavy book onto my lap and opened the cover, that familiar smell wafting up. Ages seemed to have passed since I'd read and illustrated these pages.

I began to read to her: *"What followeth is the trew and sworne chronikles of Our Lady of Thorns, the Emperice of all Arcana, chosen to represent Demeter and Aphrodite, embody'g life, all its cycles, and the myst'ries of love. . . ."*

For hours, I read, and the words seemed to soothe her. Her eyes closed, and she lost herself in tales of murder and betrayal.

When I recounted the Empress's "most glorious victories," Gran's lips would curve and her thin fingers would clench.

I read until her chest no longer rose and fell. My grandmother was at peace.

For some reason, I turned to the last page. Gran had updated the chronicles. The first entry:

The cunning Empress has beguiled Death, until all he can see is her. He reunites an Arcana with her Tarasova, courting his own destruction.

Another entry:

They are murdering me, but the Empress turns a blind eye. Though they have tricked her, I see clearly. She won't do what's necessary, so I have put the end into motion.

She can never be with him. She has no idea what Life and Death become. . . .

What had she meant by that? And what "necessary" thing had she put into motion? The last few lines were barely legible, her handwriting declining as much as her mental state:

I left you clues, Evie. Nothing is as it seems. Midnight serpents choke the roots. The Agent. The ro—

She'd never finished the last word. Mad ramblings? Or a legitimate warning in code? Filled with unease, I closed the book and laid it under her hands.

Aric entered, his concerned gaze flickering over my face before he wrapped me in his strong arms.

My grandmother had wanted me to *murder* this man.

He pressed a kiss against my forehead. "Come." He ushered me out of the room and back to his study. This time he poured two shots of vodka; we each knocked one back. I grimaced at the burn. He poured again. Another down the hatch.

He guided me to the couch, pulling me across his lap, my head against his warm chest. "Talk to me."

"She wrote worrying things in the back of the chronicles." I told him the gist. "Do you think she could've done anything to hurt the people here?"

"There's very little that's vulnerable," he assured me.

"I feel guilty—because I don't grieve her enough. What if my grief is broken?"

"It's not, *sievā*. I suspect you might be in shock. I can't think of another person who has lost as much as you have in such a short span. In just four hundred days or so."

"I figured out that I would have attended a funeral about every month," I said. "I know I should have been with her more at the end, but I wouldn't change last night."

He rubbed my back with a big palm. "Try to recall your good memories of her."

I would. I wished these last few weeks would fade to a blur—compared to memories of her laughter as we played hide-and-seek in the cane.

"What do we do now?" I asked, my voice sounding lost.

"You will pick a place on the mountain, and we will have a funeral for her in the morning."

I sat up to face him. "Bury her here? At your home? But she was awful to you."

His brows drew together. "At *our* home. Where my wife's grandmother belongs." God, he was a wonderful man to overlook all the things she'd said about him.

Which reminded me ... "When you went hat in hand to her that night, what did you ask?"

He hesitated.

"Tell me."

"I sought her for two reasons: to give her my vow that you would be protected for as long as I lived." Oh, Aric. "And to ask if she sensed this game was ... different. Because I had."

"How so?" I quickly asked, "Do you think it can be stopped?" When would I accept reality?

He shook his head. "I believe I sensed *this*"—he gestured from me to him—"our upcoming union. The marriage of Life and Death."

The marriage that felt forbidden on every level. "What did Gran say?"

"She said this game *was* somehow different. But one aspect would always remain the same." He pulled me back against his chest. "Only one can win."

39

THE HUNTER
Closer still . . .

"Climb," Matthew said, pointing to the top of a rise. "If you want to see her."

Though we couldn't be far from Fort Arcana, he'd insisted on stopping here. I figured this peak must be where Evie had radioed me the last time we'd spoken.

Her roses covered the face. And they were still *alive*.

When we'd first gotten here, I'd said, "She must be close! Is she at the fort?" Over all the time I'd spent with the Fool, no amount of threats or coaxing could make him come off her current whereabouts.

"Some time ago," he'd answered. "No longer."

So how had her flowers lived since then? I couldn't imagine the power she must've used creating so many. It was almost as if she'd left part of her ability here as a generator.

I swiped rain from my face. Even in the dusky light, the bright red and green were stark against the ash. "If I get myself up to the top, you'll finally tell me how to reach her?"

"Gaze out from the peak. Get a new viewpoint." Then he started fiddling with his bug-out bag, ignoring me.

I wore my brace, was still limping with my crutch, muscles weak. But you better believe I would push my body and my leg to scale this mountain. In a worsening storm.

'Cause I was desperate to get to my girl.

I hooked my crutch under my pack to free up both hands, then set to climbing. Soon sweat mixed with rain, dripping in my eyes. Each time that brace pressed on my wound, pain sang through me, but I white-knuckled my way upward.

When I reached the top, I lurched, nearly tumbling backward. I yanked my crutch free and steadied myself. Then I gazed out with disbelief. Black rock and roses stretched from this peak all the way to the next.

Just when I had clawed my way back to the land of the living, Matthew had sent me to the valley of the dead.

My gut churned, and I almost threw up.

Unable to stop myself, I started out over the lava rock. Felt like I was stepping on graves in a cemetery.

Then came the scent of . . . honeysuckle? I followed the smell, limping farther across the rock toward the middle of the valley.

Vines began to tangle among the roses, but in the distance was a clearing. I hurried toward it, ignoring the pain in my leg. Within the clearing were two grave sites with epitaphs. One was circled with ivy, the other with blooming honeysuckle.

Evie had created these memorials. I read:

Selena Lua
The Moon
Treasured friend, ally, and guardian.
Loyal and strong to the end.
You will be dearly missed.

To the end. Had Evie known Selena sacrificed herself to save my life? Just like Clotile had done a year ago.

Each day after the apocalypse stretched out like a month of life before it. I felt as if Selena had watched my six and fought beside me—for years.

Fitting that her memorial was beside . . . mine.

> *Jackson Daniel Deveaux*
> *The Hunter*
> *Beloved son, brother, friend, leader,*
> *and intended husband.*
> *I love you.*

I dropped to my knees.

Evie smelled like honeysuckle whenever she was happy with me. She'd wanted it to bloom on my grave forever.

All my life, I'd figured I would die young, buried in a forgotten paupers' cemetery somewhere. I never thought I would have been loved like this. She'd made me sound as if I'd made a difference, as if I'd be *missed.*

I reached for the stone to trace those treasured words. As soon as I made contact, visions appeared in my head.

From Matthew? The Fool was giving them to me, as he often had with Evie! I saw her in the days after Richter's attack; I heard her thoughts.

In one scene, she was *missing an arm,* clinging to a tower. Her head whipped up as she lit on the idea of going back in time and saving me. All she had to do was find Tess. Evie's grief transformed into a frantic determination.

More scenes played out. She stole from survivors and abducted another Arcana. She knew she was turning into a black hat, but she was ruthless to get to Tess.

To save me.

She made it to the empty fort. *A shell of what it once was.* I thought of all the work that had gone into building it—all the blood, sweat, and dreams I'd poured into that place. And I hadn't even been able to provide a light to guide Evie's way inside.

Within those walls, she dug up a grave. Tess's. The girl had tried to reverse time to save us all—and she'd died from it.

Evie appeared to die right with her, rocking the girl's withered corpse. All of Evie's hopes of bringing me back from the dead had been pinned on reaching Tess. . . .

I grazed my fingers over the words on my memorial: *I love you.* She had been crazed as she carved this rock, this gravestone.

She was broken: *Jack and I had marveled at the snow.*

The vision faded. I clenched my fists and yelled to the sky. How the fuck could Matthew let her suffer like that? Filled with rage, I staggered back across that rock, then stumbled down the mountain.

He was waiting for me.

I lunged at him. "What the hell you thinking?" My fist shot out, connecting with his mouth.

He went reeling, but struggled back to his feet.

"I should kill you!"

Holding his jaw, he spat blood. "I broke her smile."

I yelled, punching his face again. "Goddamn it, *coo-yôn!* Why?" I barely pulled myself off him.

He gave me a bloody grin. The *sosie* was back.

Took everything in me not to hit him again. "Why did you want me here? Why?"

After all the agony Evie had gone through at that gravestone, I was desperate to find her and show her I'd lived.

Then came a traitorous thought . . . *maybe she* should *think I'm dead.*

Was this the new viewpoint Matthew had promised? When I'd told him to take me to her, he'd said, *if you make it.* He hadn't been talking about my recovery. He'd been talking about my chances of never reaching her—by my own choosing.

Fifty-fifty, which way I'd go.

Fighting for breath, I said, "Can she be happy with Domīnija?"

"Can anyone be happy A.F.?"

I rubbed my hand over my forehead. "Is she with her grandmother?"

"Tredici gave the Tarasova to her."

So Evie had reunited with her last living relative—what she'd wanted most. The two had been delivered from the Ash, tucked away in a place with food and heat and luxuries.

Safe at last.

No, no, what the hell are you thinking, Jack? A life without Evie wasn't worth living. *You really believe you can go on without her?* I tried to look at this coldly: she was critical to my survival; survival was everything A.F.

Not to feel her with my every step? *J'tombe en botte.* I fall to ruin.

And no one could love her more than I did—*no one.* She'd known what she wanted, and she'd chosen me. *I* was her intended husband. I would put the choice to her again.

Which would mean opening up all her wounds. My gut twisted. In that vision, more than her smile had been broken. What if my return from the dead pushed her over the edge for good?

Besides, she hadn't chosen me only for me. She'd chosen the future I'd offered her. Now I couldn't offer her a goddamned thing. I thought of my empty pack, of starting all over again.

I had nothing.

Nothing.

I was right back to where I'd been before the Flash, slowly strangling to death 'cause I wasn't good enough for her.

Matthew watched my eyes, as if he knew exactly what was going on in my muddled thoughts.

I'd believed she would be better off going with Domīnija *before* I'd lost everything. Now I knew . . . if I truly loved my girl, I'd let her go.

She would never be Evangeline Deveaux. We'd never see the bayou come back to life. It wouldn't always be Evie and Jack. My eyes blurred, but nothing was wrong with my vision.

I loved that *fille* more than my own life; this just proved it.

"I'm not goan to kill you right now, no," I told Matthew, my voice thick. "But only 'cause you're goan to swear never to tell her I survived." I swallowed. "As far as Evie's concerned, I'm buried under that rock."

Coo-yôn nodded, then reached into his pack, pulling out . . . that cell phone and the tape player! Evie's pictures, her voice.

How'd he get those . . . ? Didn't matter. The kid was giving me another crutch, right when I needed it most.

God, peekôn. Noble, for the record, cuts like a blade to the heart. . . .

40

THE EMPRESS
DAY 453 A.F.

The rain tapered off for my grandmother's funeral.

Despite her breakdown and murderous message, Gran was a Tarasova, and the other Arcana demonstrated their respect. All creatures were silent that day. The surface of the water was glass. Aric wore a dark suit. He'd cut lilies from the nursery to place on her grave.

We buried her beneath an oak I grew on the southwest side of the property.

She would forever face Haven.

If the sun ever returned, it would set for her each dusk.

I only wished I could have buried Jack beside her, so he could always see his beloved home. . . .

41

DAY 455 A.F.

What's going on with him? I wondered as I headed to a window overlooking the training yard.

Since the funeral, Aric hadn't invited me to move into his bedroom. We'd slept on the study couch, with me wrapped in his arms.

Yes, he liked his sanctuaries, and yes, he'd been furious when I'd trespassed in his bedroom before. But I thought he'd also liked sleeping in a bed with me.

Or sleeping with me in general. He'd made no overtures to have sex.

I watched him riding Thanatos through the rain, pushing them in a grueling session. Even that tank of a warhorse looked like he wanted to tap out.

My Endless Knight was training as if *possessed*, as if he might blow from tension. He was no more satisfied with our current situation than I was.

Had he decided to give me time to grieve? Maybe he thought any move on his part would spook me. Or he simply didn't know enough about relationships in general.

We'd slept together; now what? It wasn't as if either of us had a lot of experience.

But I'd signed on with him. I'd accepted him as my husband. We both had needs that were not being met. So I decided to make it really easy for him.

Knowing he would be outside for a few hours, I began moving my things into his master suite—to Cyclops's snuffling dismay. "Sorry, boy. Married life requires some privacy."

In the bathroom, I arranged my toiletries on my half of the marble vanity. His armor hung on a stand; I tossed my silk nightgown over it, just to see what he'd say.

I hung up my clothes in the closet beside Aric's and cleaned out a few drawers for my things.

In one, I kept a cherished remembrance....

Then I started making some real changes. His sole piece of furniture was a carved sleigh bed. I directed my vines to move more pieces in. Soon my laptop sat charging on the new bedside table.

His ceiling and walls were solid black, the floor black marble. I figured a couple of the walls should be mine. On one, I created a vertical garden, styling blooms into a red infinity symbol. I began decorating the other wall using paint he'd sourced for me.

As I moved my brush, I wondered how he would react to all this. I hoped by kissing me.

On the many occasions I'd watched him training in his leather pants and chain-mail shirt, I'd lusted over him. And I'd had sensual dreams of him that hadn't arisen from the past. In one, I'd run my lips over all the runes on his chest, tracing them with my tongue before descending.

Now that I was married, there were things I wanted to try, things I'd heard about from Mel and other girls in school. And since I'd vowed to myself to have no regrets . . .

God, if Aric only knew what I was imagining right now.

I'd just finished up when I heard his spurs down the hall. His footsteps slowed. He must've smelled the blooms and the paint.

He opened the door. He was sweating and streaked with mud, looking so magnificent he temporarily blanked my thoughts.

His gaze swept over my changes: my gown tossed over his armor, my new garden and artwork. In the center of a black wall, I'd painted a huge white rose.

Like his banner.

His lips curled, and his eyes went starry. "You moved in?"

"I take it you're okay with the plan?"

"Delighted." He crossed to stand before me, then cradled my face in his hands. "I didn't want to pressure you. And I didn't know if you would want to officially mourn."

So old-fashioned. Which, considering his age, was understandable. "I thought you wanted your privacy."

He exhaled. "My own doing. I was an ass about that when I first forced you to live here."

I couldn't argue with him on that score. "I also worried that you might like sleeping in your bed alone."

"That bed is four hundred years old, which means I've spent a lot of time in it fantasizing about you. Once I have you there again, I suspect I will have little control at first. I was attempting to be a gentleman and refrain, so the couch seemed a safer bet."

"We can't wait for anything. I'm greedy for time with you."

He grinned as he ran his thumb over my forehead. Had I smudged paint there?

"Neither of us has experience with this," I said. "But if you ever have questions, talk to me, okay? If you ever need something, you have to let me know."

Nod. "If you will talk to me as well."

"I promise."

His tone grew husky as he added, "At present, I do have an urgent need." His deep voice made my heart race.

I wetted my lips. "What's that?"

"To wash this paint off my wife." He leaned down and took my mouth. How could I have already gotten so addicted to his kiss? He slanted his mouth, deepening the contact.

Between kisses, we somehow managed to strip each other and make it into the shower. We washed and explored.

His rough hands on my breasts. My palms gliding over his chest and lower.

I nuzzled his runes and licked the skin. As I had in my dream, I followed the slashing marks down.

He realized my intention, and a gust of breath left his lips. Eyes aglow, he threaded his fingers through my hair. The lower I went, the more his hands shook on my head. His breaths grew hoarse.

When I kissed, he gave a yell and bucked. Agonized sounds burst from his chest because *I* was sending him into the throes. Emboldened, I took him between my lips.

"*Sievā*," he brokenly rasped. "*Sievā!* Gods almighty!" Yet even as his body quaked, he reverently caressed my face with the backs of his fingers. . . .

⟟

"You told me we would rewrite history," he said as I lay against his chest later that night.

I was tracing his runes, relaxed and languid. Though he'd never had sex before me, he must've noted some wicked tricks over his long life.

My fingertip glided over a tattoo. "I dreamed of kissing these, following each one down your body. Even when I hated you, I had sexual dreams about you."

"Welcome to my entire existence," he said wryly. "When I got these marks, I never imagined they would guide your beautiful lips toward my delight. Tell me, was that a stray impulse?"

"I was imagining it as I painted the wall."

"Again, you premeditated!" I slapped his chest, and he chuckled. "If you give me the name of the contraceptive shot you had, I will source for more of them. I am keen that nothing interrupts our enjoyment of each other." His tone indicated the understatement of the millennium.

"It's called Depo-Provera. It's supposed to last three months or so, and Paul has a few more doses." When he'd injected me, I'd said, "The idea of living another three months feels far-fetched right now." He'd replied, "Better safe than sorry, huh?"

Aric nodded. "I will be on the lookout for it."

"You are not going *anywhere* without me, Reaper. The sooner you accept this as fact, the easier your life will be." Husband training a two-millennia-old man was going to be a challenge.

Aric raised a brow at that. Then, seeming to make a decision, he eased me aside to get out of the bed. "I have something for you." As he strode to our closet, I gawked at the sight of his flawless body.

The return view was even more rewarding.

He sat beside me and handed me a small jewelry box. "I want you to have this."

I opened the box, finding a gorgeous gold ring, engraved with runes that called to mind his tattoos. An oval of amber adorned the band. *Beautiful.* The warm color reminded me of his eyes whenever he was pleased.

"It was my mother's." He took the ring out. "I never gave this to you in the past. But would you honor me by wearing it now?"

I nodded breathlessly. "Yes."

"My homeland was famous for amber—from pine." He slipped the ring on my finger, and it fit perfectly. Holding my gaze, he said, "We are wed now."

First priest I find, I'm goan to marry you. Jack's words. I recalled the love blazing from his gray gaze before I stifled the memory. "Aric, th-this is so beautiful. Thank you."

"I'm pleased you like it." He lay down again, pulling me against him.

I laid my palm over his heart, gazing at my wedding ring. "Of all the stones . . ." The symbol of his parents' marriage had been derived from trees. Another waypoint.

"The amber's significance wasn't lost on me." He grazed his fingertips up and down my back.

I bit my bottom lip. "I don't have a ring for you yet." However, I did have an idea where to get one. . . .

"I would wear yarn tied around my finger if it told the world I was taken by you."

"If I'm your lawfully wedded wife, shouldn't you call me by my name?" He parted his lips to speak, but I cut him off: "You're about to tell me that my ever-changing names don't matter, and maybe they didn't in the past. But Evie is the Empress who was smart enough to give you a shot. E-V. Just toss the idea around and get back to me."

He grinned. "I will toss the idea around."

"And one more thing," I told him. "I want you to read my chronicles."

His hand stilled. "You mean that."

"Of course. Even though I'm worried they'll make you hate me again."

"Impossible."

Then I recalled some of Aric's recent barbs. "On second thought, I should probably hold them back—since I'm not in your alliance and all."

"What are you talking about?"

I shrugged a shoulder. "With Circe."

"I was wondering if I could get a rise out of you."

Rise and walk.

"For the record, you and I are not allies," he said. "We are one entity now. Everything that is mine is yours."

In a quiet tone, I asked, "Is my need for revenge yours as well?"

"Yes, I vow to you we will kill the Emperor. Which means training for you. Be careful what you wish for, *sievā*."

42

"Strike with both," Aric snapped, swatting my ass with the flat of his sword.

I was pouring sweat, exhausted, and in *no mood.*

"The oak and the vines—at the same time. Come now, wife, I've seen you do this before. I've *felt* you do this before."

I put my hands on my knees, gazing at the oak I'd barely managed to grow, much less control. Between breaths, I said, "I think this is . . . one of those situations . . . where actions look easier . . . than they are."

He expected me to practice on him. And he was too freaking quick. That hadn't been the first time he'd swatted me.

The man hadn't been kidding when he'd promised training. Every day for the last month, drizzle or downpour, he would escort me to the yard and then push me to the limit.

He pointed his sword toward the river. "Circe is brimming, and Fauna builds her army. If you want the Emperor dead, you must become stronger as well."

The Priestess's moat grew broader and deeper by the day, overflowing more of the countryside, creeping up the mountain. We were officially an island.

Lark continued breeding her creatures, our island population swelling.

Aric and I helped with them whenever she searched for Richter and

Finn. She still hadn't lost hope that she'd find him. He might have died, but without the Arcana calls, we couldn't know.

Aric and I had recently delivered Maneater's litter of six war-wolves. Lark said Scarface was the father, but I refused to believe it. I'd told Cyclops, "You old dog, you've still got it going on, don't you?"

Though I'd cooed at the (huge) squirming bundles, Aric's gaze had gone distant. "She grows more formidable each day."

Now I waved at the castle, telling him, "I'm not doing too shabby with my powers." Ivy and roses draped the walls. Inside, vines ran along every hallway, climbing over ceilings. Past Circe's moat, my thorns covered acres of uplands. They would act as more sentries—because I could sense through them—and possibly help ensnare an advancing Bagger army.

Yet something was definitely *off* with my abilities. Had been for a while. They seemed muted.

Aric rested his sword over his shoulder. "But you can do more."

I straightened. "Like you? You're faster and stronger than ever before." Each time I watched him train in his sexy chain mail, with his sword raised as he controlled his massive warhorse, I would disbelieve he was mine. The actual Grim Reaper.

Whenever he caught me checking him out, he would cast me a smoldering look, his eyes promising wicked things for later. He always delivered. . . .

Now he yanked off a glove to cup my cheek. *Never enough touch.* "I attribute my strength to you. Now I have something to protect."

In return for everything Aric had given me, I showered him with affection. If he'd been arrogant before, now he was growing breathtakingly cocky.

He'd begun to change in other ways as well. He no longer drank, unless the two of us shot vodka. He grinned a lot. Even laughed.

All he'd needed was a companion, someone to call his own. The Endless Knight had been no more equipped to handle solitude than I would be.

Circe had commented, "He's *disgustingly* happy, Evie Greene. As if he's not even an Arcana anymore. It grows *embarrassing*."

I was succeeding in at least one of my missions. Making Aric content distracted me from grief. From the past. Whenever we had sex, I lost myself in him, finding oblivion, my mind blanking. . . .

He gazed down at me now. "I will *always* protect you." He'd told my grandmother that before she'd died. Like Jack had died. And my mom.

Aric leaned down and pressed his lips to mine.

Oblivion. I sighed, going soft against him.

But when he deepened the kiss, I somehow remembered to draw back. We tried not to flaunt our relationship in front of Lark's creatures or Circe's river.

"Very well, little wife. I'll endeavor to wait until tonight. Seems you're more in the mood for training."

I almost groaned.

He stepped back from me. "Throw the seeds from your pocket and grow them in midair."

"No way. I'm not strong enough for that right now." I would pass out.

In a measured tone, he asked, "Why do you think that is?"

"Aric, what if those Bagman bites . . ." I hesitated, then said in a rush, "permanently damaged my powers?" There. My secret fear was out.

He shook his head. "Not a chance. You wouldn't be this healthy overall. You have boundless energy when you dance."

A few times a week, I would dance for him in the studio—which usually landed me back in our bed as soon as my skin grew damp from exertion. "Then what is it?"

"I'm not certain yet. I'll let you know once I work out a theory."

When the drizzle intensified to a downpour, I pulled up the hood of my poncho.

"Come." Aric took my hand. "This was enough for today."

We started back toward the castle, both lost in thought.

I was looking forward to a hot shower—with him. We rarely

showered alone. To be fair, who wouldn't conserve water after living through the Flash?

Then we would eat in his study, holing up in front of the fire to read the chronicles he'd acquired over the last three games, including the Lovers'.

Aric was almost finished translating theirs. When I'd pressed about the contents, he'd admitted there wasn't much to help us. The entries were basically stream-of-consciousness murder fantasies—and I starred in every one.

I'd assumed those pages would, you know, *make sense*. Or be *helpful*. But even the Lovers' father had admitted their chronicles were a revenge contract. No wonder Aric hadn't wanted to share the deets.

He'd also read my own book. The information within had filled in blanks that had plagued him for centuries. Among a dozen other mysteries, he'd wondered how I'd defeated the Centurion, how I'd survived the Tower and the Angel's fire, and what I'd done with the Magician's chronicles after I'd killed him and Lark (burned after reading).

He'd also suspected Lark could create animals, but he'd never been able to verify that ability until now.

Just as he'd never been able to verify the Minor Arcana. Which made sense. The Minors had probably steered clear of him, letting him do his deadly thing. Would they repeat that strategy in this game?

Even after all these weeks, I still couldn't shake my ominous countdown feeling; maybe I sensed *their* approach?

Tick-tock. Tick-tock. If not them, then what threat loomed . . . ?

I'd told Aric about my sense. He'd replied, "We can't possibly do more to prepare against enemies, so try not to focus on it too much. Remember: this game will *try* to make you insane."

He'd scratched his head at Gran's cryptic writings in the back of my chronicles, promising to keep delving for answers.

Since she'd passed away, I'd tried to focus on good memories of her. She had taught me a lot about my abilities, and not all of the information had been geared toward killing.

She'd told me an Empress could fashion wood into whatever shapes she liked; in my pocket was a wedding ring for Aric that I'd painstakingly crafted.

I'd figured the band would need to be as resilient as metal, so I'd chosen one of the strongest trees in the world: lignum vitae. Latin for *wood of life.*

Aric would like that detail.

After secretly measuring his ring finger—I'd used a tiny vine as he slept—I'd created prototype rings, honing my ability.

Once I was satisfied with the band, I'd reinforced it with everything in me, making the wood as strong as steel. I'd darkened the grain and smoothed it, until the band was gleaming black.

I might not be wielding the earthshaking plant powers I'd had in the past, but I could make a mean wedding ring.

It would be as enduring as he was.

But for some reason, I kept hesitating to give it to him.

Because of Jack? I didn't know. I tried not to think about my first love at all, figuring I could keep the tourniquet on a little longer. That noose around my heart might be limiting what I felt for Aric, but I probably couldn't handle anything stronger than the crazy love I already had for him. . . .

When we reached the front door, he stopped and pulled my hood back, assessing my face. "Perhaps you're simply fatigued from lack of rest."

Sometimes the tourniquet slipped. Especially when I slept. "Yeah, maybe." I still wasn't free from nightmares about the Emperor's attack. Last night, I'd shot up in bed screaming. Aric had been right there for me.

"It was just a dream." He pulled me against him. "You're safe, love."

I shook in his arms. The Emperor had to be stopped. I believed Circe—Richter would usher in hell on earth.

"Sievā, shh, shh," Aric murmured, rocking me. "I've got you."

"Jack used to say that." I tensed, couldn't believe I'd uttered that aloud. Where's your head at, Evie? *"I'm sorry."*

"Don't be sorry," Aric said firmly. *"You* should *talk about him. He was a big part of your life."*

"I don't want to hurt you."

Aric pulled me back to face him. "Do you try not *to think about him?"*

After a hesitation, I nodded.

"Jack saved your life and protected you when you were vulnerable. You and I would never have this time if not for him."

"I ... let's not talk about that." I reached for Aric, seeking that oblivion. "Kiss me...."

Now I assured him, "I'll get more sleep tonight." Maybe I'd been too mentally damaged by everything. Maybe I should have taken more time to grieve Jack.

No, no, I couldn't have. I wanted—needed—to make Aric happy. And we were on *borrowed* time....

I had believed dying in a fight against Richter would be easier than simply accepting what he'd done. Now I knew what would be harder than both.

Losing Aric.

I couldn't stifle a shudder.

"*Sievā*, is there anything more distracting you?"

I shrugged. "Just thinking about Richter a lot."

"We should train more in the coming weeks. We'll add an hour each day." He wrapped an arm around my shoulders, drawing me against him. "You have to be ready to fight. If anything happened to you ..." He swallowed thickly. "I think I would lose my mind."

Bingo, Aric.

That's exactly what happens.

43

"No male ever had roommates like this trio of females," Aric said drily.

He and I lay in bed, gazing at each other by firelight, trying not to notice how the entire mountaintop trembled.

Circe's moat sloshed with whirlpools and eddies, like barely contained violence. In fact, the river often swelled up into rapids, the castle all but waterfront property. Last week, she'd sent a geyser a mile in the air.

All that pent-up energy, just waiting to be unleashed.

I lowered my voice to say, "I caught you eyeing the river earlier with an uneasy look. She could swamp us as an afterthought."

Even worse? I'd seen the Priestess's girl water-form moving in the fog—walking *among* us, like a ghost. When she'd gone still, she'd turned fully transparent. I'd looked right through her.

The other night Aric and I had found wet footsteps leading out of the indoor pool, but no steps leading in. Circe had hydro-ported from one body of water to another, then had been loose inside the castle.

He exhaled. "Swamp us? Or possibly erode the mountain right out from under us?"

"Whoa." I hadn't thought of that. "I believe she genuinely cares about you. Looking back, I can see she was doing anything she could to help get us together. But will the heat of battle make her strike?"

"She has garnered a lot of control over the games."

"Like you."

He inclined his head. "Yes. In any case, she's never betrayed me."

"But *I* have betrayed her." I'd finally gotten him to explain what had happened between me and Circe in the last game.

After convincing her that I was different—from the previous times I'd backstabbed her—we'd become friends. But when I'd murdered my ally Fauna, Circe had grown suspicious. Before she could slip away to safety, I'd abducted her, chaining her in my cellar, delaying the kill so Death wouldn't hear of it or see a new icon.

Aric had found her down there—directly after I'd tried to poison *him*. He'd saved her life, earning her loyalty.

I bit my lip. "Maybe she'll only target me." Had my countdown feeling been about Circe? Maybe I shouldn't be waiting for the other shoe to drop; I should be waiting for the wave to crest.

"*Sievā*, targeting you *is* targeting me."

Some beast roared in the night. The animal calls and cries were a constant reminder of Lark's growing arsenal.

"The longer the game stretches on, the stronger we each become."

Except me. "Does Richter?"

"Yes," Aric said quietly. "And Fortune and the Sun."

"Sol said he would be able to light up the entire world, controlling millions of Baggers. Could he?"

"Possibly. But if Fortune alone realizes her full powers, then she has already defeated us."

"What do you mean?"

"Her luck-energy manipulation," he said. "She could blindly affect a battle—before it even started. Her ability could guarantee that her alliance would win any conflict."

"The odds would always be fixed in their favor?"

He shook his head. "Not odds. Fixed *outcomes*. We would have no odds."

Maybe *she* was the root of what I'd sensed. Damn it, *something* was coming! I grabbed Aric's shoulder. "I want you to wear your armor as much as possible. Please. If you died . . ."

He clasped my face. "I need you to understand something. No matter what happens in the future, no matter what this game brings, these months with you have been worth all my loneliness and pain." He gave me brief, hard kiss. "I would repeat those millennia, just for this taste of life with you."

"Again, I love you too, Aric. Now, wear your fucking armor."

His thumb brushed over my cheekbone. "I'm likely to fall in battle."

"You haven't in two thousand years." Then I frowned. "Do you no longer expect us to have a life together?"

"A long one?" He shook his head. "I told you the odds of us both living to eighty in this world was exceedingly slim, especially if the game toils on. We're soldiers, and we're at war. But we will return."

"Where will players come from in the future?" I asked. "Most of us have no family left."

"But every Arcana has a closest relative somewhere in the world. That person will continue the line."

Digesting everything he'd told me, I said, "If we're soldiers at war, then let's go out in a blaze of glory—*together.*"

"Should both of us lose, how will we know not to kill each other in the future? The mere idea that I might hurt you again..." His eyes flickered with emotion. "We could write to our next incarnations, but who will deliver such a missive?"

"When you asked me to be with you months ago, how had you planned for this?"

"I would have trusted Lark to carry letters on," he said. "Now we each have a target on our back."

"I couldn't ask you to do another seven-century stint." He'd told me and Jack that immortality was the *utterest hell.* "But I couldn't handle it either. I'm not built to be alone. Aric, if something happened to you... I couldn't..." Losing them both? There was no tourniquet tight enough. "Winning the game would be my absolute worst nightmare."

Voice gone gruff, he said, "You truly mean that."

I nodded. "We need to figure out another way to preserve our memories."

"We could bargain with the Fool—"

"Out of the question." I inhale a breath, then softened my tone. "What about Circe? Maybe we could ask her to cast a spell."

"Though we might not even trust her not to kill us?"

Good point. "Beggars can't be choosers."

"We'll talk to her." He reached for me, pulling me closer. "Come here."

I went into his arms, and for a time, I didn't have to think at all. . . .

44

"The unclean one!" Lark called when I stopped by her room. She was sitting on her bed, in the middle of a pile of animals.

Aric was finishing up some other translations, so I'd told him I would go check in with Lark. Secretly I wanted to make sure she wasn't planning our murders with all her animals and such. "Are you taking a break?"

"A few minutes. Just to rest my wings. I mean, my falcon's wings." She waved to the bed. "Cop a squat."

I waded through animals, then scooted a grumpy badger family out of the way so I could sit beside Lark.

"You're making the boss happy," she said. "Like a thousand times more happy than when you two hit it off before. I heard the man *whistling* the other morning. For real?"

"For real." I reached over and plucked feathers from her hair.

With an irritated growl, she shook her mane out.

I insistently tucked her hair behind her ears. "Your ears are getting pointed."

She slapped her claw-tipped fingers over them and hissed at me.

"I think they're adorable."

With a wary expression, she lowered her hands. "Whatever." Fretting her lip with a fang, she said, "Do you think Finn'll be cool with my changes?"

"I do. In past games, he loved your animal attributes. I have a memory of him telling you so."

"Really?" That got her to smile. "I'm so ready to get back together with him. When he was at Fort Arcana, we passed letters via falcon, really getting to know each other. I'm a goner for that boy."

"Cyclops was supposed to lead him to you." As soon as Finn's leg had healed enough for him to ride. "What happens now if you find him?"

Fidgeting with a claw, she said, "My falcon can reel him in."

"Reel him in . . . where? Back *here*?"

More fidgeting.

"Oh, shit. Seriously, Lark?" Aric would have an aneurism.

She finally met my gaze. "Where'd you think we'd go? Either Finn stays or I leave. You wanna get rid of me?"

"No, not at all." I sighed. "I don't know what I was imagining. Maybe that he would have a pad nearby, one as tricked out as his old one. You two would date." If he was even still alive.

"Will you help me with the boss?"

"Once you find Finn, I'll try to talk to him. But I can't promise anything."

"Thanks, Eves." She grinned widely, flashing her sharp fangs, reminding me why Aric would balk hard at this. Finn might be my ally, but he was still an Arcana. "So what's it like to, uh, live with someone?"

"I thought it would take some getting used to, but it's been easy." Because Aric and I fit together seamlessly. Plus he was turning out to be a perfect husband, no training necessary.

This morning, I'd awakened to find a bloom in a vase beside the bed. He'd grown the rose himself, had planted the seed two months ago.

Roses could be difficult to grow from seed, so for him to have made the effort . . . and to bring forth a bud . . .

He'd given me the very first one.

A white rose, like the one on his flag. I'd painted it; he'd grown it.

Symbols, waypoints. The rose connection between us had spanned centuries and was ongoing. Just like Lark and Finn's infinity connection endured.

I tilted my head at her. "You're not really asking me about living together, are you? You're trying to girl-talk with me. About sex."

"Duh." She rolled her eyes. "I've never done it—girl-talk *or* the deed—and you have, so . . ."

"So you want to know what sex is like?" Aric and I did spend a lot of time at it.

Early on, he'd coaxed me to describe in detail every sexual dream I'd had about him—so he could recreate them. Last week in the dance studio, he'd fulfilled another one. After I'd danced for him, he'd peeled off my workout clothes, lifting me atop the barre so he could lick my damp skin, wedging his hips between my thighs. . . .

I told Lark, "It's exciting." Understatement. As he and I discovered what our bodies could do together, we experimented a lot. Just this morning, that white rose had led to some kissing and then more.

Much more.

I nearly fanned myself, quickly diverting my thoughts from that memory. Clearing my throat, I said, "Imagine the thrill you get from flirting—when your stomach knots and your toes curl and you can't catch your breath—and multiply it by a thousand."

Lark got a dreamy look on her face.

"I think Finn will make you really happy."

Her pointed ears twitched. "Are *you* happy with Death?"

I was madly in love with him. So why was his wedding ring *still* in my pocket?

Yesterday I'd headed to the training yard early, determined to give him the ring. He'd been on horseback, looking as devastating as ever. . . .

His body went tense when he caught sight of me. That's my husband. *He dismounted and stalked toward me, spurs ringing, his gaze gleaming in the dark like a shower of stars. "I missed you, wife." His expression was possessive—and intent.*

Pulse racing, I stepped back. He moved closer. There I was, stalked by Death, and I had to fight the urge to run into his arms.

He maneuvered me till my back met the stable wall. He dipped down to kiss my neck, having quickly discovered how sensitive I was there.

I sighed, just about to give him the ring . . . when snow started to fall.

He felt me stiffen and pulled back to search my face. "What is it, love?"

I gazed up at him and lied: "Not a thing."

Now I told Lark, "I'm crazy about Aric."

"That's not what I asked, Eves. Are you *happy*?"

"When I'm with him and I can forget everything that's happened, then I . . ." I *what*? "Then it's good."

Her expression said she didn't really believe me, but she was going to let it go. "When I get Finn back, I wanna sleep with him. A lot."

"Paul's got contraceptive shots."

"Sweet! I'll leave the breeding to my animals."

I made a sound of agreement. *Sing it, sister.* "Why *are* you breeding them so much?" She'd been committed to it before, but never like this.

"I'm nervous all the time, and it makes me feel safer. It's like stress-eating. Consider it stress-breeding."

"Why are you nervous?"

"Because we've got freaking *Poseida* out there, threatening to tsunami us! I'm not pointing a claw or anything, but I'm pretty sure the river ate one of my tigers."

"Come on, no, it didn't." I scoffed, but did I really know? Probably not a good time to tell Lark that Circe was . . . moving among us.

"The Priestess might like you and the boss, but who am I to her? I don't want to go the way of that tiger."

"The fictional tiger victim that was fictionally eaten?"

She raised her chin. "If the water gets much higher, the menagerie will flood."

Waves did lap at the compound gates. Each time Aric had planned to talk to Circe about working a spell for us, the water had frothed. I'd held him back.

"You saw her tidal wave," Lark said. "How big was it?"

I admitted, "As tall as a skyscraper."

"What's to stop her from destroying us all? From destroying all my animals?"

"Nothing." The Priestess could swat us like flies. "There's nothing we could do to stop her. But we trust her not to hurt us. Just like I trusted you not to rip out my throat when Cyclops slept in my bed." Sometimes he still scratched at the door at night and whimpered in vain. I spoiled him with treats to compensate.

"Trust, huh?" Lark said, adding in a strange tone, "That's about all we have."

"What does that mean?"

"You're not exactly packing a big punch these days. Not like when you fought off Ogen. And you don't have the Fool or Jack watching your back. Or Selena and Tess, or Joules and Gabriel. We don't have Ogen." She shook her head. "And Death . . ."

"What?"

"The boss isn't thinking about killing; he's thinking about you."

I narrowed my eyes. "Which you always planned on, right? You strategized for us to get together."

She shrugged. "On Day Zero, he and I had a talk about how he was going to kill me in a few years. I plotted from that moment forward to find his weakness." Utilizing her single-minded determination.

"How did you know what he was truly like? He could've been some homicidal maniac."

"He *is* a killer. But every killer has a weakness."

If my grandmother was to be believed, we were all killers. All treacherous and disloyal.

Lark buffed her claws. "I went from the underdog to top dog—in months."

"Do you really want to win the game?"

"Somebody's got to repopulate the world's animals. I could do a lot in a few centuries, especially with my animal regeneration."

I'd explained her untapped ability to her. Once she'd located Finn and Richter, she was going to start practicing it.

Lark's eyes suddenly flashed red. Every animal in her room froze and went silent, like statues. "Can't talk anymore. My falcon might have picked up a lead."

"Oh. Sure thing." I rose and waded back through creatures. Over my shoulder, I said, "Let me know immediately if it's Richter." As I ducked out of her room, I considered heading down to talk to Circe, but when I looked out a window, the river churned. She seemed in no mood to chat.

Sooner or later, Aric and I would have to approach her about the spell.

I made my way to his study. He called it *our* study, but I would always consider it his alone—the sanctuary where my scholar/warrior husband curated his treasures.

He stood as I entered. Such a gentleman.

When I'd initially come to this castle, he'd always kept the desk between us. Now he wasn't happy unless we touched in some way.

I took his offered hand, and he tugged me to sit on his lap, his fingers interlocking with mine. "I've missed you, little wife." His voice was husky, sending shivers through me. "I had trouble concentrating on work, kept replaying this morning."

I blushed.

"In theory, that position promised to be rewarding," he said with a sinful grin. "In practice . . . *earth-shattering.*"

My body was already singing for his touch, my glyphs shivering. He noticed and cast me a look of pure masculine pride—so sexy my breath hitched. Desire banked between us, sparking.

Possessive gaze on my face, he leaned into me, taking my lips as if he hadn't seen me in weeks, as if he'd never get enough of my kiss.

I couldn't get enough of his. My palms traced up his chest to rest at his neck, my fingers twining in his tousled hair.

He teased me wickedly, till I would do anything to ease this ache. I wanted him to lose control, to be as lost as I was. Finally I wriggled over his lap, pleading against his lips, *"Aric . . ."*

He drew back, eyes blazing. He stood, setting me on the edge of the desk. With one sweep of his arm, he sent all his papers flying, clearing the way for me to lie back. Well, clearing everything except for the poppy that still grew.

He used his speed to strip us just enough. Not at all like a gentleman.

He was fierce with me on that desk.

And then on the couch.

And then up against the bookshelves with my legs around his waist. We were *both* fierce, the force jarring books from their shelves.

When they went crashing to the floor, I cried, "Your books!" They meant everything to him.

He laughed, his face *glorious.* "Let them fall!"

"But these are your treasures."

Voice rough with lust, he said, "I have one treasure." He slowed, pinning my gaze with his starry one. "And she owns my soul."

Between breaths, I said, "Does she, then?"

He nodded. "She keeps it right here"—he pressed his palm over my heart—"next to hers. . . ."

Afterward, as my pulse tried to return to normal and I basked in his tender kisses, I asked,

"You're truly not mad?" I recognized his favorite book on the floor— *The Prince.* The one written in the original Italian.

With his forehead resting against mine, he said, "In the past, I never had anything more than the game and my books and relics. No longer. I have a wife I adore. I am more than a mere killer and a collector. I am a *husband.*" He rocked his hips, ready for more. "And if I'm not mistaken, I'm a damned good one."

⫱

"I have something for you," I told Aric after we'd showered and dressed. "Will you sit there and close your eyes?" I waved him toward the bed, determined to give him the ring I'd secretly pocketed again.

Brows raised, he sat. "I'm not a lover of surprises, *sievā.*"

"Especially not from me, huh?"

With a half grin, he closed his eyes.

He'd said he was a damn good husband. God, I agreed. So what was I waiting for?

As I reached for the ring, the wolves started howling at something. Lark's zootopia was going to drive us insane before it was all done. I tried to ignore them, telling Aric, "I hope you like it."

The wolves got louder and louder.

I'd just worked my hand into my pocket when a scream came from somewhere in the castle. Lark?

"I FOUND FINN!!" The mountain echoed her with a thousand animal calls.

Aric was on his feet in a flash. "Shall we reconvene later for my surprise?"

"Yes!" We both hurried to find Lark. She was in the entry hall, with a train of creatures following her.

"Well, where is he?" I asked, thrilled that Finn was alive. "Did he tell your falcon what happened to him?"

She nodded excitedly. "Over the last few months, he teamed up with Joules and Gabriel. Since there haven't been any Arcana calls, the three of them have been attacking the Emperor in guerrilla raids. Once the falcon found Finn, he split from the other two. He scored a car, so he can follow—"

"The Tower and the Archangel?" Aric interrupted her. Voice dropping to a menacing pitch, he said, "Are you leading the Magician in this direction?" At her terrified nod, he snapped, "To *this castle?*"

She swallowed. *Gulp.*

"Stop the falcon this instant!"

Her eyes went red. Moments later, she blinked. "Finn's pulled over."

I got chills from Aric's expression. "What's wrong?"

"At best, the Magician's friends are using him—to find us. At worst, he's in league with them."

Joules had been gunning for Aric ever since Aric had killed Joules's girlfriend, Calanthe. In self-defense, but still . . .

"Boss, I swear Finn's not!"

Furious, Aric added, "Even if he's innocent, how do we know Fortune and the Emperor aren't following the Tower and the Archangel? Or that the Sun isn't keeping tabs on their location through his Bagmen? That falcon could be leading a trail of Arcana directly here." Gaze shifting to me, he rasped, "Endangering what I hold most dear." He turned back to Lark, towering over her. Voice booming, he said, "And when in the hell did I give leave for the Magician to call on this castle?"

Lark shuffled her feet, on the verge of tears, so different from her usual swagger. "I wrote him . . . I thought . . . you might let him . . . live with us—"

"*LIVE* here?"

I squeezed between them. "Finn is my friend and ally," I told Aric. "At Fort Arcana, he told me about his and Lark's plan to reunite, and I gave my full support. Lark checked with me earlier about Finn living here at the castle. If this place is truly my home too, then *I* invite him to stay here for good."

Aric narrowed his eyes. "I don't suppose your husband gets to say anything about your *invitation*?"

I jutted my chin. "No, he knows better. Because he's a *damned good* husband."

45

"This is the most ill-advised thing I've ever done," Aric informed me as he drove us through Circe's river opening. "Which is saying something, considering my age."

I was barely listening, too busy staring up at the towering walls of water. *So much power...*

Aric and I were in his Range Rover, leaving our horses behind. We needed speed to reach Finn as quickly as possible.

Once we'd driven a few miles, Aric said, "And to bring you? Sheer lunacy. I truly can't deny you anything."

"Well, obviously you *can*—since you're not wearing your helmet." I held it at the ready in my lap.

He'd only grudgingly agreed to wear the rest of his armor. "As fast as I've become, I won't need protection from the Tower or the Archangel."

And the Emperor? Part of me clamored to face him, to get my revenge at last. Part of me knew we weren't ready. "Yet bringing me is lunacy?" I glared at Aric. "I thought I was a powerful goddess who didn't need any hand-holding." He'd told Jack as much.

"Your powers are being... recalcitrant at present. In any case, there's no *need* for you to go with me."

Lark had wanted to come along as well, but Aric had drawn the line: "If the Magician is plotting, Fauna, I won't have you there trying to save him from me."

So she'd directed Finn to a rest area that we could map to.

As Aric and I had loaded up the car—with the two bug-out bags I'd insisted on bringing and tanks of extra fuel—Lark had packed food because Finn hadn't eaten in ages.

Just before I'd hopped in the truck, she'd handed me her music player for the ride, muttering under her breath, "Finn isn't plotting."

"I believe that. Aric's just being careful."

"Eves, please look out for my guy."

I nodded.

She'd leaned in to whisper, "Am I killing Finn to want him here?"

I hadn't been sure if she'd meant that Aric might ultimately murder the Magician—or that Circe might.

I'd wondered if I should warn Lark that something big was on its way into our lives. *Tick-tock.* I'd decided against it, since Finn was already in jeopardy. "He's starving, Lark. He won't last long out in the Ash." Outside of our spaceship. "I'm going to do everything I can to bring him back to you."

Now I told Aric, "Even if there's no need for me to come, I don't want us to separate. When we waited for Circe to part the river earlier, I think you wondered for a second if she was going to let us out. What if you left by yourself, but she refused to let you *back in*? How would I get to you?"

"Yes, I did wonder. Because she is an Arcana." He increased his speed, flying down an abandoned highway, weaving around Flash-fried cars and eighteen-wheelers. "Say the Magician is innocent of conspiring with the other two. And say we're able to extract him cleanly and bring him to our home. We'll be feeding and sheltering another player who can turn on us."

"Finn would never do that."

"Yet you expect Circe to turn on me?"

Good point.

"And what about convergence?" he demanded. "More Arcana *bring* more Arcana."

"When I first got here, there were four of us. This is just one extra. In any case, do you really want to be the card that keeps Lark and Finn apart? What if karma paid you back in the same way?"

His voice a growl, he said, "The thought *has* occurred. That's one reason I'm making this trip."

My lips curled at his surly demeanor.

"What are you grinning about, wife?"

I shrugged, all nonchalant. "I like your truck."

"Good. Apparently, it's half yours."

For a hundred miles or so, we listened to Lark's playlist, lost in our own thoughts. Slowly I became aware that Aric was sliding me looks and drumming his fingers on the steering wheel—not in time to the music.

I turned down the volume. "Spit it out, Reaper."

"I think I know why you're struggling with your powers."

I raised my brows.

"You need to grieve."

"And how should I go about that?" Release the tourniquet and bleed out? What would be left of me?

He opened his mouth to say something. Closed it. Another try: "My nightmare is losing you. I've told you more than once that I can't imagine life without you. But I realized that you might have said the same to Deveaux. And now you're *living* the life you couldn't imagine. The nightmare came true for you."

I balled my fists in my coat pockets. *Twist, tighten, constrict.* Once I'd gotten my emotions under control, I said, "Life with you is hardly a nightmare, Aric." Our existence was a good one; I should be happy. "You're the perfect husband."

"When we get back, you're going to talk to me about Deveaux. You're going to tell me about the red ribbon and why the snow makes you sad."

I swallowed. "You . . . you expect a lot from me sometimes. Do you really want to see me cry over another man?"

"I want to be there for you through anything. *Sievā*, you can't keep stifling this."

I shook my head. "I would never want to hurt you."

"Before the last two months, seeing you grieve for him might have hurt. But now I know you love me. I *feel* it. And I know you loved

Jack." He offered his hand on the armrest. "So that proves your heart is big enough for two."

I drew my left hand from my pocket and laced my fingers through his. He'd proved something to me as well. I met his gaze. "I've never loved you more than I do right at this moment."

His expression grew proud, and a calmness flowed over me. By the end of this night, we would either die retrieving Finn—or I would give him the ring.

"Blondie!" Finn's face lit up to see me when I hopped out of the truck.

He'd been waiting for us in the rest area parking lot, leaning against his scorched sedan, the falcon perched on the hood.

Aric had pulled up not far away, strategically parked for a fast exit. He stepped out, seeming on high alert.

I glared at his lack of helmet. Damn it, I'd just handed it to him before I got out. "Really, Aric?" Okay, maybe he still needed some husband training.

He hiked his shoulders. "Stay close to me, *sievā*." I had a flash memory of Jack saying, *". . . like a shadow, you."*

Tourniquet.

I hadn't seen Finn in months, but the Magician was still using a crutch, hobbling over to hug me. He looked like he'd lost a twenty pounds, and his clothes were threadbare.

I hugged him, shocked by how skinny he was. "I missed you, Finn." I truly hoped he hadn't plotted against Aric. "How did you part ways with Joules and Gabe?"

"Told them I needed to see my girl." He shrugged. "And that I wasn't really cool with ganking Death, since the Reaper's gonna let me crash on his couch for the rest of my life and all."

Aric scowled. "By whose goddamned leave?"

"Don't mind him." I believed Finn, so I ushered him to the truck. When I opened the back door, the falcon swooped inside.

Lark didn't want to take her eyes off her guy. Aww.

Finn hesitated at the door. "Really sorry about Jack, Eves. The Cajun was a class act. One of the best guys I've ever met." Finn had spent months out in the Ash with him, Selena, and Matthew, scrabbling together a home. I knew the Magician would've given his life for Jack.

I managed to say, "And Selena. She was right by his side till the end." *Twist, tighten, constrict.* I felt Aric's gaze on me. Was he wondering why my eyes didn't water? They would soon, if he had his way.

"Yeah. She was. I miss 'em." Finn brushed his long dirty-blond hair off his forehead. "You ever hear from Matto?"

Aric suddenly drew one of his swords. "We aren't alone, *sievā*. Get into the car."

Not likely. I shoved Finn into the back, then turned and readied for a fight. My thorn claws sharpened, and I bled vines into the broken pavement.

Out of the murk, a streak of light shot toward Aric. A javelin! "Aric, watch out—"

Like a blur, he'd ... *caught* it with one hand—before I'd even finished my warning. I gaped at his speed.

"Obliged for this, Tower!" he called. "You can never have too many." He spun the gleaming, silver javelin in his palm, and it retracted into a baton.

Holy shit! We'd scored another lightning javelin! My eyes went wide with realization, and I said, "You *planned* this."

He winked at me, then gently tossed me the baton. I fumbled before dropping it. He grinned, as if he found my clumsiness endearing.

"Bite me," I muttered, picking up the baton and slipping it into my coat pocket. "Hand-eye coordination is not *my* power."

"Just so." Expression gone cold, he yelled, "Show yourself, Tower!"

Joules swaggered out from the remains of a building, twirling another baton, his skin sparking with hostility. Gabriel descended in a dark rush of wings. He bowed formally to Aric and myself.

They looked like hell. They'd been missing meals too, and their clothing was ragged. Even Gabriel's old-timey suit—normally so immaculate—was bloodstained and tattered.

I noticed Tess's icon on the back of his hand. He noticed me noticing, and his face fell, his leaf-green eyes full of sadness.

"I knew you'd use the Magician to find me," Aric said. "Was your plan to kill solely me? Or the Empress and Fauna as well?"

Joules said, "We only got to the part where I electrocute you."

Finn stuck his head out from the backseat, falcon in his arms. "What the hell, dudes?" He was genuinely wounded. "You guys were following me? Freaking harsh, man. *Harsh.* I thought we were friends."

Aric cast me a look. *See?* Most Arcana couldn't be trusted.

"Oi, Empress, I'll be havin' that javelin back," Joules said. "Even if I have to fight you for it."

"I do believe you gave your vow never to hurt her," Aric said. "In any event, you'll have to go through me."

Joules turned to Gabriel. "What do you think, Gabe? Should I—" Joules hurled his next javelin at Aric with shocking speed—and a *second* one that I'd never seen from his other hand!

Aric caught one javelin, even as his sword flashed out to deflect the second strike.

Before I'd had time to blink.

From the truck, Finn breathed, "Duuude."

Aric smirked. "Ever wonder where the phrase *lightning-fast reflexes* came from?" God, he was so cocky. I loved it.

I caught the baton this time. We'd scored a pair of javelins!

Joules gave a strangled yell. "I don't care how long it takes. I will kill you!"

"Concentrate your minuscule talents on the Emperor and his allies. Or die."

I told them, "We should *all* be concentrating on Richter. Where is he?"

Finn said, "He and his alliance have a lair, but we haven't been able to find it. Especially now . . ."

"Why now?"

"Zara kind of scored the sickest military attack copter ever." She'd traded up after the crash? "She and Sol fly in it. It's tricked out with machine guns and even missiles."

Fortune's arsenal was growing more powerful, like Lark's. I wondered if Zara had discovered the full extent of her luck manipulation. "Is Richter still with them?"

Joules's dark eyes flashed. "*Right* with 'em. That fecker learned how to ride waves of lava." Just as I'd read in my chronicles. "Even if we could target him with lightning, Zara's always there to provide cover."

Aric looked furious. "You allowed her to acquire an attack copter? *After* you'd been raiding them?"

In a blustering tone, Joules said, "I've struck and fried every sittin' helicopter, at every base, every airport, and every hangar we've passed. Even parts of helicopters, so she couldn't do repairs. But she's been hidin' this one."

"That craft employs infrared vision," Gabriel said quietly. His speech and accent were as old-timey as his suit, even as he spoke about infrared. "Such technology thwarts even the Magician's illusions. And there are few heat signatures left in the world—no engines, scarce animals and humans—for us to blend with. No trees provide cover." He unfurled a silky black wing. Multiple bullet holes riddled it. "How do you suggest we *concentrate* on them? You have wisdom, Endless Knight. Impart it. I will heed you."

As much as I would love to fly, those wings truly were a weakness. He'd had a bullet hole in one the last time I'd seen him. And Aric had stabbed through one not too long ago.

"Step one," Aric said, "do *not* lead them to the alliance that could actually stop them."

"We broke clean from 'em," Joules said.

"What about Bagmen?" I asked. "They scout for Sol."

"Gabe would've scented any Baggers." Joules waved off my concern. "Hell, *I* would have."

Gabriel cocked his head. "*Wait.*"

"What do you hear, friend?" Joules murmured, producing another baton. Though he usually sounded like a streetwise bruiser, sometimes when he spoke to Gabriel, he seemed younger, not as coarse.

Made me wonder what the Lord of Lightning had been like before the apocalypse. Before Calanthe's gruesome death.

"A . . . helicopter is, in fact, approaching us," Gabriel told him. "Somehow, Zara has our location."

"Leave me, Gabe."

The Archangel shook his head. "If I had a dollar for every time you have said those words . . . And I give you my customary reply: Never."

I frowned at my feet. A tremor? I heard the copter in the distance and . . . crackling asphalt? The need to fight and kill *blistered* me inside, the heat of battle burning as hot as the flames I'd nearly walked into four months ago. But without a plan and prep, we couldn't take on a military copter and earthquakes.

Aric snapped, "Into the truck, *sievā*!"

I hurried toward it. Across the lot, fissures forked out like Joules's lightning. My jaw dropped as Finn's abandoned sedan plummeted into one. An explosion rocked the area.

I reeled, clutching the door handle. Aric appeared behind me to shove me into the truck. As he raced to his seat, the back door opened on my side.

Joules and Gabriel piled in! The falcon screeched when Joules elbowed Finn to move over.

Aric slid behind the wheel, his demeanor lethal. In a low tone, he said, "I've been known to grant Death wishes."

Gabriel retracted his silky wings, but they were still huge in such a confined space. "We respectfully request a truce." As Matthew had called an Arcana truce.

Another quake. More fissures snaked around our truck.

Four voices cried to Aric, "Go!"

With a muttered curse, he gunned the engine. "If we escape, I will be tossing you from this vehicle, and when I do, I'll most likely slit your throats."

46

Aric sped through the parking lot, his quick reflexes adjusting our course as quakes continued. He expertly veered toward the exit, then out onto the highway. The engine roared as the truck raced forward.

He narrowed his eyes at the rearview mirror, telling Joules, "One of Fortune's missiles takes out five of us. *Five.* She will unleash everything in her arsenal to hit this truck."

"Looks as if you drive like you do everything else. So don't bloody *let* it take us out!"

Finn cast his former friends a glare, then turned from them, speaking to the falcon in a hushed voice.

Joules swiped a hand over his face. "How the feck did they find us? The Sun's Baggers?"

"I didn't scent any," Gabriel said. "They have a very distinctive scent."

Joules asked Aric, "Can the Sun disguise it?"

Aric glanced at me. "Empress?"

"Maybe. If he washed their skin. The slime is what stinks."

"Oi, what makes her the expert?"

Eyes on the congested highway, Aric absently answered, "She spent several days in the Sun's company."

"Damn, Empress. You move fast."

I stiffened.

Aric grated, "You *do* wish to die, Tower."

A new crevasse opened up not two feet away from the truck. "Uh,

Aric." I stared down. "Fissure directly to our right." It ripped along as fast as we drove.

He answered, "And one on my left."

I craned my head around and got my first look at Zara's terrifying new weapon. The helicopter's shape was angular and sharp, with huge guns mounted beneath it. The painted nose looked like a dragon's roaring mouth, fangs glinting.

Zara hovered above the fiery remains of Finn's car. "She's checking out the explosion. Maybe she'll think some of us were in the car...." My words trailed off.

The copter smoothly rotated in a controlled circle, like a roulette wheel. *Where she stops, nobody knows.*

Carousel. Roulette. Tourniquet.

Symbols. Waypoints ...

The copter stopped swiveling, the creepy nose pointing straight at us. "Floor it!" I cried. "They've seen us." The nose dipped down as the copter accelerated.

Gabriel's black wings twitched. "What's that sound?"

I blinked, disbelieving my eyes. "She's fired a missile!"

"Hold on, *sievā*." Aric's intent look scared the hell out of me.

I faced forward. "Cars, Aric." A pair of wrecks were too close to each other—no way he could squeeze through that tight opening. Yet he accelerated as he headed right for them. His expression was cold focus, his jaw clenched.

Oh. Shit.

"Out of me way!" Joules cried, scrambling for the door.

Falcon in his arms, Finn dove for the back.

Joules lengthened a javelin. Before I could warn him, he'd cracked open the back door and tried to lob a bolt—

Metal on metal shrieked. Side mirrors tore away. A shower of sparks lit the night, and the door slammed shut on Joules; his javelin recoiled and jabbed Gabriel's wing.

Zara's missile struck the wreck on the left, sending pieces high in the sky. Aric dodged a plummeting wheel. An axle.

From the third-row seat, Finn said, "Sick driving, dude!"

Joules sputtered, "You tryin' to get me killed?" He collapsed his spear. "Gabe, you all right?"

"I will be fine anon."

"Shut up and make yourself useful," Aric told Joules. "What's your range?"

Shoulders back, he replied, "Far enough."

"Whatever it is, they'll know the distance from your previous attacks—so she'll never fly *within* that range. If she fires again, you're going to have to hit the missile." Aric pushed a button on the dash, and the extended moon roof opened above us. "Let it get close before you strike it."

"Feck me, you want me to nail a speeding target? *From* a speeding target?"

Aric sighed. "Do try to get the javelin *out* of the vehicle this time."

Joules's eyes went wide, his face sparking with rage. "Oh, you bloody—"

"Tower, let us remain on point," Gabriel interrupted.

Aric glanced back at Joules. "Give some to the Archangel."

"Nobody but me can throw these and make them go boom."

I said, "Actually ..."

Joules shrugged and tossed Gabriel a couple of batons; then he popped up through the moon roof. "That's right—give the Lord o' Lightnin' some room." He created another javelin, then rolled his head on his neck.

Aric said, "Archangel, blast cars. Often. We need other heat targets."

With a nod, Gabriel stood up in the backseat beside Joules, his furled wings fluttering.

When the copter jerked and smoke puffed from the bottom, I said, "I think she just—"

"—fired another!" Gabriel finished.

"Jaysus, incoming!"

Gabriel and Joules bombed every car we passed, but the missile was still on our ass and closing fast.

"Take it out, Tower," Gabriel said. "Now!"

Joules hurled a javelin . . . it zoomed away . . . An explosion behind us! "Pegged that fecker!"

Even Aric appeared surprised.

Joules cackled with delight. "And I've still got time to moon her. You think me arse'll show up on her infrared?" The streetwise bruiser was back.

"Missile!" Gabriel said.

Joules hurled another javelin . . . and took that one out as well! "I can do this all night, Fortune!"

If we could stay alive long enough, we might get her to blow her entire arsenal.

"Conserve some power," Aric said. "She might send two next time."

By the light of the fires, I could see the copter falling back. "Why's she slowing down?"

"To give her missiles time to accelerate. The Tower won't be able to hit them at full speed." Aric caught my gaze. "When I give a signal, I want you to leap from this car."

"No! If you go out, I go too. That was the deal. Tell Joules how to do that lightning field."

Joules ducked down. "What lightning field?"

Aric gritted his teeth. "And when he wields that power against *us?*"

"Kick the can down the road, Aric! We'll deal with that later."

"Roll before you hit," he told me. "Then run for water."

"What are you talking about—"

He reached over me to yank open my door.

A vine shot out from my forefinger, and I lashed myself to the oh-shit handle. "Don't even think about it!"

He slammed the door. "Stubborn woman!" He made a sound of frustration, then asked Joules, "Can you throw two javelins with accuracy?"

"In me sleep."

"Throw a pair to land at the exact same time, about a hundred feet apart. Lightning will combust between them. *If* you are as accurate as you say."

"No shite?" Joules got into position.

"You can do this," Gabriel told him. "You must."

The Tower took several rapid breaths, then lobbed a pair of javelins at the same time. . . . The bolts landed, but nothing unusual happened.

Aric veered around a motor home. "At the *exact* same time."

Gabriel cocked his head again. "She's fired. *Two*. Picking up speed!"

Joules let loose another pair. Two more strikes. No combustion.

Aric said, "You are capable of this, Tower. I have *seen* you do it before."

Joules gave a yell and hurled two more. I held my breath. Could already see the pair of missiles streaking toward us.

A web of lightning exploded into the sky. Sizzling electricity unlike anything I'd ever seen.

The missiles exploded in the electric net.

"Oi, now we are cookin' with gas!"

"That chick's got to be out of missiles," Finn said. "I only saw four last time."

Aric maneuvered around more wrecks. "She hasn't fired bul—"

Bullets bit into the highway on both sides of us. "Get inside!" I cried.

Joules and Gabriel dropped down.

Aric swerved, narrowly missing a convertible with two Baggers still seat-belted in. Another spray of bullets sent pieces of that car at us, but he evaded the debris. With his cold focus, he threaded two big rigs, then dodged a locomotive that had fallen off an overhead rail bridge.

Heart racing, I said, "And to think I once wondered if you'd ever driven a car."

"I can't outrun those bullets much longer."

More pitted the ground inches away. Ricocheting pavement busted my window. "Shit!" Wind rushed into the truck. My hair whipped, my eyes watering.

"Are you hurt, *sievā*?"

"No, I'm good." A Bagman on the side of the road caught my attention. As if in slow motion, I watched it . . . wave at me. Not good. *Going crazy.*

We passed a second one. It placed a slimy hand on its chest, as if making a pledge.

Either I was going insane . . . or Sol was screwing with us. Another Bagman up ahead raised its arm, indicating to the right—where there was a turnoff onto a smaller road.

Or was Sol *helping* us?

The Evie of old would swear she and Sol had shared a moment, that some kind of bond had formed. The Evie of late would say, "Trust no one. Kill first; ask later." As Gran had repeatedly said, Arcana were *all* treacherous and disloyal killers. Aric too had little trust in other players.

Which Evie would I choose to be?

Just as the line of bullets veered toward us, I said, "Aric, take the next right!" Damn it, I would create my own symbols. I would fill in my own new slate.

He wheeled a hard right, and we skidded onto the smaller road. "Are you familiar with this area?"

I didn't answer. At the next junction, another Bagger pointed left. "Go left."

We fishtailed left, the line of fire stitching the pavement where we'd just been. The road began to curve through canyons. Bullets struck the rock walls, instead of us; I just prayed they wouldn't ricochet the wrong way.

"Much better terrain, *sievā*. Is the Fool speaking to you?"

Gabriel said, "Will the calls return?"

I shook my head. "Um, the Bagmen are directing us. I think Sol is using them to help us."

Aric did a double take.

"Jaysus! The Empress has gone mental. As can happen when you're *diddlin' Death*."

Gabriel laid a hand on my seat, his talons digging in to the leather. "If he is leading us anywhere, it will be into a trap—or off a cliff."

"Why would he help his enemies?" Finn asked from the back.

Joules blustered: "Sol's the one in the feckin' helicopter shootin' at us! He's not goin' to try to kill us *and* try to save us."

Aric murmured to me, "I can't disagree with their logic."

"Sol has to make it look like he's still allying with Zara."

Joules turned to Aric. "You're listenin' to this?"

Finn added, "Eves, the Sun is not a good dude. He's evil."

Yes, at times. But I had been too. Now I was different. "He's *layered*," I said, using Sol's word. "Up ahead, there's another Bagman pointing left."

Aric eyed me. "Are you sure? If you believe this is the right course, I will follow it."

"You will?"

"I trust you with my life."

I'd made so many mistakes, tragic ones, that I hardly trusted myself. Then I pictured Sol at the edge of the lava gravestone. He'd been conflicted. "I believe Sol is helping."

Aric turned left at that Bagman.

Joules bit out another curse. "I understand she's the only tart for you, but no piece is worth dyin' over!"

Aric's shoulders tensed. "And yet you keep risking Death because of the one you lost."

Joules's skin sparked anew, his hand dropping to his boot.

Did he have a knife stowed in there? "Don't even think about hurting him, Joules! Or I'll poison you where you sit."

To our left was a tunnel. A Bagger pointed to our right. Aric went right.

"Look down there," Gabriel said. "The canyon leads to a city, one with standing buildings." That valley had mountain-to-mountain structures. Fires burned in places. Smoke billowed. Lots of things to confuse infrared vision.

Aric raised his brows at me. "Perhaps the Sun *was* aiding us. If we reach that city, we could lose Fortune." He took my hand on the console.

Joules coughed. "Is that a wedding band I spy with me little eye? Already married, Empress? Jaysus, the Cajun's just months cold in the grave. Actually, he never was *cold*, now, was he?"

Joules might as well have struck me.

Aric's voice turned menacing. "If you ever speak about Deveaux again, you will use respectful words—or I swear to the gods, I will spit you on one of your javelins."

Finn, Gabriel, and Joules looked shocked by Aric's defense of Jack. Even I was surprised.

Joules muttered, "Talk about singin' a new tune."

The street shook again, vibrating the truck. "The Emperor's getting closer."

Aric accelerated even more. "We must make that pass before he takes out the road."

I peered out the window; a fracture was opening up beside us, racing us. But we were pulling ahead. "We've got it. We're beating it."

Aric suddenly slammed on the brakes. I jerked my gaze forward.

A skin-and-bones horse trotted in front of us. We all gaped to see an animal—

Fissures forked across the road leading to the valley. The horse disappeared into a crevasse not ten feet from us. Our escape had been sabotaged.

47

Aric whipped the truck into reverse. "Wings down, Archangel." When Gabriel tried in vain to lower them, Aric punched out his window, leaning out as he steered.

"Where do we go?" I asked.

"Fortune is coming up behind us. There's only one other way."

The tunnel.

Aric backed up to the turnoff, then slammed the truck into gear. Though Richter could bring down that mountain on our heads, we raced through the tunnel entrance. Aric killed the lights, speeding into the pitch dark. In the center of the tunnel, he braked. "Listen."

Swoop swoop swoop. Zara's copter. "She's flying over. She'll be waiting for us on the other side."

Aric nodded. "She might have a missile left. Even without one, she could use her guns to set off a rock slide, trapping us until the Emperor arrives."

"Some of us know how that feels, Death," Finn said quietly. Because Aric had told Ogen to batter a mountain—while my allies and I had been inside it.

Aric said simply, "Yes."

To Joules and Gabriel, Finn added, "And you two are not the friends I wanted to spend my final moments with." He petted the falcon, straightening its little helmet.

"I'll see you soon, Cally lass," Joules said, again seeming so young, almost . . . innocent. He even crossed himself, reminding me of Jack. . . .

I turned to Aric. If this was the end, I was grateful for even two months with him.

Making a sound of frustration, he gazed over his shoulder at Finn. "Magician, you need to disguise this truck."

Finn looked surprised that the Endless Knight was addressing him. Adjusting the bird to see Aric better, he said, "Zara will still be able to detect the heat from the engine."

"Conceal that too."

The falcon gave a low cry, as if to say, "Listen."

"Uh, I only create illusions. Like pictures, you know? I ride the pine for the big stuff."

As though the words were pulled from him, Aric said, "You're a magician. You wield magic. Work a cloaking spell to make us *truly* undetectable. Not an illusion."

Finn perked up. "For real? I can do that?"

"You can, and you must. I don't know the exact incantation, but it started with the words . . ." Aric recited something that sounded Latin-y.

I had no clue what he'd said, but Finn tensed, as if jolted by Joules's electricity. "Dude. I've dreamed that."

"It means: *I command and conjure.* Begin the invocation, imagine what you want to happen, and the rest should follow."

Finn's illusions distorted reality for others, but not necessarily for the people he worked his magic on. We would still look the same. The truck would. "How will we know if he's done it?"

Aric met my gaze. "If we make it past Fortune alive."

Finn repeated Aric's words, then looked shocked when more mysterious commands followed. His breath blurred as he spoke his Magician's language. He started to sweat.

"That's it," Aric said. "Concentrate."

Finn's body quaked; the falcon fluttered.

The little hairs on my nape rose. *Something* was happening. Magic seemed to swirl all around us. Joules and Gabriel shared a look. They'd felt it too.

After another minute or two of speaking, Finn paused. "I feel like I completed a spell, or something. Could be that a white rabbit's appearing in a black hat somewhere on earth." With a grimace, he added, "But whatever spell I worked, I'm definitely fueling it."

Though we had no idea if he'd produced an illusion, much less a total concealment, Aric eased the truck toward the end of the tunnel—and straight into Zara's spotlight beam.

From here, we could see the copter up close.

"She has one missile left," Gabriel murmured.

"What's your plan?" I whispered to Aric.

"To drive under her."

I hissed, "There's not enough room!" The moon roof was still open; I didn't know if I wanted to see how close it would be.

The spotlight was blinding as we emerged from the mountain. If Finn's power wavered . . . if Zara floated lower . . .

Aric inched toward the helicopter.

Then *under* it.

We all craned our heads up, holding our breath. . . .

Joules muttered, "Jaysus, the skids are too close."

If the copter descended by a hair, it'd meet the racks on the truck roof.

"Faster, Reaper," Joules grated. "Get us bloody out of here."

"*Quiet.* Faster means more heat and sound; I won't increase either." Though everything in me clamored to flee, cool Aric continued gliding forward. A few feet more . . . almost there . . .

Clear! A chorus of exhaled breaths.

Finn shook, dripping sweat. "Guys, I-I don't know how much more I've got in me."

"Just a little longer, Magician," Aric said.

We'd driven about half a mile away when Zara floated higher—and launched her last missile.

The tunnel imploded, collapsing half the mountain, the impact shaking the truck even at this distance.

Almost to himself, Aric said, "Such a mistake, Fortune." Then he told Finn, "We're almost concealed behind another mountain. If you can maintain the spell till then, they'll assume we're trapped in that rubble, slowly dying."

Though Finn looked like he was about to pass out, he gave a pained nod.

As we curved around a bend, Gabriel said, "Look back to the left. That is the road we *were* on, heading toward that bridge."

I followed his gaze to a mangled suspension bridge. "It's been out for a while." It reminded me of the one I'd leapt off to escape Death. Joules, Gabriel, Tess, and I had battled Aric and Ogen. How long ago that seemed. *Talk about a new tune. . . .*

Aric slid me a look. "If we hadn't followed where the Sun led us, we would be dead." To Finn, he added, "We're clear."

Finn's exhalation must've lasted a minute.

I cast him a grin. "You're one badass Magician."

"Thanks, blondie." Clammy and pale, he weakly smiled. "And thanks, Death, for the recipe. That was real. And it was fun. But it wasn't real fun."

Joules slapped the back of Aric's seat. "Oi, you cut that close. You got bloody nerves of steel, Reaper, I'll give you that."

Gabriel added, "Well played, Death."

I nodded. "I never would've had the discipline to ease under that helicopter."

Aric caught my gaze. "I never would have had the faith to trust the Sun."

All of us had contributed powers tonight—except for me—but my belief in Sol had helped save us.

We'd gone a few miles when I spotted another Bagman. This one stood beside the road with his thumb out like a hitchhiker.

Aric raised his brows at me.

"Sol has a *unique* sense of humor. Can you slow down? I want to say thanks." And maybe face one of those creatures up close. To face my fear.

Aric slowed, but remained tensed for action.

I sliced my thumb and grew a flower for Sol as a token of gratitude. Battling memories of my attack, I handed it to the Bagger, addressing Sol through the creature: "A yellow rose, fit for a sun god."

With a horrifying smile, the Bagman took the rose—and gave me a formal bow.

"Sol, you *are* layered. Thank you, Illuminator."

Aric drove on into the night.

"Guess what this means?" I told the guys. "We've got a man on the inside."

48

Groaning silence reigned as we continued down the highway. "Now what?" I asked Aric.

"I find a place to dump our unwelcome cargo."

Gabriel and Joules didn't look excited about the prospect.

I told them, "We've got some supplies in our packs. You can have them." In a lower tone, I said, "Before we go, I want you to know I'm sorry about Tess and Selena."

"And we are sorry about Jack," Gabriel said and even Joules nodded. "I wish Tess had waited for you. But we thought you'd been killed either by Richter or Circe. Tess wanted to bring you back most of all."

I hadn't deserved that much of the girl's respect. To save Jack, I would have sacrificed her.

More groaning silence.

Aric flashed a glance in the rearview mirror at Joules. "Why did the two of you and Temperance target me?"

Joules shrugged like such a tough-guy, but his voice broke as he answered, "Cally said that as long as you live, we're just walkin' corpses anyway."

"True."

Joules's face sparked, a bluster session on its way.

"Can we please not fight anymore?" I asked them. "The Priestess said that if Richter wins, there will be hell on earth. Mankind will be doomed."

"We have already been seeing that," Gabriel said. "Any supplies Fortune can't chopper to their hidden lair, he *burns*. Starvation in this region is worse than it has ever been."

No wonder Sol had broken ranks. He'd dreamed aloud of feeding thousands. "We're all going to have to work together to take him down. I'm ready to die; are you?" I gazed from one to the next.

Joules glared at Death as he replied to me, "Like I told you on our first meetin', Empress: what I want is on the other side."

"I'm in," Finn said. "Richter can't get away with what he did to Selena and Jack and all those people. . . ."

Suddenly his words sounded fainter; I felt light-headed. I frowned when warm moisture dripped onto the back of my hand. Was that blood spilling over my icons? From my nose?

I swiped my sleeve against it, but the blood kept coming. Dizziness hit me, my vision getting fuzzy. "Aric?"

"*Sievā*, you're bleeding?" He skidded to a stop. "Gods, were you hurt?"

I remembered Jack balling up his shirt to press against my nose. Even over the blood, I'd savored his scent.

—*Empress.*—

I tensed. Was that . . . Matthew's voice? Why would he be in my head after all these months? How dare he contact me now! *Leave me alone!* A buzz in my ears grew louder and louder, like white-noise on steroids.

—*Have a secret. He doesn't want me to tell you.*—

His eerie tone gave me chills.

Aric hurried around the truck, snatching open my door. He leaned in, cradling my face in his shaking palms. He was speaking to me with dread in his eyes, but I couldn't hear a word.

Get out of my head, Fool!

—*Listen.*— A different voice carried into my mind: —*"What kind of danger is she in? Damn it, tell me! What's coming, coo-yôn?"*—

I whimpered. *Jack??? Is that you?* He sounded so close.

Blood kept pouring. My breaths shallowed till I was hyper-ventilating, on the verge of blacking out. But I was desperate to hear more of his voice. *Jack, please say something!*

White-noise answered me.

Please, please, PLEASE—

My eyes rolled back in my head.

49

"There she is," Aric said when I blinked open my eyes. He sat beside me, stroking my hair.

I was in our bed? So foggy.

Why did Paul have a blood pressure cuff on my arm? "Everything checks out," he told Aric. "I'm sure the posttraumatic stress from that attack didn't help things."

Aric said, "Thank you, Paul."

With a "Get some rest, Evie," the medic left.

My eyes went wide as memories returned. *Matthew, answer me!* I bolted upright, growing dizzy again.

Aric grasped my shoulders. "Easy, slow down. What's wrong, love?"

That buzz in my ears was back. I shook so hard my teeth chattered. *MATTHEW, please answer me! I'm begging you. Is Jack alive?*

Matthew had never actually said he was. The Fool might have been channeling something Jack had said before he'd died. Maybe Matthew was trying to drive me crazy. If so . . .

Kudos, the plan's a success.

I rubbed my temples, muttering to Aric, "I-I don't know." What if I'd imagined Matthew altogether? Imagined Jack's voice?

Oh, God, of course. I'd been remembering a detail about Jack, and then his voice popped up?

257

In a solemn tone, Aric said, "There is something we need to talk about, *sievā*."

Now what? I could've been out for days. In that time, he might've uncovered something new and dire.

So why was he looking at me so strangely? Almost like *I* was nuts.

Maybe I . . . shouldn't tell him what I thought I'd heard. Not until I knew more. How exactly would I put the revelation anyway? *Jack's alive, but apparently he kept that little detail secret. Ah, but Matthew spilled the beans!* Buying myself time, I waved Aric on.

I was scarcely listening as he began talking about Paul, of all people. How the EMT had grown worried when I'd been shut in with my grandmother for so long. How I had lost weight and become listless. The man had pleaded with me to get a checkup, even offering to source contraception after Aric and I had started sleeping together.

Wait. I glanced up. "After?"

Aric nodded. "He said you told him you had no need of contraception."

The hell? "I went to him and got a shot *prior* to us getting together. I told you about it."

"As I told him in turn, but he swears that never happened."

Real? *Un*real? Had I . . . imagined my meeting with Paul? I'd already feared gaps in my memory; Gran had told me things that I'd had no recollection of. Was I now *inventing* memories?

Had I invented Jack's return?

In a soothing voice, Aric said, "I'm not angry, love. Just talk to me." He wasn't the first person to look at me as if I'd gone insane, like I was trouble with the possibility of rubble.

Won't be the last.

No. I refused this. I *had* heard Jack, and I *had* gotten that shot. "It did happen, which means Paul's a liar." *But* why *would he lie?* "I'm going to confront him." In time. Right now, all I wanted was to hear from Matthew again.

Yet I frowned as a thought occurred. "Why would you be talking to Paul about contraception?"

Aric tucked my hair behind my ear. "*Sievā*," he said gently, "do you not know you're pregnant?"

Tick-tock.

AFTERWORD

As many of you know, I've written each book in the Arcana Chronicles with a Tarot card guiding the plot and informing the theme. In addition, every card mentioned or appearing within the pages will also be symbolic (even those played in a passing card game between Death and Evie).

Book / Card / Theme

Poison Princess / The Empress / Growth
Endless Knight / Death / Change
Dead of Winter / The Lovers / Choice
Arcana Rising / The Ten of Swords / Loss

Dead of Winter foreshadowed the importance of the Ten of Swords—Tarot's most forbidding card—in *Arcana Rising*. The card's image is grim: under a swath of black clouds, a body lies sprawled on the bloody ground with ten swords jutting from his or her back. It represents total devastation that strikes without warning or mercy.

But the Priestess Card is also pervasive in *Arcana Rising*, bringing enlightenment and insight. She signifies mystery, intuition, and most importantly, trusting in oneself.

I believe Circe's take on the Ten of Swords is one of the greatest lessons to be learned from Tarot: when you can't change your rock-bottom situation, when you can't remove the ten swords in your back, you still have to rise and walk. Not necessarily to bounce back at once, kick ass, and triumph, but to *endure*.

To put one foot in front of the other; one may be down, but never out.

Ultimately, a person can rise stronger than ever before—for the battle still to come.

I hope you're enjoying Tarot's immense influence on this series. Although the Arcana Chronicles will come to a close in 2017, the cards will always live on....

**Turn the page for the cover and title
of the penultimate installment in the Arcana Chronicles.**

Coming Spring 2017

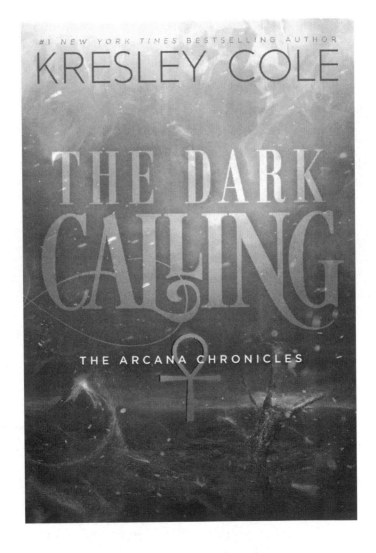

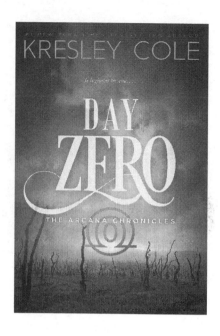

If you haven't read DAY ZERO yet, grab a copy to find out:

How Death first explained the basics of the game to Lark.

Why Jack shudders at the memory of removing his mother's rosary.

How Lark's wolves got to be so big and scarred.

Why Zara is such a skilled pilot and markswoman.

How Gabriel learned to fly.

How Sol, Joe, and Bea planned to celebrate their anniversary.

Plus eleven other DAY ZERO stories from your favorite characters.

Read on for a new excerpt from DAY ZERO,
and get ready for secrets to be revealed!

THE PRIESTESS (II)

Circe Rémire, Ruler of the Deep
"Terror from the abyss!"

A.k.a.: The Water Witch

Powers: Water manipulation, including tidal wave generation and flood creation. Hydrokinetic combat, shapeshifting, and constructs (can form water objects). Hydro scrying (can perceive through water). Hydroportation.

Special Skills: Spells and hexes. One spell enables her to remember past games.

Weapons: Water, trident.

Tableau: A priestess—with water for hair and tentacles for legs—looms over a sacrificial victim at a bloody altar.

Icon: Trident.

Unique Arcana Characteristics: Iridescent blue scales on her arms, with a small fin at each elbow.

Before Flash: A grad student from Bermuda, attending the University of Miami. Her focus: Atlantean mythology and the Bermuda Triangle. Engaged to a computer programmer and instructor there. Member of campus Wiccans.

"Are you tipsy?" I asked my soon-to-be husband. I was sitting with my cheek pressed against the door. He was sitting on the other side. It was well past midnight, so we weren't supposed to see each other.

"I might be a tee bit wispy, luv," he said, his voice as jovial as ever. No one had ever made me laugh like Ned. "But my wipsiness can't be helped. My family kept raising their glasses to me. They think I'm a boss for landing a woman as beautiful as you." His crisp British accent got more relaxed when he'd had a drink or two. "My sister said if a movie were made of our lives, it'd be called *The Siren and the Nerd.*"

Siren. I frowned as some memory tried to surface. *The ocean's siren song....* I raised my hand to my head as a wave of dizziness overtook me.

Over the last week, the wedding festivities had been going great—until I'd received a long, mysterious wooden box. The accompanying note had been just as puzzling.

Priestess,
Hail Tar Ro. I believe this is yours.
Death

Ever since I'd touched the contents of the package—a golden trident, engraved with cryptic symbols—I'd been having bouts of dizziness, and nightmares about being trapped under the ocean.

I hadn't been able to shake the feeling that something bad was going to happen, as if I was on a countdown clock. And my symptoms were getting worse.

I'd confided them to my grandfather, my best friend. He'd worried that I wasn't ready to marry.

But I am! Ned was the one for me. We were soul mates. I was lucky to have found him.

In a fit two nights ago, I'd taken the trident to a headland cliff and tossed it into the waves. But my issues continued—

"Circe, dear?"

What had he been talking about? Oh, yes . . . "Siren and the Nerd?" I feigned a huff. "They only commented on my looks?"

"They *might* have mentioned your early PhD candidacy, but I told them you were going to cut out all that scholarly rubbish after our nuptials."

I grinned, pressing my palm to the door. I loved this man like a drought loves rain. "My family also spoke a lot about you tonight— about how you went out on the water without your seasickness patch." My brothers had taken him fishing. They'd reported back that they'd never seen anybody throw up so much and live to laugh about it. "*And* without your sunblock." They'd also said they'd never seen anyone burn so fast.

"I did that part on purpose, for my Larry the Lobster impression at the reception. I'm method that way."

Laughter burst from my lips. I'd never known I could laugh this much before Ned. No, there'd been another time. . . . In a dark forest, a green-eyed girl and I had laughed till our bellies ached.

"You can't deny the lobster-red hotness of my skin. No, seriously. My skin is literally hot."

I tsked. "And you'll be bright red for all our photos tomorrow."

"We can always hope I'll be *peeling* by then." Ned sighed. "How you put up with me is a mystery."

A voice in my head murmured, *Mysteries from the deep.* The nightmares. *Shake it off, Circe.*

"You're brave to want kids with me, luv. Three no less."

I'd told him I wanted to get started once I'd earned my degree. He'd saluted me, replying, "I shall enthusiastically contribute to this endeavor. You will know what the word *commitment* means."

Now he asked, "What if they turn out to be nerds who get seasick?"

"Then you'll know you're the father."

He laughed. "You give as good as you get. God, I'm ready to get this wedding business sorted, so we can get back to *us*."

"I know. I feel as if I haven't seen you in weeks."

"I don't like sleeping in different beds. Custom or not, if you have another nightmare, you need to come get me."

"I will," I lied. I'd had several each night since that package's arrival. Yet those nightmares had felt more like . . . memories. Maybe I was losing my mind. "You know how much I love you, right?"

"Ah, but the merest fraction of how much I love you."

"I'm serious, Ned." I could all but *hear* him frowning. I glanced at my arm. For an instant, my skin appeared to glitter. Like a fish's scales. "I knew the night we met that you would be mine." I'd been giving a campus lecture on the Bermuda Triangle and Atlantean folklore, presenting pictures of Circe's Abyss, the deepest spot in the Triangle.

The abyss I'd been named after.

A deep-water oceanography team had recently completed the imaging of it. Those images had captured an underground aquifer—*below* the abyss.

And inside the aquifer was a rock formation so exact that it had to be man-made.

If the formation was a structure from a sunken city—such as Atlantis—how had it gotten into an aquifer?

Like a ship in a bottle. . . .

Though Ned, a brilliant computer programmer, was devoted to hard science, for some reason he'd attended my lecture. He'd grasped anything I could throw his way, asking observant questions. He hadn't scoffed when I'd told him of my Wiccan leanings.

Afterward, coffee had turned to drinks. Drinks to dinner. Since then, we'd never separated a single night. Until now. "I thought you were adorable," I said. "Your cheeks flushed whenever I looked at you."

"Because I kept saying to myself, *I think I'm bloody in love with her.* I didn't know how it could be possible, but there it was."

I murmured, "There it was." I imagined his palm pressed against the door, opposite mine.

Strange how the wood burl beneath my hand looked like a whirlpool. I shivered. Clearing my throat, I asked, "Will you finally admit why you came to my lecture?" He'd teased me with different reasons: Because he'd ducked in out of the rain (it'd been clear that day). To sample the free lukewarm coffee. To kill time until his superhero gig started.

"The truth? What would you say if I told you a mate made me a wager?"

I made my tone scandalized. "A *wager*? What were the terms?"

"He bet me a hundred quid that the woman hosting this Atlantean lecture would be the most beautiful creature on earth." He exhaled. "Best hundred I ever lost."

I squeezed my eyes closed. "Everyone calls you a comedian, but I think you're really a romantic."

"God, I'm going to enjoy teasing *and* romancing you for the next eighty or so years of our lives."

"Do you really think we'll live that long?" That wood burl on the door appeared to spin.

"Of course. Laughter and love keep a body young."

I inhaled a deep breath. My big day had finally come. *I can do this.*

I'd sent everyone in the bridal party away, needing time to compose myself before the sunset ceremony. In the few hours I'd dozed after talking to Ned, the nightmares/memories had come on full-bore. All morning and afternoon, I'd battled anxiety. Again, I sensed a countdown ticking.

Toward what?

I shook my head hard. I just needed to get down the aisle and reach Ned. He would make me feel better. His eyes would light up when he saw me in this gorgeous strapless dress. I would muffle a laugh when I saw the tips of his ears and his nose peeling.

Bouquet in hand, I took a step.

In the wrong direction. Left was toward the chapel ceremony; right would take me to the beach. Another step to the right.

I strained every muscle to get to Ned, but my feet wouldn't obey me. *I'm losing my mind, losing my mind!* My eyes went wide when I opened the door and headed outside—away from the chapel—from the man I loved.

I wanted to call for him; no sounds would pass my lips. When I reached the pink-sand beach, the sunset gleamed over the placid water. My arms fell limp by my sides, my bouquet dropping soundlessly in the sand.

Tears of frustration welled. What force had taken me over? Would Ned think I'd run away? That I didn't want to marry him?

I struggled to scream, "I love you!" Yet couldn't speak at all.

The sea had always called to me, but now . . . now its siren song was undeniable. Suddenly, I knew where I was going. Toward that abyss.

I had *always* been headed toward the abyss.

Tears streamed down my face. *Ned will think I left him.* I reached the water, and the gentle waves lapped at my ankles. A glimmer beneath the surf caught my eye.

Somehow the trident had returned to me.

As I dipped to collect it, a tingling sensation flowed up my forearms, and light-blue scales appeared there, like long, iridescent gloves. They sparkled in the sunlight. My elbows itched maddeningly. I scratched them, and my skin sloughed off—to make way for jutting blue fins.

I sobbed. How could Ned ever want me like this?

Those cryptic symbols on my trident were now legible to me. They read: *The Abysmal Ruler of the Deep.*

In a daze, I cradled the weighty gold weapon in my arms and waded into the water up to my knees. To my waist. To my neck. I did not stop until I was submerged.

I expelled my last breath, awaiting the burning suffocation of water filling my lungs, but instead I . . . *became* the sea.

The weight of my trident made me sink. The pressure didn't bother me. The temperature had no effect. I could see, hear, feel, taste, even scent through the water. This jumble of new sensations made me giddy, as if my soul was soaring—instead of sinking.

Deeper and deeper I dropped. Although it should have been pitch black as the waning daylight faded above me, somehow I could see. Luminescent sharks darted through me. Plankton and crustaceans tumbled within me as if buffeted by an island breeze.

I descended till I'd reached the bottom of Circe's Abyss. Rocks parted, revealing a vortex that led beneath the seafloor shelf. To the aquifer?

I was swept into the vortex, then sucked even lower through a tunnel—as if down a drain. Or down Alice's rabbit hole.

The water turned fresh. Before me was the structure from those pictures! I flowed around the stone exterior.

Swarms of phosphorescent creatures teemed on the walls, illuminating carvings in the rock. The symbols were in the same language as the words engraved on my trident. I read:

Abysmal temple of the Great Priestess, the Ruler of the Deep.
All who hear the Priestess's call will fear her catastrophal powers.
TERROR FROM THE ABYSS.

This structure, these markings, those creatures . . . I was seeing things no normal human had ever beheld. All my life, I'd been obsessed with the sea, with Atlantis.

I *was* the sea. Was I also an Atlantean?

Live coral adorned an entrance, each branch ending in a trident shape.

Curiosity driving me, I flowed through the opening. Inside was an airlock with steps rising out of the water. I instinctively knew how to regrow my form, to become a woman again. Trident in hand, I arose from the sea and climbed the steps.

Shafts of that phosphorescent light beamed inside. Shadows rippled.

Ancient mosaics decorated the walls. I ran my fingertips over the damp tiles. The eerie scenes depicted tidal waves engulfing helpless lands, and monstrous sea life—giant sharks, whales, squids, a kraken—attacking ships. The shadows made the scenes appear to move.

Chills skittered up my back when I came upon a bloodstained altar, liberally carved with trident symbols. I glanced at my own weapon.

Could this be *my* temple? Hadn't Death called me "Priestess"?

As I eased farther inside, memories from my dreams arose. This place *was* mine.

I got the sense that my temple was a refuge. But also a . . . jail? Somehow I knew I would quickly die on land, but *slowly* die here in this lonely, echoing abyss.

Solitude would be my punishment, and fear my jailor. What crime had I committed to be cursed like this?

No, I didn't care about my fate; one way or another I would return to Ned! He would accept these changes in me. I believed in him.

I ran to the airlock and became the sea once more. I'd almost reached the top of the tunnel when the seafloor above began to quake.

The water was heating. I gazed up from the tunnel opening, disbelieving my vision.

A giant submarine was hurtling down, far too fast to be a normal descent through the depths.

Past the vessel, I could see lights in the sky—as if the ocean above me had disappeared, the water sucked out.

Though it must be night, the sun seemed to be shining. And I thought I saw a sky full of . . . flames. I was riveted. Until that light went dark—snuffed by the submarine crashing down atop my only exit.

I was trapped.

In my lonely, echoing abyss.

WITHDRAWN

$12.99

LONGWOOD PUBLIC LIBRARY
800 Middle Country Road
Middle Island, NY 11953
(631) 924-6400
longwoodlibrary.org

LIBRARY HOURS

Monday-Friday	9:30 a.m. - 9:00 p.m.
Saturday	9:30 a.m. - 5:00 p.m.
Sunday (Sept-June)	1:00 p.m. - 5:00 p.m.

98852731R00167

Made in the USA
Lexington, KY
10 September 2018